"You're one of the prospective brides?"

Leah wanted to grab on to Daniel, but held her desperation in check to simply nod. "Yes. Yes, I'm a widow."

His expression changed, confusion turning to understanding. "I see. I'm so sorry."

You have no idea. I never want you to know. "Thank you."

"What about your family? Your father?"

"They're gone, too." *Gone* seemed an insufficient explanation for her grief, but of course he would understand the pain behind those words. It was an all too common story. The war had stolen so much from all of them. "Nothing is as we remember it."

His eyes clouded with sympathy and something more. Regret. Anger. And then incredulity. He did understand. He extended a hand as though he wanted to touch her to see for himself if she was real, but he drew it back, self-consciously. He shook his head. "And after all that, here we are."

* * *

Cowboy Creek: Bringing mail-order brides, and new beginnings, to a Kansas boom town.

Cheryl St.John's love for reading started as a child. She wrote her own stories, designed covers and stapled them into books. She credits many hours of creating scenarios for her paper dolls and Barbies as the start of her fascination with fictional characters. Cheryl loves hearing from readers. Visit her website at cherylstjohn.net or email her at saintjohn@aol.com.

Books by Cheryl St.John

Love Inspired Historical

Cowboy Creek
Want Ad Wedding

Irish Brides
The Wedding Journey

The Preacher's Wife
To Be a Mother
"Mountain Rose"
Marrying the Preacher's Daughter
Colorado Courtship
"Winter of Dreams"

Visit the Author Profile page at Harlequin.com for more titles.

CHERYL ST.JOHN

Want Ad Wedding

HARLEQUIN® LOVE INSPIRED® HISTORICAL

Special thanks and acknowledgment to Cheryl St.John for her contribution to the Cowboy Creek miniseries.

Recycling programs for this product may not exist in your area.

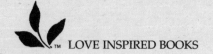

LOVE INSPIRED BOOKS

ISBN-13: 978-0-373-28355-2

Want Ad Wedding

www.Harlequin.com

Printed in U.S.A.

And God is able to make all grace abound toward
you; that ye, always having all sufficiency in
all things, may abound to every good work.
—*2 Corinthians* 9:8

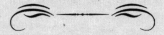

The steadfast love of the Lord never ceases.
Your mercies never come to an end;
they are new every morning,
new every morning:
great is Your faithfulness, O Lord,
great is Your faithfulness!

Chapter One

Kansas, April 1868

A plaintive train whistle shrieked in the distance, scattering dozens of heath hens that pecked along the tracks. Daniel Gardner experienced a sharp pang of anxiety. A murmur of excitement passed through the crowd on the station platform and among those waiting along Railroad Street, the road separating the tracks from the town. Indicative of the population of Cowboy Creek, only a few females stood among the motley gathering of drovers, cattlemen and shop owners who eagerly awaited the arrival of the first bride train.

Daniel and his friend Will had convinced the other town leaders that brides were the answer to the growth and survival of this boomtown they'd overseen from the ground up, but four women were a paltry drop in the bucket. His gaze moved from D.B. Burrows, owner and editor of *The Herald*, his angular face rapt with serious intent as he scribbled notes, over dozens of other bystanders, before finally landing on a sunburned young drover who sported a stiff new pair of dungarees, a red shirt and a silly crooked-toothed grin. Right about now Daniel was imagining the reactions of those much-anticipated prospective brides when they stepped off the train and got their first look at this throng of menfolk starved for the sight of a woman.

"Well, this is it." Beside him, Will Canfield squinted from beneath the brim of his brown felt bowler and leaned a little more heavily than usual on his expensive Italian-made walking stick. He wore a tailored suit coat and starched white shirt. Tall and lean, his goatee neatly trimmed as always, he was the picture of a gentleman with his sights set on a public office. Only Daniel noticed his friend was favoring his left leg, because only Daniel knew the walking stick was not purely for show. He was also relatively sure it did not conceal a derringer or a knife as was rumored about Cowboy Creek. They'd both had enough of killing during the war to last them a lifetime. Their town was populated with peace-loving citizens, eager for a new slice of life and the profits the Union Pacific Railroad and a steady stream of Texas longhorns were bringing. Women would heighten their plans to a whole new level.

"This is it," Daniel echoed. He wanted the past behind him. The town needed order, and these females would help bring it. Cowboy Creek was providing a new life and a fresh start for a good many people. The whistle screamed again. He checked his pocket watch and tucked it back inside his suit coat. "Right on time." He looked to each side and held out both arms. "Step back! Step back and give the passengers room to get off the train!"

His voice held enough authority that the eager men shuffled to the rear of the platform.

The great black locomotive hissed as the brakes were applied, and it slowed on its approach, trundling past the railroad office east of the station and coming to a halt with the passenger cars only feet from the wooden platform. Clouds of steam expressed vapor into the air. From the exit closest to them, a uniformed conductor jumped down, lowered the stairs with a squeak of metal and stood waiting.

Passengers were visible inside the car, making their way to the exit and out onto the small metal platform. Anticipation hummed around him. The first to appear was a fellow in a brown pinstripe suit and a derby, followed by a white-haired gentleman with a huge mustache. A man and his young son emerged next. Passengers disembarked from the rear of the car, and a second passenger car spilled its riders, as well. The impatient townsmen crowded around the people exiting the train until the platform became a blur of shoulders and hats. Hoots and appreciative calls blended with laughter and good-natured competition.

Daniel and Will exchanged a tense glance. Had they thought of everything?

"We started with only four brides, Dan," Will said. "Next time we'll be better prepared for the rush of bachelors."

"Or not announce the brides' arrival," Daniel replied in a grim tone. He scanned the area until he spotted a stack of crates, then pushed his way through the milling crowd and climbed to the top. With two fingers held strategically between his lips, he let out an ear-piercing whistle. He whistled again. "May I have your attention?" he shouted.

The crowd quieted and heads turned.

"Gentlemen, please make a path and escort our brides forward!"

A smattering of applause followed his request, and from the outer edge of the platform the crowd parted unevenly, allowing three figures in ruffles and flower-bedecked hats to make their way through the gathering to the stack of crates. Daniel jumped down beside Will and they stood on either side of the group of ladies.

Daniel removed his hat and every cowboy doffed his own. "Welcome to Cowboy Creek." He glanced aside. "We're still missing someone."

"Mrs. Swann was with us a moment ago," the petite young woman beside him said. "She must have become lost in the crowd somewhere."

Will took the next initiative. "Welcome. I'm Will Canfield. And this is my friend Daniel Gardner."

Daniel noted Will deliberately wasn't leaning on his walking stick while attention focused on him.

"Cowboy Creek is pleased you're here," Daniel told the new arrivals. "We have a special welcome planned for you once we have everyone accounted for and can move away from the station."

"I'm Pippa Neely." The flamboyant little gal with ginger-gold hair had enormous hazel eyes and a pert smile. She wore a voluminous lavender skirt with gold braid designs down the front and fringe around the hem of the jacket. Atop her head bobbed a brown satin bow with a lavender paper rose. "I thought we'd never arrive! What a grueling journey!"

"Pleased to meet you, Miss Neely," Daniel greeted her. In her letter to the town council, Pippa had described herself as an actress. Then he turned politely to the lady standing next to her.

"I'm Hannah Taggart," the young woman explained. She wore her fawn-colored hair severely pulled away from her face. Her gray eyes moved uneasily from Daniel to the crowd of men and back. She wore a wine-colored dress with puffy fabric at the elbows and over the bustle, ruffles everywhere, but with no ornamentation save the row of buttons at her neck. She was a tall girl, not slender, and Daniel imagined her choice in clothing added to her size.

"Miss Taggart," he said. "You're the Reverend Taggart's daughter."

She smiled easily. "He was right behind us a moment ago." She glanced into the crowd. "Disembarking was a challenge, but no doubt we all feel welcome."

"The men are a bit overzealous," Daniel said by way of apology. "I'm sure you'll forgive their excitement."

"Prudence Haywood, Mr. Gardner." The short curvy woman introduced herself with a curt nod. She had auburn hair, hazel eyes and wore a cameo brooch on her collar.

Daniel and Will acknowledged her introduction.

"Here's my father!" Hannah announced.

The beaming fellow approached and removed his hat to shake the hands of both men. "Reverend Taggart," Daniel said. "We're so pleased you're here."

"It's Virgil," the reverend said, his friendly manner a welcome answer for the unspoken question of what sort of preacher might be coming their way. He sported a narrow mustache and a wide smile that creased the corners of his eyes. "Hannah and I are excited to be here right when your town is on the verge of a population explosion."

"Can't bring women to this county without preachers

and doctors and schools," Daniel pointed out. "We've been planning this for some time. We have a lot to show you."

"I look forward to hearing all about it."

"Papa, where is Mrs. Swann?"

"She was by my side only a few minutes ago. These Kansas fellows seem quite friendly and eager to meet the ladies." He stood on tiptoe to survey the way he'd come, but the crowd had closed back around the temporary opening. "There she is. I see her hat."

"Let the lady through!" Daniel called, standing as tall as he could manage and peering above the crowd. He was thinking that perhaps he would need to get back on the stack of crates when he spotted a blue feathered hat on a pale gold head of hair. "There she is. Mrs. Swann! Let her through."

The poor woman steadied her wisp of a hat atop her head with one white-gloved hand, and turned this way and that, speaking to men as she choreographed her way through the crowd. When she finally neared the open clearing where Daniel and Will stood with the other newcomers, she turned, disengaging herself from the attentions of an overeager cowboy, and nearly stumbled forward.

Daniel caught her elbow to steady her.

"Oh! Thank you. This is quite a reception!" She glanced up. Cornflower-blue eyes rimmed with dark lashes opened wide in surprise. The world stood still for a moment. The crowd noise faded into the void. "Daniel?"

Daniel's gut felt as though he'd been standing right on the tracks and stopped the locomotive with his body. He couldn't catch his breath or find his voice. Sounds resumed and he filled his lungs with air. Finally his heart resumed its inadequate cadence, and he cleared his parched throat. *"Leah Robinson?"*

She was as pretty as ever. Prettier maybe, her face having lost the roundness of girlhood and her skin and bone structure having smoothed into a gentle comeliness. Her winged brows were pale arches over those sparkling blue eyes, and her lips were full and pink. Her green-and-blue-plaid dress with black trim was the perfect foil for her pale perfection. It was ungentlemanly of him to notice the curves…the pale skin at her throat… yet he never had been able to look away.

Mrs. Swann was Leah Robinson, one of his best friends before the war. Will had once shown him a wedding announcement from a Chicago newspaper, and all these years Daniel had pictured her just as she had been back then, full of youth and vitality, and married to the army officer she'd chosen. That had been a lifetime ago. So what was she doing traveling to Cowboy Creek with their mail-order brides?

The crowded platform was a blur of faces. Leah tasted dirt on her tongue and her eyes were so dry it hurt to blink. Cowboy Creek was as muddy as Chicago, and she'd thought that was bad. That city was systematically raising buildings, even entire blocks, above the level of the river, and it had been impossible to keep a clean pair of boots. It looked as if it would be the same here.

Daniel. Seeing his familiar face anchored her in this sea of chaos, brought back memories of home and family, eased her fears and assured her she'd made the right choice coming here. She hadn't seen Daniel in years, and yet here he was standing before her as tall and real as anything she'd ever laid eyes upon. It took every last ounce of her reserve not to throw herself into his arms and feel safe at last. Here was someone she could trust, someone who remembered her and shared her past. His tanned face and piercing green eyes revealed he was as shocked to see her as she was to discover him here under the Kansas sky.

"Daniel," she said again, feeling foolish, but so relieved that she finally felt some moisture in her eyes. "I am so glad to see you."

"What is this?" His tone seemed almost gruff. "You're one of the prospective brides?"

She wanted to grab on to him, but held her desperation in check to simply nod. "Yes. Yes, I'm a widow."

His expression changed, confusion turning to understanding. "I see. I'm so sorry."

You have no idea. I never want you to know. "Thank you."

"What about your family? Your father?"

"They're gone, too." *Gone* seemed an insufficient explanation for her grief, but of course he would understand the pain behind those words. It was an all too common story. The war had stolen so much from all of them. "Nothing is as we remember it."

His eyes clouded with sympathy and something more. Regret. Anger. And then incredulity. He did understand. He extended a hand as though he wanted to touch her to see for himself she was real, but he drew it back self-consciously. He shook his head. "And after all that, here we are…"

"You survived, Daniel." Her voice was too breathless, but she didn't care. Life was precious.

"Leah?"

She turned as a dark-haired man with a cane approached from Daniel's other side, amazement on his sculpted face. "Leah Robinson?"

It took her stunned brain a moment to sort and make sense of what her eyes were revealing. Will Canfield? Both of them here in Kansas? How could this be? Growing up in Pennsylvania, the three of them had been inseparable. "It's Swann," she said. "My husband's name was Swann."

"Your army officer?" Will asked.

Her army officer indeed. *I made a mistake back then. More than one mistake. I should have stayed in Pennsylvania.* "Yes."

"I'm sorry. A lot of good men didn't come home." Will stated a fact. Yes, her father had been a good man. Thousands upon thousands of men had been killed. And many of those who had come back returned to burned-out farms and missing families. Her story was no different from plenty of others.

She had nothing to say. That both Daniel and Will had survived was, in her eyes, a blessing at the hand of their merciful God. Awash with joy at seeing her old friends, her heart swelled with emotion. She'd been so alone and frightened. *Thank You, thank You.* She was so happy to see their beloved faces that she moved into Will's embrace and hugged him. He stiffened, but she didn't let go. She pressed her cheek against the fabric of his jacket and clung.

"Will is engaged," Daniel pointed out from beside her.

Leah pulled back and glanced from one man to the

other. "Oh, my goodness! Engaged?" She gave Will a delighted smile. "I can't wait to meet her."

"Her name is Dora Edison," he explained. "She's the daughter of the owners of the feed and grain store."

"Why, that's wonderful. Have you set a date?"

"We were waiting for a preacher," he replied.

"I want to hear all about her. And I want to learn everything about the two of you since we last saw each other. I'm curious how you both came to be in Kansas."

"We'll have plenty of time for that." Daniel's familiar mellow baritone calmed Leah's nerves. "Now that everyone's together, we'll continue to move the celebration along. We're heading over to Eden Street for a welcome gathering. Meanwhile, your bags and trunks will be delivered to the boardinghouse."

Leah tucked her hand into the crook of Daniel's arm and they made their way into town. Walking beside him was like a dream come true. She'd been so utterly alone these past months. Feeling at times like a piece of driftwood afloat at sea, she'd known all the while she had to find some way to ground herself and make a new home and a new beginning. As difficult things went, coming to an unknown place didn't rate at the top, but it hadn't been easy to get on that train with strangers. The unknown was always frightening. Now she'd found two of her dearest friends. She lifted her gaze and caught Daniel looking at her.

His courteous smile didn't reach his eyes. "Couldn't have been more surprised to see you among our brides."

"I can't say I ever imagined myself in Kansas," she answered. "I dare say I'm more fortunate than many, just to be alive and have an opportunity to start over."

Daniel glanced away. "We've all started over."

"And you, Daniel. Are you married—or engaged like Will?"

"No." He shook his head and once again met her gaze. "No. Will and I came here to join our friend Noah. He got injured and homesteaded here before the war ended. When we got out of the army, we came to see how he was doing and we liked what we saw. Back then it was land as far as the eye could see, and the Union Pacific hadn't come this far. We staked claims, bought up sections and we were here when the railroad decided this was the best place for a terminus." He took a breath then went on. "We saw the future of this as a cattle town and grabbed on to it. After that, men looking for new starts poured in. There aren't many women yet."

"But now there are four more."

He nodded. "This was a trial to see how brides would be accepted. We're seeing now how much excitement there is at the prospect. So we wait and see what happens."

"As the women find husbands."

"Yes."

"Well, it looks as though there are plenty of men to choose from."

A muscle in his jaw worked. He looked decidedly uncomfortable about that. "Looks like it."

"I was hoping to put my experience as a midwife to use." The wind gusted around them. A strand of her fair hair fell to her shoulder, and his gaze followed as she tried to tuck it back in place. "I want to be useful."

"You'll want to meet Mrs. Godwin then," he said. "Amos and Opal are a young couple who have started a boot shop just up the street and across from the boardinghouse. They're going to have a baby, so Opal will appreciate a visit from another woman, especially a midwife. We have a doctor, but I think Doc Fletcher's more suited to fixing up cuts and broken bones."

"I'll be sure to go see Mrs. Godwin."

"This welcome won't take long, and then you can get settled and rest. Is there anything you need?"

She looked up at him. *Security. Safety. A place to raise a family.* "Not that I can think of."

"Well, you only have to ask. You'll find the board-inghouse comfortable and the proprietress a good cook. If you need something, give Aunt Mae's lad a message and he will find me."

"Thank you, Daniel." *Daniel Gardner.* It couldn't be chance that she'd ended up in a town where both Daniel and Will were living. Perhaps this was how her prayers had been answered. Her clothing still hid the mound of the new life growing inside her, but she had no intentions of keeping her baby a secret. She wanted this baby more than anything, and she'd been willing to make this trip to find a new and better life for his sake. She needed a husband, but whomever she married would have to accept her child as his own.

Chapter Two

A platform had been constructed smack dab in the center of an intersection. On the four corners sat the Cattleman Hotel, a bank, the Cowboy Café and what looked like another hotel called Drover's Place. All the buildings were wood structures, some had wood awnings and most boasted glass windows with gold lettering. Men of all sizes and dress filled the boardwalks and gathered in the streets. It appeared the entire town and its outlying residents had shown up for this momentous event.

A cowboy band played "Sweet Nightingale" with dulcimers and fiddles as the four women and Reverend Taggart were escorted to the platform. The song reminded Leah so much of home, of afternoons and evenings in the company of her family, that her throat grew thick with tears. Her gaze met Daniel's, and he signaled the band. The strains of that song faded away, and they played "Lincoln and Liberty." Men's voices joined the instruments and swelled until the singers drowned out the musicians.

"Hurrah for the choice of the nation!
Our chieftain so brave and so true;
We'll go for the great Reformation—
For Lincoln and Liberty, too!"

The song ended and the crowd cheered.

Will moved to the front of the platform. Leah searched the gathering of men, easily spotting a pretty dark-haired young woman watching with rapt interest. Was she Will's fiancée?

"Our newest residents have had a long trip," Will began. "So we're going to get them settled in their rooms at the boardinghouse. Their belongings should have been delivered by now." He turned back to their guests. "Welcome to Cowboy Creek, ladies and Reverend. We hope you'll find your accommodations comfortable. Our town is safe for women and families. We enforce a no-gun law in town, so if any of you are carrying a weapon, you will have to check it with Sheriff Davis."

A rumble of male laughter rolled through the crowd at Will's announcement. A broad-shouldered, lean-hipped fellow with a huge mustache gave a mock salute from the corner of the platform.

"That's our sheriff, Quincy Davis," Will continued.

Willowy little Pippa Neely made a show out of patting her pockets and checking the roll of reddish-gold hair on the back of her head as though searching for weapons. She peered into the beaded reticule that dangled from her elbow, then shrugged and shook her head. Even traveling by train she'd managed to make her hair and clothing look lovely. Leah had felt rumpled and dirty since the second day out of Chicago.

The men in the crowd loved Pippa's pantomime and laughed uproariously. The vivacious young woman had been great fun on the trip west. Always cheerful and often playful, she made the best out of every situation and had bolstered the spirits of the other passengers when the trip grew long and tiresome. Reverend Taggart just shook his head and grinned at her antics. He'd grown accustomed to Pippa's mischievous showmanship.

"How about you, Reverend?" someone called from the crowd. "Are you packin' a gun?"

The reverend raised both hands in the air as if prepared for a search.

Daniel stepped forward. "We figured you'd be tired after the long journey, so the Cowboy Café will bring a meal to each of your rooms. After today, Aunt Mae will be planning on your eating at the boardinghouse, unless you tell her differently. Let's go get you settled."

The crowd applauded as the newest residents made their way down the stairs onto the boardwalk and headed to the next block. Eden Street boasted several businesses. On the right was a telegraph, a barber and a doctor's office. They passed the sheriff's office and a newspaper office before reaching Aunt Mae's boardinghouse. It wasn't a fancy structure, but it was two stories with an abundance of windows and two sets of stairs, one leading to a balcony that covered the front of the whole upstairs and the set on the side leading to a second floor entrance. The building was freshly painted and someone had planted fledgling rose bushes on either side of the entrance.

The short stocky woman who greeted them was every bit of sixty, with a square face. Her gray hair held a few remaining streaks of reddish brown. She wore a green dress with a white collar and white trim. When she smiled her cheeks folded into wrinkled pleats to match her lined forehead.

"Welcome! Welcome to Cowboy Creek. Oh, just look at the lot of you. You're as welcome here as a rain on an August day. Tell me now, who is who? You're the reverend, of course."

"Pleasure to meet you, ma'am."

"Shoosh now, not ma'am. Just Aunt Mae."

The women introduced themselves and Aunt Mae greeted them as though they were family, exclaiming over their dresses and hair.

"You'll meet my permanent boarders soon enough. Gus and Old Horace spend their days sitting on benches in front of the mercantile, but they never miss a meal." She explained about meal times and continued, "There's a bathing room beside the kitchen. You can heat water on the kitchen stove. I have a lad who brings in wood and empties the tub. I figured you'd all want baths today, so I have water ready and will keep the kettles full."

Aunt Mae gave them their room assignments. "Mrs. Swann, you're on the south corner in front. Miss Hannah, you're right beside her. The fellows carried up your trunks. There's soap and toweling ready. If you need anything else, just let me know."

Hannah, looking especially tired, thanked their hostess and trudged up the stairs.

"I'll help you settle in, dear." Aunt Mae gathered the hem of her skirts and followed. Pippa thanked everyone and climbed the stairs behind them.

Leah met Daniel's piercing green eyes. Looking at his tanned face and chestnut hair bleached gold from the sun, she noticed a few lines that hadn't been there last time she'd seen him. He was broader and more muscled than Will, his strength unrestrained by the fabric of his neatly pressed shirt, but his features were harder, leaner than she remembered. The war had seasoned his still-handsome face, but it was now a man's face. No doubt they'd both lived a lifetime in the years that had separated them.

Overshadowing her relief at seeing his familiar face was a rush of regret and loss. As youngsters the three of them had been close until Will had declared his feelings for her. He had seemed a good choice for a husband. His family were merchants, and he had a head for business and figures. Daniel had been the adventurous one, the one talking about heading west and starting a ranch. Back then thoughts of the unknown seemed reckless and frightening. She'd sought only security and familiarity.

She'd had no idea what was coming. None of them had.

When the two friends had joined the army, she had implied that she would wait for Will. Time and distance had quickly come between them, and through sporadic letters they'd agreed to end their courtship. That's when Leah met and married an academy graduate. At the time a future in the east, living the life of an officer's wife, had seemed safe, protected—glamorous even. However, Charles had turned out to be shallow and self-centered. His assignments had taken them to truly uncivilized parts of the country.

She'd been terrified. In the ensuing years, she'd had plenty of time to regret her choices. She'd come here to make a fresh start, but how could she plan for the future or hold on to a shred of dignity when she had to face both men who'd known her when she'd still had hopes and dreams? That had been a lifetime ago. Everything was different now—everything except the fact that she was still looking for security, but this time for two.

Daniel gave her an awkward nod. "Send for me if you need anything."

"I will." She wanted to bury herself in his strong embrace and seek comfort and safety, but she had no right. They'd once been the best of friends, but now they were estranged friends with years between them. She was going to have to move on as planned.

He exited the boardinghouse, and she felt as though a light had gone out. Turning, she made her way up the stairs.

Aunt Mae had shown Hannah to her room and now opened the door for Leah to enter hers. "It's freshly cleaned and gets morning sun."

"It's perfect, thank you."

Leah was strong and determined. She would find work. She would select a kind and thoughtful husband. Feelings were too complicated, and she couldn't trust them. She was here to rest and take care of herself. Because this baby was going to live. She would take no risks. No more travel. Cowboy Creek was her new home, and she was going to make the best of it.

Daniel entered the Cattleman Hotel and glanced into the restaurant. Will sat at a table with Reverend Taggart, so he joined them. The reverend stood and shook his hand. "That was quite a welcome, Mr. Gardner."

"Call me Daniel, please. And we're honored you and

your daughter chose our town. How is your room at the boardinghouse?"

"It's more than adequate, thank you."

"Will and I want to show you the church. We've been meeting on Sunday mornings, and those willing to take turns have led services. It will be good to have a real preacher. Your house is being finished and should be ready to move in to by the end of the week. Maybe you or Hannah would like to pick out the furniture."

"I'm a simple man, and my daughter won't be staying with me for long once she finds a suitable partner. I don't need much, but if it makes your job easier, I'd be happy to select a few items."

"There's an adequate furniture store at the corner of First and Grant," Daniel said. "Select what you need and put it on my account. Irving will know you're coming."

"That's mighty generous."

"It's our job to take care of the man God has called to our town. We appreciate your willingness to come."

"When we saw the advertisement for brides, Hannah and I felt we should write you. I didn't want to send her off alone, and she was determined to come. It felt right."

"Did you have a church in Chicago?" Daniel queried.

"Indiana, actually. Lafayette."

"Wasn't that where a man set out in an air balloon to try to make it to New York City with mail several years back?" Will's eyes lit with interest.

"Yes, indeed. That was quite an event. Due to weather, the fellow landed in Crawfordsville, however, and the mail was delivered the rest of the way by train."

"Have to give him credit for trying," Daniel added. "Would it work for you if I show you the church and your house tomorrow morning?"

"That sounds good. I'll meet you outside the boardinghouse?" The reverend stood and extended a hand.

Daniel nodded and both he and Will stood to shake his hand. The reverend left the restaurant.

"He seems like a good choice," Will commented.

"He does." A stocky young man poured Daniel coffee and took his order. As soon as he'd walked away, Daniel looked at his childhood friend. "What are we going to do?"

"About what?"

"About Leah, of course. Her lieutenant husband died and she's a widow." He shook his head, still stunned by her arrival. "*Leah's* a widow. Her folks are gone, too. It pains me to think of her being alone and feeling so desperate that she answered our ad."

"All of the women who answered the ad were desperate," Will replied with perfect logic. "We have to figure that much. Most places have very few men of marriageable age left."

"I know. The women all have their reasons. But this is Leah."

Will tilted his head in concession. "You're right. It may not have worked out for the two of us, but she's the closest thing either of us has to family."

And family was the most important, yet rarest commodity these days. "Like you said, it's safe here," Daniel said.

"The streets are not dangerous for a woman," Will agreed.

"But we don't know every last man. You can bet those gals will be buried under invitations to dinners and invited for rides and asked to picnics and all manner of social things. It will probably be confusing to have so many different men as husband prospects."

Will raised his eyebrows. "We can't choose for any of them."

"I know. But maybe we could give Leah our guidance." They sat in silence until Daniel's meal arrived. He picked up his fork. "We need to talk to Noah. I wish he'd come today."

"You knew he wouldn't. He didn't want any part of it. He only comes to town when he has to."

"After I eat, I'm going to see him. Come with me."

Will took a sip of his coffee and grimaced. "Cold. All right. I'll go change and head for the livery."

Will had Daniel's brown-and-white skewbald gelding saddled when he arrived. They headed west. A few miles away from town, they encountered a small herd of buffalo. Interrupted from their grazing, the beasts lumbered away. Daniel and Will sat astride their horses and watched. As they stayed there without moving, several turkeys strutted out of the long grass and pecked at the ground. Daniel patted his horse's neck, then slowly drew his rifle from its scabbard on the back of his saddle, aimed and fired. The horse beneath him didn't flinch. One of the birds flopped on the ground and the others scattered.

Daniel got down to retrieve his kill. "I'll take this to Noah for dinner. Maybe we'll make a night of it."

Will leaned on his saddle horn. "You know he'll get cantankerous when he figures out we're hoping he'll want one of those brides."

"Yep." He used a leather thong to tie the bird to his saddle.

Will tipped his hat back and looked at Daniel. "Maybe he'll take a shine to Leah."

"Maybe." Daniel didn't like the arrow of discomfort that pierced his thoughts and made him turn away to look at the sky. He relived a brief moment of jealousy, remembering the hug Leah had impulsively given Will. His friend had appeared startled and exchanged a glance of confusion with him over her golden head. Daniel prayed he'd either get used to thinking of Leah with someone else or the good Lord would send him his own wife to change his confusing feelings about her.

Before the war Daniel had stood back and watched as Will courted Leah. She had shown his best friend favor. Daniel had never told either of them how he felt about her, but Will had figured it out. Things had been tense at first, and they hadn't talked about it at length, but Daniel had assured Will that if he made Leah happy, so be it.

After the men had joined the army, Will and Leah's separation had made communication difficult, and eventually the two had ended their courtship. Daniel and Will had come to terms with the past a long time ago. Life was too uncertain to hold grudges stemming from circumstances that were out of their control. They'd seen each other through days and nights with little to no rations, dug graves side by side, mourned comrades left where they'd fallen and bolstered each other's grit and determination when death had seemed the easy way out. Leah's arrival might muddy the waters in respect to their plan for brides, but her presence wouldn't come between them. He'd see to that.

They spotted Noah digging a post hole. It appeared

a section of fence had been broken or trampled. "Did buffalo do that?" Will called. "We saw a small herd."

Noah squinted at them from beneath the brim of his hat and leaned on the handle of his shovel until they got close. His hat shaded his face and eyes from the sun, and beneath the brim his collar-length hair was dark with sweat. "What brings you two out here? Wasn't this the big day?"

"It was." Daniel got down and hobbled his horse. Will did the same.

"Everything go as planned?"

"Cowboy Creek has a friendly preacher and four new marriageable women," Will told him.

"That's what you wanted." Noah gripped the shovel and continued digging the hole.

Will went for one of the posts in the back of Noah's wagon and Daniel grabbed a sledgehammer.

"So, it all went well and you came out here to be ranch hands this afternoon?" Noah still had a Virginia drawl. The burn scars on the side of his face stood out white in contrast to the rest of his face, which was red from exertion and the sun. The scars extended down his arm and on his chest, as well, and were the biggest reason he stayed to himself and rarely went into town.

They'd met the southerner when the 155th Pennsylvania Regiment had marched to Washington. Opposed to slavery, Noah had left behind his home and family to fight for his beliefs and joined the army at the Potomac in '62. Only a year later, as they joined the fray at Gettysburg, Noah's gun backfired at the Battle of Little Round Top and ignited a fire that left him badly burned.

His discharge from the army had been all the more difficult for him because Noah had always believed that as a born southerner he had to fight harder than any northerner. His bravery had been an example to all the men who fought with him, but he'd been forced to leave due to his injuries. That's when he'd come to Kansas and staked his claim.

"I shot a turkey for supper," Daniel said. "Thought we'd stay."

"Daylight's burnin'." Noah's reply was terse as always.

Daniel and Will glanced at each other and bent to the task.

Near sundown, the fence repairs were finished and the men headed to Noah's cabin. Noah's black fierce-looking companion, a cross between a dog and a wolf, greeted Noah and watched the other two men dismount. Wolf accompanied Noah to town on the rare occasions he went, and folks were wary of him. Like Noah, Wolf came across more dangerous than he was.

The men washed at the pump in the yard, and Daniel prepared the turkey, splitting it and roasting the meat over a fire pit. Noah brought turnips from his root cellar and Will baked biscuits in a skillet. It was dark by the time they ate under the stars.

"You remember us telling you about Leah Robinson?" Daniel asked.

Noah tossed a turkey leg to Wolf. The dog snatched up the meat and trotted several feet away to eat. "Wasn't that the woman Will was engaged to before the war?"

"That's her. She showed up today on the bride train."

Noah looked at them with a quizzical expression. "I thought she got married."

"Her husband died."

"In the war?"

"I assume so."

"So she's looking to remarry."

"She is, and I'm concerned about her." Daniel removed his hat to rake a hand through his hair and then settled it back on his head. "The three of us grew up together. I don't want her to make a wrong choice. She needs to find the right husband. Someone who will take care of her like she deserves."

"Too bad Will's got himself a fiancée. He could marry her."

Daniel's supper felt like lead in his belly at the thought.

"We were barely more than children when we were engaged. Like it or not, the war changed us all," Will objected. "Besides, Leah isn't cut out to be the wife of a politician. Dora is well aware of my ambitions, and she shares my vision. What about you?"

Noah tossed a bone into the fire and rubbed his hands together. "Don't need a woman. There's nothing wrong with my life the way it is."

"You have a great life out here," Will agreed. "But companionship is a good thing."

"Don't need a companion, and don't ask me again."

"All right, all right," Will said in exasperation. "Don't get your tail feathers all ruffled." He glanced at Daniel. "How about Owen Ewing then? He has a flourishing business. He's a fine cabinetmaker."

Daniel cast him a dark scowl. "He's also the undertaker. That would never do. Not for Leah."

"You're not getting squeamish on us, are you?" Noah asked.

"I wouldn't be the one marrying him. Leah is a lady of refined sensibilities. She can't live in a home where there are bodies in the basement. The other ladies would snub her."

"He might have a point," Will said.

Noah shrugged. "Quincy's a good man. Honest as the day is long. Hardworking. He's only in his thirties. He looks like a man women would take to, doesn't he?"

"A lawman's job is too hazardous," Daniel objected. "He's not salaried, you know. He gets paid by the arrest, so he's motivated to get himself into some tight spots going after criminals. A wife would worry about a man in that position. And, worst case scenario, he might get killed. You never know. She's already lost one husband."

Will and Noah both nodded, and Noah poured them cups of coffee. "This is like the old days, the three of us eating under the sky," he commented.

"Except the food is better and there's more of it," Will said.

They sipped their coffee and discussed a couple more candidates that Daniel rejected for one reason or the other.

The firelight flickered across Noah's scarred cheek as he peered at Daniel. "Seems the best choice for Leah's new husband is you."

Chapter Three

Daniel's last sip went down the wrong way and he choked. He coughed and cleared his throat. "Me? I don't think so."

"Why not? You don't have dead bodies in your basement. You aren't a lawman, so your life isn't at risk. You have an old father to take care of and you don't scratch your neck all the time." Noah listed all the reasons for which Daniel had just rejected the last husbands under consideration. "She knows you. She is fond of you, am I right?"

"She's fond of him," Will supplied. "She tucked her arm right into his and chatted with him all the way to the boardinghouse."

"That doesn't mean she'd want to marry me."

His friends raised their eyebrows at Daniel's ardent objection.

"She doesn't see me like that. Never has."

He'd thought of nothing but that walk to the boardinghouse, about the delicate curve of her cheek and the sweep of her lashes. She was still the prettiest thing he'd ever seen. She'd been wearing her pale hair caught up on her head, but he remembered it curling around her shoulders as a girl. Leah had always been full of life. She'd ridden with them, run alongside the riverbank barefoot, practiced shooting at tin cans and held her own.

Some nights during the war while he'd been sleeping on the ground in the cold and rain, he'd dreamed of seeing the sun glint from her hair as it had that afternoon. He'd heard the sound of her full-throated laughter that turned his insides to warm honey. And then he'd awaken and the present would grasp him in its cold, unforgiving fingers. The notion that she was here in Cowboy Creek now, looking for a man to marry, tied him in knots.

Will tossed the dregs of his coffee into the fire and it hissed. "You're one of the three wealthiest men in Cowboy Creek, probably in all of Kansas."

"I wouldn't want her to marry me for my money."

"You're reasonably handsome. To a woman," Noah added.

Daniel signified his annoyance with a snort.

"You already have a house ready and waiting for a wife," Will said. "Don't try to say you didn't build that house with a woman in mind. You want a wife. She needs a husband. You can help establish her in town."

"That seems so…" Swallowing hard, Daniel sat with elbows on his knees and rubbed his chin. "Calculated. Impersonal."

"Any marriage she makes now will be calculated," Noah pointed out. "And marrying you is more personal than marrying a stranger. You're already friends."

To her they were friends. To him she was the woman who had always been just out of his reach. This idea seemed like a backhanded way of fulfilling his boyish dreams. But the war had changed him. He was no longer the naïve, lovelorn boy he'd once been.

"Who else do you trust with Leah?" Will asked.

Daniel scraped a knuckle on his jaw as he thought. No one. He didn't trust anyone with her welfare…her future. Nor did he *want* her marrying another man. "I'd…" He stopped short and considered. "I'd have to propose to her. Court her." He glanced up and regarded the two men. "Would I have to court her?"

Will grinned.

He would have to swallow his pride to ask her to marry him. And even if he did, there was no guarantee she'd have him. "What if she won't have me?"

"If she won't have you, then *I'll* court her," Noah said. Which told them all how profoundly he believed Leah would marry Daniel. "Let her decide for herself."

He would do it. He would ask Leah to marry him. He would lay out all the reasons why he was the best choice. And then he'd let her decide.

Daniel felt something more than he'd felt for a long time. He didn't want to let himself think of Leah in the big house he'd built on Lincoln Boulevard just yet. He didn't want to picture her in the rooms he'd walked through when the house was a mere shell, before burnished flooring, paint and fixtures had made it a home. He'd always had a faceless woman in mind. As he'd surveyed the land and overseen construction he'd planned that one day he'd share the home with a wife. But Leah's image, with her bright blue eyes and soft pale hair, was all he could envision now. He had his doubts about the wisdom of this decision, but along with his reluctance he felt more than he'd felt in a long time.

He felt hope.

* * *

Leah woke early and ate breakfast in Aunt Mae's dining room with the other brides and the full-time boarders. Gus Russell had stark white hair and still stood straight. The lines at the corners of his wise dark eyes were evidence of his years in the sun. "Cowboy Creek got a windfall when you young gals showed up," he said.

Old Horace wore his long gray hair pulled back with a leather thong. He had been tall in his day and was still lean, but his back was hunched so he was always looking up. "Why if I'd a knowed these fillies would be so purdy, I mighta got a haircut and throwed my hat in the ring."

"Wouldn't any of these young ladies want a dried-up old coot like you," Gus countered.

Old Horace bristled. "I still got my charm. Down in Mexico I was quite a ladies' man."

Gus stabbed a piece of sausage from a platter. "The Mexican War was over twenty years ago and you were an old man then."

"Did you fight for the annexation of Texas?" Hannah asked.

"For two years," Horace replied.

"Mr. Gardner is showing me the church this morning," Reverend Taggart said to his daughter. "I thought you might like to join us."

"If you don't mind, I'm still tired from the trip," she answered. "Is it all right with you if I rest this morning?"

"That's perfectly fine," her father replied. "You rest. I imagine you'll want to check out available locations for your shop when you're up to it."

She gave him an affectionate smile. Hannah was a talented seamstress and made all of her own clothing.

Leah cast her a curious glance. "You're planning a shop?"

Hannah nodded. "I've always wanted to have my own dressmaking establishment. This place seems like the perfect opportunity, with new businesses cropping up everywhere and more women arriving. I might not have many customers at first, but I'm sure business will flourish as the town grows."

Which reminded Leah of her own plans for the morning. She was going to visit the newspaper about an advertisement. "The newspaper office is right next door to us here, isn't it?" she asked.

"I'm heading there right after breakfast," Prudence replied. She wore a plain brown dress, with her ever-present cameo at her throat.

"We might as well walk over together then," Leah suggested.

"Actually I went late yesterday, too," Prudence said. "I got a position."

"My, my, isn't that news?" Aunt Mae exclaimed. "What if you get a husband who lives outside town, dear?"

Prudence glanced at the others around the table. "I will choose one who either lives in town or nearby."

Old Horace squinted at her. "Do you have newspaper experience?"

"D.B.—er, Mr. Burrows has assured me my help is quite welcome."

"Perhaps Mr. Burrows is in the market for a wife," Aunt Mae added with a wry lift of one eyebrow. "Wouldn't that be convenient?"

Prudence pursed her lips in exasperation. "I don't think so."

"Well, I'm significantly impressed you've found a position so quickly," Pippa said. "Perhaps you could employ your curious side and find the latest news on all the residents."

"We got news for ya," Old Horace chimed in.

"*Facts* are what we need," Gus reminded him "That newspaper has a reputation for blowing the truth out of proportion. Why, this town was still a row of clapboard buildings and tents, and *The Herald* was already calling it a boomtown."

"It is a boomtown, you old fool," Old Horace rebutted.

"If you'll excuse me, I'll be going." Prudence set down her napkin and stood.

Leah watched her go. She was the least friendly of all the women who had traveled west together. Leah understood Prudence was widowed, as well, so perhaps she was still grieving and not ready for friendships. Everyone handled grief their own way. "May I help you with the breakfast dishes?" she asked Aunt Mae.

"Goodness, no. You're a paid renter, even if the town is paying your rent for a few weeks. The dishes are my job."

"Thank you. It was a nice meal." Leah took care of a few last-minute things, and then walked next door.

D.B. Burrows was a tall fellow with muttonchop sideburns and pale skin. He was standing at a worktable when she entered. "Morning," he offered.

"Good morning. I'd like to place an ad, please."

"Miss Haywood will get all the information," he told her.

Leah hadn't seen Prudence sitting behind a partition until she stood and reached for paper and ink.

Leah recited what she'd planned for her ad.

"There aren't many women around here yet," D.B. said.

"I understand that," Leah answered. "Hopefully, people will read it and remember me when my midwife services are needed."

D.B. wiped his hands and moved to stand beside Prudence. He stood a little too close in Leah's opinion, but the young widow didn't seem to mind as she showed him what she'd written. "That's good," he praised.

This seemed awfully quick, but maybe theirs would be the first marriage, just as Aunt Mae had suggested. Or Leah was reading more into their new employer and employee relationship than was there. She paid for the ad. "Do I remember seeing the doctor's sign on this street?"

D.B. nodded. "Keep walking the way you came here and on past the jail. Across the street on the corner is Doc Fletcher's place. If he's not in, there's a chalkboard."

"Thank you."

Quincy Davis spotted her as she passed, and he came out to greet her. "Morning, Miss..."

"Mrs. Swann," she supplied.

"Mrs. Swann. I trust Aunt Mae has made you comfortable?"

"Yes, indeed." She glanced across the street and spotted Gus and Horace settling onto chairs in front of a building. The sign above the door read Booker & Son—Purveyor of Dry Goods from Nails to Cloth.

"Is that the mercantile?"

"It's one of 'em. The largest, in fact. Gus and Old Horace loiter there all day, except when they go back to the boardinghouse for lunch. Sometimes if I don't see them, I can hear clanging and I know they're playing horseshoes behind the store. There's a lot between the store and the church."

She continued on her way and found the doctor in his office. He was rail thin and his hair was balding on top, but he still had gray fringe around his ears.

"How do you do?" Leah said. "I'm Mrs. Swann."

"Welcome to Cowboy Creek." He had smile lines in both cheeks and his dark eyebrows were thick. "You're one of the widows? You ladies are the talk of the town, you know."

"Yes, sir. I've come to introduce myself and tell you a little bit about me. I've had midwife experience and I'm hoping to put my knowledge to use."

"I'm sure you'll be quite useful," he replied. "As soon as we have more women and babies on the way. Right now there is only Opal Godwin here in town, but I know of two more women on nearby ranches who might appreciate your services."

"I wanted to make sure I wasn't stepping on your toes before I called on Mrs. Godwin," she said.

"Goodness, no. I'll be happy to be relieved of those duties. I have more than enough to keep me busy with all the rowdy cowboys, snakebites, scrapes and cuts, and the occasional construction accident."

"That's good to hear. Not the part about the snakebites and the accidents, of course. The part about you being relieved to turn over some of your cases." She paused and he studied her. "There is one more thing I need to mention."

The doctor waited.

Leah's nerves fluttered. She hadn't told anyone yet. Saying the words aloud brought back her past losses. "I'm going to have a baby myself."

"I see." He nodded. "Best you find yourself a husband soon then."

"Yes," she agreed. "But I'm concerned for my baby."

"Of course you are."

"No. What I mean is, I've lost two babies before it was time for them to be born."

"I'm real sorry to hear that, ma'am. Would you like me to check your health now?" he asked. "How did you fare on your trip?"

He did a routine exam, asking questions about the circumstances leading to previous issues and finding her healthy. "I see nothing that would warn us of a problem," he said.

"This time feels different," she said. "I don't know how to explain it, except I don't feel the same way I did the other times."

"I trust your intuition, but I caution you to get plenty of rest and not overtax your body."

"That's my plan," she assured him. "I don't want anything to happen this time."

"I think you should come see me every few weeks," he suggested. "We'll keep a close watch."

"Thank you, Doctor Fletcher."

"Now head back to your room and rest." He grinned. "Doctor's orders."

Leah said a silent prayer of thanks. This time was going to be different. This time she would have a child to hold in her arms and love. Her heart ached with the joy of gain and the sorrow of loss. One crucial component remained—the reason she'd come to Cowboy Creek. She still had to find a father for this baby— a husband.

Chapter Four

Daniel and Will had spent the night at Noah's and lit out at first light. Daniel gathered clothing and headed for the bathhouse, then around the corner to the barber for a shave. He met Will and Reverend Taggart outside the boardinghouse and couldn't resist glancing up at the room where Aunt Mae had mentioned Leah was staying. He'd lain awake most of the night, and it hadn't been the other men's snores that had disturbed his sleep. It had been thoughts of Leah and how she would react to what he was going to ask this morning.

The reverend was appreciative of the white frame church building on Second Street, with its steeple and fresh paint. The interior smelled of new wood and plaster. The council had voted for and commissioned twelve stained glass windows that lined the east and west walls, six on each side. The morning light streamed through those windows and reflected colorful rainbows on the polished wood pews and floor.

Reverend Taggart walked up the middle aisle in devout silence, examining every beam and board of the interior as he slowly reached the front. His steel-gray eyes were moist when he turned to face the other men. "God is so good and merciful. This is more than I ever expected. I know our Creator can use this building, and I pray He can use me to minister to the people of this community. I wish my wife could have been here to see this."

"When did you lose her?" Will asked.

"Five years ago. It's been only Hannah and me since then."

"Let's go have a look at your house," Daniel suggested.

Virgil Taggart nodded. "I can't wait to come back here."

Daniel dropped two keys into his hand. "It's yours and God's."

The parsonage had a front porch and a yard large enough for a garden. Daniel settled his hat back on his head. "There are three bedrooms, a kitchen and small dining room. The workers are finishing up the plaster and paint this week. They're digging a root cellar. You'll share a well with the church. For now we've planned for your meals at the hotel, but I hope to hire a cook and housekeeper for you."

"I'm a simple man, Mr. Gardner. Hannah and I have been on our own for some time. Once she's married I can look after myself."

"You can, but your time is better spent looking after the people," Will said.

"You should be able to move in at the end of the week," Daniel explained. "Monday at the latest."

"That will be fine. The boardinghouse is perfectly comfortable until then."

They parted in front of the parsonage, and Daniel

headed up Eden Street toward Aunt Mae's. Removing his hat, he held it against the front of his coat. He took a deep breath and rang the bell. Pippa answered the door.

"Mr. Gardner! It's so nice to see you." She wore another fancy dress, this one in green with puffy sleeves at the shoulders. Beads at her throat and dangling earrings glistened in the sunlight that filtered through the window on the landing above. "Aunt Mae is making a pot of tea. Would you like to join us?"

"Thank you, but I've come to see Mrs. Swann."

"Oh, of course. She's upstairs. I'll run up and get her for you."

A few minutes later, Pippa descended the stairs. "She'll be right down."

He waited impatiently, pacing the foyer. Each time he came up to the framed mirror, he looked at his intense reflection and reminded himself to relax his features and smile. It wouldn't do to scare the poor woman away.

A stair squeaked. "Daniel."

He glanced toward the landing. The light caressed her hair through the panes of glass and turned it to spun sunshine. She wore a white dress with sprigs of tiny blue flowers and light blue trim. Ivory lace stood up around her throat. Blue fabric buttons on the jacket matched another row of buttons on a flounce that covered the hoop skirt. She reminded him of a fresh floral breeze on a spring day.

"This is a nice surprise," she said with a soft smile. "I thought you'd be busy working."

"There's something I want to show you."

"Oh. Well, all right."

"We won't be long. You won't need anything. Are you up for a short walk?"

"Yes, of course. That sounds nice. How far?" She came down the rest of the steps and he held open the front door for her.

"Only a block to the east."

"I'm intrigued."

Leah was delighted to see her friend. He offered his arm and she tucked her hand into the crook of his elbow. Daniel looked dashing in his gray jacket and black tie. His polished black boots sounded on the boardwalk that ran in front of the businesses on Eden Street, around the corner and down two steps. The side street had only a dirt path for walking, and she was thankful it wasn't muddy.

Across the street was a saddle shop. A minute later, the sound of a hammer ringing drew her attention. A square building was under construction on the street behind the boardinghouse.

"That will be the schoolhouse soon," Daniel told her.

They reached the corner of the block, and across the street from them on the opposite corner sat a large gray three-story house, trimmed in white, with arches above the windows, two chimneys and trees no taller than the first floor planted at intervals in the yard. "What a beautiful home."

"It's Second Empire architecture," he said. "And the porch is colonial, but together it has a Victorian look without being frilly, don't you think?"

She nodded. "I guess so. I don't know much about architecture."

"I saw this style used in Boston, so I studied it. The style evolved from seventeenth-century Renaissance buildings. The house has eleven rooms."

He led her across the street and toward the house.

"Do you know the people who live here?" she asked.

His gaze moved from the house to her face. "I live here."

"It's *your* house?" She stared up at the stories above as they approached.

He used a key in the lock and opened the front door. "Please come in."

Leah stepped into the enormous foyer and studied the ceiling with plaster-designed leaves and scrolls, and a sparkling chandelier. Their heels echoed on the shiny wood floor. Only one small table and an umbrella stand occupied the space. He led her through a wide doorway into a parlor with crown molding, wood embellishments, built-in window seats and a beautiful blue-and-white-tiled fireplace. Curtains had been hung at the windows, but the room was bare of furniture.

He showed her each room, pointing out special features. She sensed his assessing gaze on her several times, but when she looked up at him, he went on with the tour. Only one room was completely furnished, but he showed her his bedroom from the doorway.

"And that's it," he said.

"It's lovely," she told him honestly. "It's even nicer than any of our homes back in Pennsylvania. You paid attention to every detail." And it was his attention to detail that revealed his intent. She pictured him returning from war, joining Will to create a town, and taking on this project that held so much hope and meaning. He'd chosen everything so carefully and overseen the construction. He intended to share this home with a wife. Raise a family here. Perhaps he had his eye on one of the brides with whom she'd traveled. It was entirely possible his intended wife would arrive on the next bride train.

"I did," he agreed in the deep, smooth voice she remembered well. "I wanted to get it just right."

She opened the front door and walked to the end of the porch. "There's plenty of room for gardens. And the trees will shade the porch. You've planned everything."

"Almost everything."

She looked up at him.

"Leah."

Their gazes remained locked.

"Let's sit on the steps for a few minutes." He took one hand while she used her other to smooth her skirt under herself and sit. "I'm sure you recognize that I built this house for a family."

She nodded. "I can see that."

"Nothing is as it used to be. The war changed this country. It changed its people. There is opportunity for so much here in the North. Industry is flourishing because of that wretched war. A lot of people are getting wealthy. The railroad changed this land, too. And the cattle are making Cowboy Creek rich."

He raised his chin a notch. "Riches sure aren't everything, and we all know that. But they're a way to be comfortable now, to make a good life. We can have good lives here."

"New lives," she said. "That's why I came. I need a new start. There's something I need to tell you, Daniel."

"Before you say anything, Leah, I'd like to speak. I have been thinking a lot about the future."

"All right." She already knew, of course, that he was making plans for a wife and children. His ambition and planning were remarkable, actually. Leah had always known him as the one who suggested fishing spots, foot races and expeditions into the woods. She fondly recalled the two of them sharing evenings around a roaring campfire, telling tall tales, laughing. Always laughing. She wouldn't have pictured him here in this town, intent on building a community and securing a family. If she'd imagined what he'd be doing, she would have pictured him settling down on the ranch he always talked about.

But he was right. Nothing was as it used to be. And Daniel was a grown man now. A man who'd experienced things she couldn't imagine. Stability and security probably sounded pretty good to him, too.

"I would be a good husband. You already know what kind of man I am. I can provide for you. I can give you this home. And a family. We could raise children here. I own the stockyards and a lot of the property and even homes. I'm building more all the time."

He'd be a good husband and provide for her? They could raise children, he'd said. His words penetrated her reminiscent musings and registered with more than a little surprise. She purposely kept the astonishment from her expression, but rested a palm on her chest, where her heart had skipped a beat.

"I've hired workers to build the houses," he continued. "And I'm selling them to the arriving families. Besides having a respected position in the community, I'm rather well off. You can have your fresh start and never have to worry about anything again."

All that information about the property and obvious money would have mattered more before. It still mattered, of course, because he was talking about securing her future. He was looking right at her, in that intense way he had when he felt strongly about something, his green eyes bright. But the words that rang in her head were those that offered her heart's desire. A new start with nothing to worry over.

She'd hoped for a decent man to ask for her hand in marriage. She'd prayed for someone kind and God-fearing. She'd asked the Almighty for His protection for her child and a husband she could tolerate.

She had nothing to fear from Daniel Gardner. He was gentle and kind—a man of his word, a man of integrity. He wanted to marry *her* and have children together. Her mouth was dry.

She stood and moved down to the stone path, where she turned and looked back up at him sitting on the top stair. "Daniel Gardner, you're asking me to marry you."

"I'm asking if you will allow me to court you."

Raising a trembling hand to her forehead, she shaded her eyes from the sun and gazed down the street at the schoolhouse that would soon hold children. Their cheerful voices would be audible from this porch, perhaps their singing would even reach the kitchen window. The imagery stole away her breath and pierced her heart with want and loss.

Daniel had a dream. He'd survived the horrors of war and traveled to this place with hopes. He wanted children of his own. He deserved a selfless young wife who would love him as he deserved.

An ache grew in her chest, an ache like a gnawing hunger. She felt as though she'd lost something perfect and beautiful. An ache so big and ugly she couldn't bear it spread to her belly. She didn't want him to change his mind, but once he knew the truth, she didn't want him to marry her out of duty or obligation—and most of all not out of pity.

"Daniel, I'm going to have a baby."

His bright green gaze immediately flickered over her dress and back to her face. A line creased his forehead. "Now?"

"Not this moment," she said in a wobbly voice. "In a few months. I'm carrying a child. My husband's child."

He appeared to turn that information over in his mind before speaking. "He didn't die in the war?"

"No. He died five months ago."

Daniel straightened and came down the stairs. Standing beside her he seemed taller and broader. The faint scents of cedar and starch touched her nostrils. She looked up into his face, rethinking her image of him, rethinking her options. Either her options had just become a whole lot more appealing, or her losses had become even greater—if he didn't want her baby.

Nerves fluttered in Leah's chest. Her mouth was dry.

"Your suffering's the same no matter how or when he died, Leah. I'm sorry you lost your husband."

You have no idea. I don't want you to know. "Thank you, Daniel."

"I understand the hurt is fresh." His tender, caring tone brought tears to her eyes. "And I know you're doing what you must do in order to move on and make a life for yourself. For your child."

She blinked and looked over his shoulder at the long narrow double windows reflecting the sky.

"I'll take care of you and the baby. I'll raise him like my own. He'll never want for anything."

Oh. There it was. The promise of a good man. An earnest and kind man. The one requirement from which she couldn't be budged. Tears burned behind her eyes. "I believe you," she managed. "You're a man of your word. A devoted man. You have ambition and foresight. And you're good-hearted." She reached for his sleeve and rested her hand on his arm. "Most importantly, you're *kind*."

His hesitation was barely perceptible. "Will you marry me?"

She looked up into his piercing green eyes and searched for sincerity. He wouldn't be human if he didn't share her uncertainty. He masked his tension well, but she knew him better. This wasn't a choice to make lightly. But marriage was a practical decision. Like he'd said, they weren't strangers. They already knew they had things in common and would be compatible. If she said no, she couldn't know who would ask her next. Obviously there were plenty of options, with all the single men vying for a wife, but she would never do any better than Daniel.

She'd married Charles, believing he would provide a home and security. Daniel's beautiful home and standing in the community would have meant everything to her at one time. Now the house was superfluous, like pink sugar sprinkles on iced tea cakes. She wanted the provision he promised for her child. She needed to feel safe. But she was hungry for kindness.

She'd lost her faith in mankind, but she still believed God loved her and was watching out for her. Why else would Daniel Gardner want to marry her?

"This marriage would be a practical partnership," she said at last. "I can promise to be a good wife. You have a standing in town, and I would make every attempt to uphold that and make you proud."

He raised his chin and gave a conciliatory nod. "Of course."

"I may not be able to assume a lot of household duties right away," she told him. "If that's a problem I understand. I must be honest with you."

"Of course," he said again.

Her stomach dipped as she formed her next words. "This isn't the first time I've carried a child."

He lowered his eyebrows in question. "No?"

"I lost two babies before. I am going to be very careful and get a lot of rest so I can bring this child safely into the world. I won't take any risks."

"Of course, Leah. Of course you must take every precaution. I'll take care of everything. I'll make sure you have help with the house, and later with the baby."

She took a shaky breath. "This is almost too good to be true."

He took her hands in his. His fingers were large and warm, and she felt undeniably safe in that moment. "We can't lose hope, Leah. We've lived through difficult times—the worst of times. We've lost so much. But there's still good in the world. God's still on His throne, watching over us, guiding us, loving us. He knows our hurt and our hearts."

"I believe that, too, Daniel. Otherwise, how would I have ended up here at this time? Seeing you and Will yesterday was like finding family I'd lost."

He nodded in understanding. "Say yes."

This was the sensible thing to do. She hadn't expected this opportunity and she'd be a fool not to seize it. "Yes."

Chapter Five

They'd decided to tell people quickly, so everyone would know Leah was no longer an eligible bride. There was a welcome function planned for after church on Sunday, so they decided to make their announcement then. Daniel had barely had time to register the monumental life change he faced and talk to Reverend Taggart about a ceremony when a commotion snagged his attention the next morning.

Through his office windows on Eden Street, he caught sight of half a dozen men riding past. He got up and went to the door.

A rider reined a horse to a stop in front of his building and jumped to the ground. He tossed the reins over a post and stepped onto the boardwalk. His clothing, face and hair were coated with dust. "You Mr. Gardner?"

"That's me."

"Theo Pierce's outfit is about four miles out," the fellow said. "Herd should reach the valley within the hour and we'll camp there overnight. Mr. Pierce sent me ahead to tell you we'll be heading for the yards at first light tomorrow."

It was the first drive of the season and cause for celebration. "This is good news," Daniel said. "I'll buy you breakfast and ride back with you to look over your cows."

Daniel got his horse from the livery, they had a quick meal at the Cowboy Café and then headed out.

"Looks like a fine, healthy herd," he told Theo Pierce. The two men sat atop their mounts assessing the longhorns.

"We started out with two thousand head," Theo replied. "Lost a dozen in the Red River, a couple to snakebite and let the Kiowa and Comanche have a few to keep them off our trail."

"We'll do a count as we lead 'em through the chutes tomorrow," Daniel said. "You didn't lose many. Sounds like a good trip."

"Not complainin'."

"Remind your men about the no-gun law before they go into town tomorrow. They can check their weapons with Sheriff Davis. Another laundry opened on Fourth Street, besides the one across from the tracks. Bathhouse on Second, and three places to eat along Eden now. The townspeople will be happy to see them."

A rider joined them, a young fellow wearing a fringed buffalo-hide vest. "A calf ran off yonder. Dutch is after 'im. His mama's cryin'. Other than that, they're pretty calm."

"Keep an eye on his mama 'til Dutch brings 'im back," Theo said.

The rider acknowledged the order by turning his horse abruptly and heading back to the herd. The state of Texas had been quilled in Indian beadwork on the back of his vest.

"That's James Johnson. He's my point man," Theo explained to Daniel. Being point man required experience. He determined course and set the pace for the drive, keeping the lead steers headed the right direction.

"I've heard that name. Thought he usually rode with Stone's outfit."

"Not this time."

"I'll book a room for you at the hotel. Plan to join me and my partners for dinner tomorrow evening," Daniel said. "Tell James he's invited, too."

"That's mighty generous."

"We appreciate you bringing your herd to Cowboy Creek. Spread the word that we treat you well and pay top dollar."

"We'll see how the sale goes tomorrow," Theo answered.

Daniel agreed with a nod and rode back to town. He hadn't made it to the livery when Sheriff Davis caught up to him on horseback. "Daniel! Don't put your horse up yet."

Daniel reined in beside him in front of the Fourth Street laundry. "What do you need?"

"There's something you have to see."

He accompanied Quincy down Lincoln Boulevard, past his own house, south a few blocks, and rode across the tracks to a row of railcars that awaited unloading. Quincy pointed to an empty flatbed car. "That one was stacked with your lumber."

Daniel glanced at it. "I had a crew deliver it to a building site to the west today."

Quincy shook his head. "'Fraid not. When they got here the lumber was gone."

"There's a night guard. What does he say?"

"They found him tied up in one of the other cars. Said someone got the jump on him last night and he doesn't remember anything."

Daniel frowned. "Someone stole the lumber?"

"Looks that way."

Daniel's first reaction was more confusion than anger, but the more he thought about it the more irate he got.

"Were those supplies for one of your houses?" Quincy asked.

"No, that was town property. Lumber for section twenty to the west." They hadn't even named the new street yet. The council planned to do that at the next meeting.

"I sent out a couple of deputies and I'll be searching, as well. I found tracks leading away from town, but they were covered by others and I lost 'em. We'll figure it out and hopefully catch the thieves."

Daniel nodded. "I'll take a look, too. Which way did the tracks head?"

"East."

"Thanks, Quincy." At the livery he gave his horse feed and water, then rode from the rail station east, following the tracks Quincy had discovered and losing them, but picking them up again a couple miles farther away.

He'd gone half a mile farther when the smell of smoke touched his nostrils and he scanned the sky, spotting a thin thread of black twisting into the horizon. He headed toward it and met two riders coming his way. As they neared, he recognized Timothy Watson and Buck Hanley, two of Quincy's part-time deputies.

Timothy wore his hat tipped back on his head. "Found your lumber, Mr. Gardner!"

"Somebody hauled it out here and lit fire to it," Buck supplied.

Daniel absorbed that grim news. "We'd better stay and watch it," he said. "Last thing we need is a prairie fire. This is a pretty stupid thing to do."

Buck's somber expression showed concern, as well. "Surprised a spark hasn't caught the grass afire yet."

"Got anything we can scoop dirt with?" Daniel asked.

"I got a tin pan in my saddlebag," Timothy offered.

"I have one, too," Buck said.

"I have a knife," Daniel informed them. "I'll loosen dirt and you toss it on the fire."

A couple of hours later, only a few embers still glowed. Even though it was spring, the three men were hot and dirty under the Kansas sun. Daniel yanked out the questionable boards and kicked dirt on them. They stayed until there was no threat of the fire spreading.

"I appreciate you both sticking around to see this through," Daniel told them in a solemn voice.

"We have a stake in Cowboy Creek, too," Buck said. "I'm doin' the deputy job and working for Owen Ewing so I can save up and start my own business."

"What do you want to do?" Daniel asked Timothy.

"I put a deposit down on a building. I've been watching to see who comes along to see if I can find a partner. Not sure, but my options are open."

"Let me know if I can help you when you decide on something," Daniel said.

"Will do."

The three of them mounted their horses and headed back to town. Uneasiness settled over Daniel and didn't let loose. Someone had stolen that wood and destroyed it, not caring who or what was hurt in the process. A prairie fire could spread for miles, decimating everything in its path—wildlife, crops, farms. The motive for such an act escaped him.

He'd talk to the town council about immediately hiring another guard for the station and railroad yards. It was better to take preventative measures than be sorry later. Daniel didn't intend to let anyone undermine what they were working so hard to build. There was too much at stake.

Leah joined the other young women on their walk to church. It was a beautiful morning, warm and filled with sunshine. The perfect day for a joyful announcement. She wished she felt more jubilant than cautiously relieved. Her future wasn't as uncertain as it had been a week ago, but apprehension still wound its cold claws into her conscience. Daniel Gardner had always been a close friend, but when it came to pondering a husband she'd never so much as considered him. Maybe she'd been too close to him and had foolishly overlooked what was right in front of her. Now that the war had cut her world into pieces like a jigsaw puzzle and she had to fit it back together again, he was the best option she had.

She felt guilty for thinking that way, as though he hadn't been a choice back then, but now he was good enough. But it wasn't that way at all, and she sure didn't want him to have the impression he was her last resort. He would make any woman a good husband, and she was truly blessed that he'd asked her to be his wife.

When they reached the new church building, Aunt Mae stood outside the door with Reverend Taggart and a dark-haired young woman who, by the size of her swollen belly, could only be Opal Godwin. Aunt Mae smiled from ear to ear. She wore a lavender-and-cream-striped dress with ruffles on the cuffs and hems of the jacket, skirt and overskirt. Lace at the neck cut into her abundant chins, and the matching buttons down the jacket front looked as though they might pop at any moment.

Opal, who was painfully thin by contrast, wore a loose dress with white lace-trimmed bodice and sleeves and a gray pinstriped skirt with black trim. Pleats draped the round protrusion of the child she carried. The colors washed out her already-tired complexion.

"You're all here!" Aunt Mae beamed. "I left early to help set up for the celebration after the service, so I didn't get to see your lovely dresses. I hope your breakfast was adequate."

"It was tasty and satisfying," Hannah replied.

"Welcome," Reverend Taggart greeted them. "Darling." He kissed Hannah's cheek.

"Opal has been looking forward to meeting you," Aunt Mae said, addressing Leah.

"And I her." Leah took the hand Opal extended and placed her other hand over the back. "I hope to be able to call on you this week, Mrs. Godwin. I'm a midwife."

"I've heard all about you, and I'm relieved to know you're here. But, please you must call me Opal." She kept her voice cheerful, but her brown eyes and the dark smudges beneath them belied her weariness.

"Your husband is a boot maker."

Opal nodded. "An extremely talented one."

"And you help him?"

"I've always helped him in the shop, but he won't let

me now, so I've been staying in our upstairs quarters sewing and doing a lot of reading."

"Your husband is looking out for your welfare and that of your child. Rest is good." She leaned forward so Opal was the only one to hear her. "I expect to be doing a lot of that myself in the months to come."

Opal raised her eyebrows in question.

"I'm expecting a child, as well. I answered the advertisement to find a husband because mine died only a few months ago and I have no family left."

Opal hadn't released Leah's hand, and she squeezed her fingers gently. "I'm sorry for your loss, Mrs. Swann. You must have been frightened and felt very alone."

A flutter of the old heartache caught in Leah's chest, and she fought it down. Opal's understanding left her feeling vulnerable. "Yes. Finding Daniel and Will here was like having family again."

"I'm glad you found your way to us."

"So am I. Thank you. And please call me Leah. How is your appetite?"

"I'm never very hungry."

"We'll have to do something about that. Your baby needs sustenance and so do you. This is an important job you have, nourishing this baby."

"Everything seems to make me feel sick," Opal admitted.

"We'll see what we can do." Leah flashed a reassuring smile. "Don't you worry, all right?"

Menfolk climbed the wooden stairs behind them, so the women entered the church. Morning sun streamed through the stained glass windows that lined the side walls, creating arcs of color across the plain-hewn pews, polished floorboards, as well as heads and shoulders of those already seated. The color and warmth lent a surreal tone to the already reverent atmosphere inside the building.

"Isn't this the most inspiring sight we've seen yet?" Pippa said from behind Leah's shoulder. "All the colors of God's rainbow right here for us to enjoy on Sunday morning. This little church couldn't be any more beautiful."

"It is beautiful," Leah agreed with a soft smile for her energetic friend.

"Who do you suppose will be the first to marry here?" Pippa asked.

Leah didn't reply, but a flutter in her chest stole her breath for a moment. It would be her. She would be marrying Daniel in this very place. *Soon.*

"There haven't been this many men in the service since the church was built," Aunt Mae said in a loud whisper. "Seems like they've all turned out to get a gander at the brides."

Hannah surveyed the crowd of men, her expression uneasy. When she looked at Leah, her gray eyes revealed what Leah imagined was fear or uncertainty. Her hair was pulled away from her face as always, leaving her expression visible. It wasn't easy to travel to an unknown place with one's future up in the air. The mail-order brides were here because they had no other choice but to take this chance.

Leah reached for Hannah's hand. "Come sit beside me. Unless you have to play the piano?"

Again something flickered in the tall girl's eyes. "No, I'm not very good at reading music. Thank you."

They noticed Will Canfield motioning and found he'd held a row for them.

After everyone had been seated and Reverend Taggart moved to stand at an oak pulpit at the front, he looked around and visibly composed himself. "Good morning."

"Good morning," the congregation greeted in unison.

"I'm Reverend Virgil Taggart. I am fortunate to have been invited to your town, along with my beautiful daughter, Hannah, and the other three brides you sent for."

An irreverent whoop filled the building, followed by claps and whistles, to which the reverend good-naturedly grinned and nodded.

Finally he raised a hand for silence. "I know. I know you're pleased. It's exciting to be here, too. I want to assure you I'm grateful for this position. I don't take it lightly, and I am looking forward to knowing each of you as my family." He released a breath, then went on. "Your gracious town has provided me with a home and ample help, so my burden will be easy. I'm going to do my best to be a friend and counselor to all who come to me. I put my trust and confidence in God to come here. He's going to show me what He has planned next, and I'm excited about it."

He reached under the podium and opened a book. "Richard Mosely has graciously offered to play the organ. Thank you, Richard. Turn with me, if you will, to page sixteen in your brand spankin' new hymnals."

Clothing and pages rustled as churchgoers reached for their hymnals and opened them.

Bless Richard's heart, he hit a couple of sharp notes before he settled into the measures of the first song. Around Leah a chorus of men's voices rose and sent a chill down her spine. She and Hannah exchanged a glance of surprise and appreciation.

"A mighty fortress is our God, a bulwark never failing.
Our helper He, amid the flood of mortal ills prevailing."

She'd never heard so many men singing at once, and their enthusiasm was overwhelming. Tears formed in her eyes, preventing her from seeing the page. But she knew the words to the ancient song by heart, so she continued.

"…on earth is not his equal.
Did we in our own strength confide, our striving would be losing.
Were not the right Man on our side, the Man of God's own choosing.
Dost ask who that may be?
Christ Jesus, it is He…"

Leah sensed something beyond the power of the moving words and let her gaze wander across the sea of men standing on the other side of the aisle. There she found Daniel looking back at her as he sang, a secret smile on his face. He looked handsome in his Sunday finery, his shoulders broad in the gray coat. A new sense of joy rose up and overwhelmed her. She'd made the right choice by coming here. She was going to be fine and her baby would be well taken care of—and loved, she prayed. She couldn't ask for more than this new beginning. After the service ended, Will walked to the front with a barely discernible limp. "Ladies and gentlemen. Please stay and join us on the lawn for refreshments and to meet the newest residents of Cowboy Creek. But bear with me for just a moment before we move outdoors. Mrs. Swann, will you come forward, please?" He extended his arm in her direction.

Daniel stood and joined him. He and Will changed positions, and Daniel watched her approach with a determined smile.

Leah's heart pounded. She'd known this was the day he planned to make the announcement, but she hadn't known where or how. Her fingers trembled on her skirt as she raised the hem away from her feet and edged her way to the end of the pew and into the aisle. She looked forward, and the kindness in Daniel's expression allayed her qualms as she reached him. He took her hand and tucked it familiarly into the crook of his arm, where the rough fabric was warm. He smelled good, like cedar and saving soap.

"This will come as a disappointment to many of you, but I do hope you will rejoice with us. Mrs. Swann and I knew each other years ago. We grew up together in Pennsylvania." He glanced at his friend, standing to the side. "Along with Will, we were close. We'd lost touch for a long while, so it was a surprise to see her on the platform the day the train arrived."

Leah observed the faces of the townsfolk as well as those of her fellow travelers. All were smiling.

"I've asked Mrs. Swann to be my wife, and she has agreed. We are officially engaged."

Silence hummed for a minute, and then a dozen groans attested to the expected disappointment that one bride prospect had been removed from the already inadequate list.

"I know, I know," Daniel said, commiserating.

And then applause broke out, softly at first, but quickly gaining enthusiasm. Shouts and whistles accompanied the outpouring of congratulations.

Leah looked toward Daniel, and when he smiled gallantly down at her, she sighed with relief. He gave her a quick hug and declared, "Now let's go eat!"

Chapter Six

Leah had already told her fellow traveling companions about her engagement, and they'd been happy for her. One by one they formally congratulated her.

Daniel took her hand. "There's someone I want you to meet."

He led her across the grass to where a muscular-looking fellow dressed in clean trousers and a plain shirt stood a distance from the gathering. He had blond hair, and when he turned wary blue eyes her way, she noted scars on his cheek.

"Leah, this is my good friend Noah Burgess. He's a farmer and rancher. He and Will and I joined up in '62." He glanced at his friend. "Noah, this is Leah Swann. She used to be Leah Robinson. Will and I have known her since we were children."

Noah nodded. "Mrs. Swann. My companions speak highly of you."

She extended her gloved hand, and he touched it briefly before releasing her fingers. "Daniel says he and Will came here to see you after the war and decided to stay. You founded Cowboy Creek."

"Well, I was here, buying horses and planting crops. Once they'd come and bought even more land, the railroad scouted the area." His smooth southern accent defined his heritage. "They thought it would be a good idea to sell and invest and build. So we did. And that's how Cowboy Creek got on the map."

"I will be happy to introduce you to my friends," Leah offered. "I might be able to secure you a private conversation with one of the ladies and give you an edge above the others."

"No," he said brusquely. "I have to get back and do chores." With that, he settled his hat on his head and turned away, heading toward the lot where horses and buggies were waiting.

Leah cast Will a nervous glance. "I guess I said the wrong thing."

"Don't fret yourself. He's not a social person."

"Or he doesn't much like me. What does he know about me exactly?"

"It's not you, Leah," Daniel reassured her. "In fact, Noah's the one who encouraged me to ask you to marry me."

"He did?"

"Yes, he did. He rarely comes to town. We pressured him to be here this morning."

"How did he get those scars? Is he self-conscious?"

"His gun backfired in a battle," he answered in a low tone. "The burns were down his chest and arm, too. I think the scars still pain him, but he won't talk about it. He was an exceptional soldier and was discharged because of his injuries."

"And a southerner, obviously."

"So he thought he had to fight harder than anyone else," Daniel said with a nod.

"He's fortunate to have you as his friend."

"The three of us got used to looking out for each other."

"I hope I will have friends like you do."

He took her hand and touched her cheek with his fingertips. "You will." His green eyes showed sincere kindness. "Until then, you have me."

His thoughtfulness blessed her. The sun glinted off his thick chestnut hair. "You make me want to be a better person, Daniel."

"You're perfect just the way you are."

She smiled. "I will let you think that."

He tucked her hand in his and they joined the gathering.

Pippa, dressed in a striking jade green dress with crisscrossing layers of ruffles across the voluminous skirt and decorative buttons from shoulder to cuff on each sleeve, was the center of attention. The color set off her vibrant ginger-gold hair and hazel eyes. Every male's attention was riveted on the petite beauty's dazzling smile.

"Leah, have you heard? There's an opera house under construction! The gentlemen were just telling me of it. Why, we can hold plays and concerts and enjoy the arts just like back east." She looked to Daniel for confirmation. "When do you expect it will be finished, Mr. Gardner?"

Daniel's gaze darted to Will and back to Pippa. "I'm afraid construction is temporarily delayed. The load of lumber designated for the opera house has been reassigned to another project with a pressing deadline. The council decided the houses take priority over the opera house. But only until a new order can be supplied."

"Some of you might have heard about a shipment being stolen from the rail yard," Quincy Davis supplied. "The lumber for the west side houses was hauled out of town and burned. The load that arrives tomorrow will need to replace that for now."

"But we've put in an order for more to replace the lumber for the opera house," Daniel assured Pippa and the bystanders.

Amos Godwin furrowed his brow. "Do you have any idea who would do something like that?"

"We don't," Daniel answered honestly. "And it's worrisome. But we've hired additional guards for the rail yard, so it won't happen again."

"On a positive note," Will interjected, "the first drive of the year is in the holding pens and will be shipping out this week."

"You didn't have t' tell us that," Old Horace said with a cackle. "We've smelled the money since yesterday!"

The crowd shared a laugh.

A while later, after they'd visited with other church-goers, accepted congratulations and eaten lunch, Daniel suggested they slip away to make plans.

Even though they'd eaten, he escorted her to the hotel restaurant for tea.

D.B. Burrows spotted them and stood beside their table. "I didn't have a chance to congratulate you. When will the nuptials be?"

"We're here to talk about that," Daniel answered.

"I plan to do a piece on your engagement in *The Herald*. Since you're the first and your decision was so hasty, it will be of interest."

Leah didn't care for his word choice. "We've known each other for a long time. It's not as though we're strangers."

"It seems Mr. Gardner had an advantage over the other men in town. You were acquainted before the war?"

"Our families were close..." she replied.

"So your parents were friendly, as well. But you were previously married to another?"

"D.B., I'll come place our wedding announcement in the paper," Daniel said in a clipped tone. "Until then, I ask you to respect our privacy."

The black-haired man pursed his lips and straightened. "Do enjoy your afternoon."

Leah watched him go. When she turned her gaze back to Daniel, he was studying her. "Why do I get the feeling he's not as interested in our engagement as in our past history?"

"Probably what makes him good at his job," Daniel answered grudgingly. "Doesn't win him any friends, though."

"What's *his* story?"

"He's mentioned he's originally from Missouri. He and his brother came to Kansas and ran a paper in a town called Harper. The town did pretty well until the Union Pacific chose Cowboy Creek for the terminus. After that the town folded. I heard D.B.'s brother died, so D.B. came here to start up a new paper."

"He's part of the town council?"

"He is. Do you have any ideas about how and when we marry? People will know you were already expecting before long, so we should probably do it as quickly as possible."

"You're right. It won't be a secret. But we don't want secrets, do we?"

He shook his head. "Not at all. Reverend Taggart will accommodate any date we choose. You do want to get married in the church?"

"Yes, of course."

"And a reception? I'll speak with Mr. Rumsford, who runs this hotel. Perhaps we can hold the reception in the ballroom. It's only a room with nice flooring and a few chandeliers. Nothing extravagant, mind you, but—"

"It doesn't have to be fancy."

"We will be celebrating," he pointed out. "And as the first couple married in Cowboy Creek and the first wedding resulting from the bride train, it will be a festive occasion. Everyone will turn out."

She absorbed the idea. "Would it be outrageous to plan the reception outdoors, but have the hotel reserved in case of rain? I'd like to keep it as simple as possible."

"I am agreeable to anything that makes you comfortable," he said with a nod.

"I think I'd be more comfortable if it's less formal."

They discussed a few more details. "Would you like to order a dress?" Daniel asked.

"Hannah is an excellent seamstress and has brought trunks of fabrics, lace and trims in hopes of operating her own shop. If I help her, I believe we can make a suitable dress in time."

"Don't spare expense and assure her she will earn more than a fare wage for her efforts."

Daniel drummed his fingers on the tabletop, uncertain how to politely discuss the other details. "And afterward you will move from the boardinghouse to my home—*our* home."

She nodded, but the way she swallowed and drew a fortifying breath indicated her trepidation at the thought of sharing a home. "Of course."

He opened his jacket, took a key from an inner pocket and slid it across the white linen surface. "Please visit as often as you like. Assess whatever furniture and items are needed. I'll help if you want my help. Let me know when you need a buggy and I'll have a driver at your disposal." Still holding her gaze, he went on. "Booker & Son across from the jail has a large selection, even mirrors and dinnerware. Abram Booker has catalogs and can order anything you don't find locally. Three blocks south of our house on the boulevard is Remmy Hagermann's mercantile. There's a furniture maker on First and Grant. Mr. Irving has pieces in stock or will build to order."

"It all sounds so expensive," she said, hesitation in her voice.

"Selling land and cattle has made me comfortable, Leah. I'd have nothing without someone to share it with. And we'll be hosting parties and guests, so don't spare anything to make our home welcoming and to represent us as citizens."

"All right." She smiled.

He reached for her hand and squeezed gently. Her skin was warm, her fingers delicate and slim. "There is one room I'd like you to save for us to do together."

"Of course."

"I'd like to select everything for the baby together."

Her blue eyes reflected her surprise at his request. She turned her hand to grasp his fingers and brought her other hand up to lie over the top. He'd hoped to reassure her of his investment in this union, and in her child.

For a moment he struggled with thinking he'd said the wrong thing. Her lips trembled almost imperceptibly before she said, "I'd like that very much."

"Are you sure, Leah?"

Her eyes were bright with unshed tears. "Yes. I'm surprised is all. Pleasantly surprised. Men don't usually show so much interest in infant affairs."

He wondered momentarily about her husband, about his participation or lack thereof. "Well, I'm interested. I want you to be at ease, Leah. In our home. With me."

Her blue eyes studied his expression with uncertainty. She was putting a lot of trust in him. He wanted to be worthy of her confidence.

"Take as much time as you need to think about things, to plan, to furnish the house. If you'd like your own room, you're free to make it a haven. All I want is for you to feel safe."

A tiny crease formed between her eyes. "Thank you for that."

"We're friends, Leah. I won't let anything change that. Friends get things out in the open."

He understood the parameters of their relationship. He planned to do everything he could to make her life easy, and see that she and the child were cared for. A home, clothing, all the necessities were easy to share with her. They were still the best of friends. Theirs would not be a bond of love. He was prepared to live with that.

But time could change many things.

Daniel was busy at the stockyards the next few days as Theo Pierce's cattle were shipped out and a local shorthorn herd was driven in. He stayed for the counting as those cows were led into the pens.

On Thursday evening, he took Leah to dinner at the hotel. "A new family arrived today," she said excitedly. "I was outside the mercantile with Pippa when they pulled up."

"Settlers looking for land or a business?" he asked.

"German settlers." Her blue eyes sparkled as she relayed the news. "They speak fine English though. They had three children, and the missus is expecting a new one. They are camped a ways out right now and looking to farm."

"Students for the new school." Her infectious excitement pleased him immeasurably. Having a special someone to share his dream made the reality all the more rewarding.

"And a mother to look after," Leah added. "Of course I introduced myself and offered my services."

"I know she was pleased to see you." He reached to tuck a strand of silky hair behind her ear, his fingertips brushing her cheek. Her lashes swept down momentarily, and then she locked her gaze on his. The impulsive gesture left them both a bit flustered. He enjoyed their time together too much for someone who was supposed to be on his guard.

Upon returning Leah to the boardinghouse, his stockyard foreman rode in, kicking up dust.

"Glad I found you, Mr. Gardner. We've got a problem."

"Go ahead," Leah said. "Handle business. Thank you for dinner."

Had she seemed eager to put some distance between them or was he only imagining that?

Israel Kinney led him to the stockyards east of town and then to a pen well away from the holding pens and chutes, where Neville Quick and another man stood. Both wore grim expressions.

"This here's Roscoe Early," Israel said by way of introduction. "Got him first, seein' as these are his cows."

"Roscoe," Daniel said.

"They all got the fever," Neville informed him. "Their bellies are bloated."

Several of the cattle in this pen lay on their sides, breathing hard. Flies swarmed around the cattle and the bloody urine in the mud.

Daniel experienced a moment of panic before thinking the situation through. "How long have they been sick?" he asked.

"A day now probably," Neville answered.

"They were fine when I brought 'em here." Roscoe's tone stopped just short of accusatory. "They're scheduled to ship out tomorrow. The longhorns were just here, weren't they? That's it. My cows got Texas fever from those longhorns."

"Let's not jump to any conclusions," Daniel said quickly.

"I ain't jumpin'. I brought in healthy cows and now they're dyin'. Used the same pastures and the same pens as those longhorns. They caught the Texas fever."

"To be safe let's keep your cows in these pens, remove and isolate the sick ones, and keep their feed and water fresh."

Roscoe wiped his face with a red bandana. "Kinda late for bein' safe if you ask me."

Daniel understood the loss. He didn't know what was

wrong with the stock, but keeping good relations with the cattlemen was imperative. "I'll split the cost of the losses with you if any of them die."

Roscoe looked somewhat mollified. He nodded.

"I'll change and help," Daniel offered.

By the next morning, six of the cows had died. Several others that had initially shown symptoms appeared to get better. But news had spread, and already cattlemen were up in arms. Splenic fever was unexplainable, but nobody wanted to take chances with it.

Daniel held an impromptu meeting of the Cattleman's Association and assured the ranchers that every possible precaution would be taken. "I've seen cattle that have died of splenic fever," he told them. "Something just doesn't seem right to me. Their eyes are yellow, and I've never seen that before."

"Are you a veterinarian?" one of the men asked.

"No, but I've worked with animals my whole life."

"I just can't take chances on your hunches."

"We'll keep them well separated," Daniel assured him. "And be safe. I'll send out men to direct the Texas herds to pastures away from your cows. We won't take any chances, but we can't turn away herds." He squared his jaw and looked out at the ranchers with an air of quiet authority. "Texans can get four dollars a head where they're from. We can pay them more because we can get forty to fifty dollars a head in the east. Our town is growing by leaps and bounds because of their cattle."

"The businessmen are getting rich," Will agreed. "And the bankers. But that passes down to everyone. The cattle bring business to all of us."

"We just have to find a way to keep the local cattle healthy," Daniel added.

The future of Cowboy Creek depended on it.

Chapter Seven

Leah hadn't heard so much as a peep from the room beside hers, so that evening she knocked. Hannah opened the door. She was wrapped in a sheet, the cuffs and collar of her nightgown appearing. She touched her unkempt hair, as though embarrassed. "Mrs. Swann."

"It's Leah, remember?"

Hannah nodded.

"May I come in?"

The tall young woman opened the door and stood back. The bed was unmade, the covers folded back as though Hannah had only just abandoned it. "I was resting," she explained. "I seem to have caught something. I worked on your dress last night."

"I'm not concerned about the dress. I'm concerned about you. Can I get the doctor for you?"

"No. No, I don't want a doctor. Don't do that."

"All right. Have you eaten?" Leah asked.

She shook her head.

"Do you think you could keep down some soup…or porridge perhaps?"

"Perhaps," Hannah replied with a tired nod.

"I'll go to the kitchen and find something. I'll be right back."

Aunt Mae was bustling about the kitchen when Leah arrived. She was sympathetic to Hannah's illness. "Shall I send for Doc Fletcher?"

Leah shook her head. "Hannah was adamant she did not want the doctor."

"The poor dear. I checked on her this morning, but she seemed to either be out or sleeping, because she didn't come to her door. Had I known, I'd have taken her something then."

"I know you would have," Leah reassured her. "Let's see if she can tolerate something light and I'll make sure she's getting plenty of liquids."

"Aren't you a darling? It's no wonder Mr. Gardner took a fancy to you right away. He didn't let a good thing get away, now did he?"

Leah gave her a modest smile. "I'm going to do the best I know how to make him a good wife."

"You knew him as a boy? What was he like then?"

She paused and thought a minute. "He was adventurous. Will was solemn and steady and focused on his studies. Daniel lived to be out of doors—riding, roping, running. On hot days he'd lead us to the stream and we'd splash and play until we were wrinkled. My hair was nearly white in the summers from the sun and the water." She touched her fingertips to her cheek and chuckled. "My mother had a conniption fit when she saw the color from the sun on my skin. Remember when that sort of thing used to be important? I was supposed to learn to be a lady at all costs."

"You grew into a fine lady, Mrs. Swann."

"Everything else is proven shallow when people are

dying all around you and you're struggling for your own life. Now I look back and wonder what use my education was. Needlepoint didn't keep anyone alive or win a battle."

"Did your mama teach you to plant a garden and how to cook?" the older woman asked.

Leah nodded. "She did."

"Well, those are the skills that are going to bring this here country back to life. We need gardens and Sunday dinners and children—and love—to get this country back on its feet. Don't count yourself short."

Leah placed the bowl of broth and a slice of buttered bread on the tray and paused to give Aunt Mae a grateful smile. "Thank you."

By the time she returned, Hannah had dressed in a loose robe and wore a shawl draped around herself. "Sorry to be a bother."

"You eat this, and then if you'll allow me I'll brush your hair for you," Leah told her.

"You don't have to do this," she said.

"Well, I want to and it's no bother, so you're stuck with me. Now try the broth. It smells delicious."

"You're right, it does. I didn't even know I was hungry until I smelled it."

Leah propped pillows so Hannah could sit in bed with the tray over her lap. She ate every bit of the food and drank a cup of sweetened tea.

"My mother used to make me tea like this when I didn't feel well," she said. They both knew what it was like to lose a mother, to lose loved ones. Far too many people knew only too well. She wondered if the poor girl was still grieving and perhaps homesick. She sympathized.

Leah set the tray aside and picked up a hairbrush from the bureau. "Turn away now and let me see to your hair. Would you like a bath?"

She removed a few hairpins, started on tangles at the ends, and worked her way up. When she got to Hannah's scalp, the girl made a sound of pleasure. "That feels so good, Leah. Thank you. I think I would like to bathe."

"I'll heat the water and ask Aunt Mae to help me fill the tub."

"I'm glad you've found a good husband," Hannah said in a soft voice. "Mr. Gardner seems like a kind man."

"He is. You'll find a good husband, too."

"I don't know. This seemed like a good idea, but now it's overwhelming. I miss Indiana. I miss our old life. This place is strange and dusty." She swiped the backs of her fingers across her cheek. "My father seems perfectly happy here though, and we believed this would be a good place to start a new life."

"I believe this *will* be a very good place to start a new life," Leah assured her. "You're exhausted and not feeling well. Probably a little homesick, as well, but I assure you things will look better soon."

"I don't see how."

"Because God loves you and is making a way for you right now. Put your trust in Him and He won't let you down. Your father loves you and you have friends who care about you. I'm here whenever you need someone, don't forget that."

Hannah cried openly then, as though her heart was broken. Leah didn't know what to do or say except put her arms around her quaking shoulders and pray. "Father, thank You for giving Hannah Your peace and comfort right now in her time of need. Strengthen her with Your joy and help her be encouraged that You have her best interests at heart. Your Word says we are not to fear because You are with us, so, Lord Jesus, please show Hannah Your presence in a real and certain way. Thank You, Father."

Hannah dried her eyes on her shawl. "Thank you, Leah."

"I'm going to go get that bath ready. You'll feel better after that."

Her friend nodded, and Leah swept from the room.

She called Hannah when the tub was ready, and Aunt Mae assured her she'd listen for her while she was in the bathing room.

Leah understood the kind of homesickness that could never be appeased. She'd spent months longing to return to the blissful days of her youth, yearning to recapture precious moments with family and friends when their lives had seemed safe and invulnerable. All that had changed when her father and every man of fighting age had gone off to war, many never to return. The greatest loss to her was perhaps her innocence, her faith in mankind. She'd seen a disturbing side of humanity that saddened her. The loss was not hers alone. She shared it with every human being in this land. Maybe Aunt Mae was right. Maybe she did have the gifts to help bring this country back. She'd lost much, but her faith had never diminished.

She refused to be afraid for her baby or herself. She wasn't going to dwell on doubts and fears. Perhaps God had guided her here to pair her with Daniel so they could accomplish something good together. She didn't want to be someone he felt sorry for or obligated to. She wanted to be worthy of his choice in marrying her.

Life would never be like it was before, but it could be good again.

The following day Leah was somewhat reassured and yet wary to discover that Daniel had not changed entirely from his audacious ways. He had planned an afternoon outing for them, along with Will and his fi-ancée, telling her to dress comfortably and casually. She wore a simple cotton dress with a jacket she could remove if the sun was too warm, and took a bonnet.

Will and Daniel came for her in Will's buggy, and they stopped at a house west on Second Street for Dora. Dora was the young woman Leah had seen in the crowd on the day she arrived. She had dark curly hair and almond-shaped blue eyes. Her lower lip was decidedly fuller than the top, and when she smiled it pulled down and showed her teeth. Leah felt herself under sharp scrutiny whenever Dora looked at her.

Daniel had scouted a location ahead of time and pitched a canvas awning to shade them from the af-ternoon sun as they ate. Leah couldn't have been more surprised to find he'd rolled out a carpet on the grass under the awning and purchased food from the hotel. He wore trousers and a plain shirt with galluses across his back, while Will wore his customary white shirt and tie.

The enormous basket contained china plates, glasses and pressed white napkins. Daniel set out molasses pails and jars containing chicken, pickles, smoked fish, cheese, olives, figs and bread. Leah stared at the display of food. "Daniel, what is the occasion?"

Kneeling, he sat back on his haunches and placed his

hands on his thighs. He glanced at her, his expression relaxed and carefree. "It's a celebration of life, Leah. A celebration of life."

She looked over the elegant spread and thought a moment. "Well, I like it."

Daniel studied her expression, grinned at her words and chuckled. She adored his enthusiasm and unflagging spirit. They looked at each other and broke into laughter.

Dora glanced from Daniel to Will. "We've never been on a picnic together before, have we?"

Will settled his cane on the rug beside him and adjusted his weight on the ground. Leah suspected the position was uncomfortable. "Daniel is the one with the extraordinary ideas. If you're not careful, he'll have you out there in the Smokey Hill River diving for fish."

Daniel laughed again, and the sound warmed Leah's heart. She grinned. "Now, you know you're every bit as good at grabbing fish as Daniel," she chided. "Better, because you have more patience."

She regretted her teasing the minute she realized the cold water would likely be painful for Will's injured leg.

"You have actually done that?" Dora asked, glancing from one to the other.

"We were children," Will said quickly.

Leah reached for the forks and handed one to each person. They filled their plates and tasted the food. Leah closed her eyes and sighed. "I haven't had cheese this good in years."

Dora looked at Leah curiously. "What did your father do in Pennsylvania?"

"He was a constable," she answered. "And on the town council, as were Daniel and Will's fathers."

"So your family lived comfortably?" Dora asked.

Leah stared at her plate. That all seemed so long ago. "We did."

"And your first husband," Dora queried. "What was his occupation?"

"He attended West Point and became an officer in the army," she replied.

"And you traveled with him?"

"I did." Her meal formed a lump in Leah's stomach.

"I've read about lavish parties and officer's clubs. That sounds quite exciting."

"I assure you it was not. We were fortunate to have a roof over our heads at winter quarters, because mainly the accommodations were musty tents."

"But someone did your laundry and prepared your meals," Dora suggested, as though life had been easy. "Your husband was an officer."

Leah looked at her, wondering how much of the population was as oblivious to the rigors of war as this woman.

"My husband was sometimes gone for weeks at a time, and I never knew if he was coming back or not. I worked with the medical officers to treat the wounded, and I ate whatever they ate. When they were out in the field, I helped teach the children. There was no soiree on Saturday evenings, I assure you."

Daniel rested a hand on Leah's arm, arresting her attention. She looked aside to find his expression tender.

Clearing his throat, Will reached for a jar of olives. "After we finish eating, let's go for a walk along the river."

Dora smiled amenably at him. "That sounds lovely."

Daniel changed the subject to a new shipment of lumber expected that day, and they finished their meal. "I'll pack up. You go ahead," Leah told Will and his fiancée.

"Thank you, Leah," Will said with a nod.

She gave him an easy smile. "Daniel will help."

Together she and Daniel wrapped food and placed lids on jars. He stored it all in the shade and covered the basket. Leah removed her jacket, and Daniel folded it carefully and laid it over the basket.

"Do you want to walk?" he asked. "Or maybe sit in the sun for a while."

"Let's just sit."

He reached for her hand and helped her up. They strolled to a patch of grass and made themselves comfortable. "How's the dress coming?"

"Hannah hasn't been feeling well, but I'm sure she'll be much better soon. I think perhaps she's more homesick than anything. She's probably sewing today."

"She's fortunate to have her father. He leads a good Sunday service, doesn't he?"

Leah agreed.

"And you?" he asked. "Are you feeling well?"

"Surprisingly well. And Doc Fletcher assured me everything seems perfectly normal. Perhaps my caution is unnecessary, but I am taking no risks."

"Your caution is justified and wise," he replied. "We're going to do everything we can to see this baby safely born. If shopping for the house is too much, remember it can wait. Nothing is more important than your health and safety. You should get as much rest as possible."

"I'll remember. So far a little walking and shopping seems to be exactly the exercise and activity I need. I feel good."

He nodded slowly, looking relieved. "The dining room table and chairs arrived yesterday."

"Do you approve?"

"I do. I inquired and you hadn't ordered a buffet or china cabinet."

"Well." She glanced at the sky. "I have no china. If you have some plates in the kitchen, we'll get by."

"We'll get by," he agreed. "But I ordered the matching pieces of furniture. As I mentioned before, eventually we will entertain. Nothing elegant, just hospitality for cattlemen and friends."

"I haven't thought about any of that for a long time," she said. She hadn't thought much beyond surviving for a long time. There was much more to think about now, like the position she would be stepping into as Daniel's wife. Like the wedding, and a gift for him. What could she possibly give to this man who had everything and seemed to need nothing?

She studied him as he watched a hawk circling overhead. His chestnut-brown hair shone in the sunlight. At the corner of his eye and into his eyebrow was a scar she didn't remember from before. She leaned toward him and touched it with one finger.

His gaze immediately moved to hers, his green eyes intense.

"How did you get this scar?"

"It was early in the war." He leaned back, palms flat on the grass and extended his long legs, crossing one ankle over the other. "One of those humid windless days when the smoke was still hanging thick in the air from the previous day's battle. It was nearly impossible to see ahead. My eyes and nose burned." Obviously the memory was vivid. "My brigade moved in formation through a trench alongside a stone wall the rebels were using as cover. When we climbed out of that trench, we only got a couple of shots before our muskets were empty, and there was no time to reload."

Leah imagined the tired soldiers fighting for their lives, and her chest ached. She remembered well the paralyzing fear of being under the attack of rebel marauders.

"So we fought hand-to-hand." He touched the scar. "Took the butt of a musket to the head."

"I'm thankful to God you weren't killed."

"You know what a hard head I have."

"No one's invincible."

A muscle ticked in his jaw. "No."

"I'll understand if you don't want to talk about things like this."

"I hadn't until now," he admitted.

"It's difficult for me to talk about what happened, too."

"Any time you want to, I'm here."

She deliberately avoided thinking about the losses she'd suffered. She didn't want to talk about them. Leah smoothed her skirt over her knees and plucked a blade of grass. It was reassuring to know there was someone who cared, but she didn't want to open herself up to those memories. "I'm not used to generosity and kindness."

"You deserve it."

Leah shook her head. She would have to be cautious around this man. He had the means to reach inside her and draw out feelings she didn't trust or want. She might want to confide in him, but making herself vulnerable would never be wise. Common sense and wisdom were her guides from here on out.

* * *

Saturday was as clear and bright as a bride could hope for on her wedding day. It looked as though the entire population of Cowboy Creek had turned out to witness the nuptials. Hannah had outdone herself on Leah's dress. The two-piece cream silk design with a small bustle in the back and overlapping bodice in the front cleverly disguised her pregnancy. People would know soon enough, of course, but today she didn't want them speculating or gossiping. Knife-pleated sashes, elbow-length ruffled sleeves and a deep ruffle at the hem made the gown elegant without being flamboyant.

Hannah and Pippa helped her dress and escorted her to the church in a rented buggy. Daniel was tall and dashing in a three-piece black suit, white shirt and tie. His presence was comforting and his broad smile allayed her last-minute concerns.

Reverend Taggart performed the ceremony with eloquence and a reading from the book of Ephesians.

Pippa, accompanied by Richard on the organ, sang "All Things Love Thee, So Do I" in her clear, lovely soprano voice, which brought gooseflesh to Leah's arms. She kept her song sweet and understated, so as not to draw attention away from the couple.

"Fruit and flowers for thee.
Whilst the glorious stars above shine on thee like trusting love; When thou dost in slumbers lie, all things love thee so do I."

When Reverend Taggart instructed Daniel to kiss the bride, her new husband did so preceded by an apologetic wink. It was their first kiss, in front of the entire town, and Leah expected it to be perfunctory and obligatory.

Instead, Daniel surprised her by taking her hand and looking deep into her eyes. Surely it was a show for the guests, but her heart leapt regardless. His easy smile reassured her. She could feel her own pulse in her temples, in the fingers he held. His were warm, and the touch created a powerful tension between them, an unexpected thrum of anticipation.

His smile faded, and his gaze fell to her lips. Leah caught her breath. He kissed her then, a mere touch of soft warm lips, an innocent and chaste gesture. But he seemed reluctant to pull away, squeezing her hand and giving her one long last look that held an unspoken promise, a promise beyond those they'd exchanged in their vows. Until death did they part, Daniel Gardner was her husband.

And while they'd been close in their youth, they barely knew each other as adults. She suspected there was a lot to learn. Her first marriage had turned out nothing like she'd anticipated. She could only pray and believe this practical union based on mutual benefits would be more suitable.

Her future—and that of her baby—was now in Daniel's hands.

Chapter Eight

The joyous celebration was indicative of the forward-thinking climate of Cowboy Creek. The first wedding was cause for hope and even more plans, because at least one conversation Leah overheard was about scheduling the next bride train. Friends and town leaders offered warm congratulations.

Noah had attended the ceremony, and now he remained on the edge of the gathering on the expansive church lawn, talking to Will and Dora. Daniel led Leah to where the group stood. "Left your gift at your place," Noah told Daniel.

"Thank you," he replied.

"It's cuttings and starts for a garden. Some vegetables. Mostly flowers."

"That's so thoughtful," Leah said with a gentle smile. "Are they from your own garden?"

"A few. But I had most of them shipped. They arrived yesterday and they look in good condition. I set them alongside the house and watered them."

"I can't think of a better gift," she told him honestly. "We can enjoy them for years to come."

Noah nodded and turned his face away to study the backs of the buildings on Eden Street, and then glanced at the lot behind the church. "How's that house of yours coming, Will? Looks like supplies have been delivered."

Piles of brick indicated something would soon be constructed.

"Should only be a few more weeks," Will replied.

"That's a lot of bricks," Leah observed.

"It will be a big house," Daniel said. He glanced at his friend. "Greek Revival?"

Will nodded. "With four two-story columns on the front and a balcony above."

"It sounds like a mansion," Leah said.

"Or the governor's house," Dora said with a smug look at her fiancée. "Isn't that right?"

"Possibly one day," Will replied.

Leah hadn't known about Will's political ambitions, but knowing him, his goals made sense. Initially her late husband, Charles, had reminded her of Will, with his ease in all situations and his natural charm. Marriage to Charles had proven his charm was all on the surface, however. At first there had been a few social events, and Charles had displayed her on his arm like expensive jewelry. Later, as the war progressed, his assignments had taken them to crude outposts and forts, where gentlemen's gatherings didn't welcome ladies and there had been few other women. Perhaps he'd been disillusioned with her or with his army career, but in any case she had never been one of his priorities, and it hadn't taken long until he'd become neglectful and dismissive.

Leah had no idea if her marriage to Daniel would follow the same pattern, so she didn't hold any unrealistic expectations. However, she knew Daniel's character. He was kind and honest. That was more than she could have hoped for and more than she'd known before.

She had much to be thankful for. This was a prosperous, thriving town, and she'd just married one of its respected leaders. As long as her baby was healthy and safe, she could handle anything else that came along.

Daniel was having second thoughts about the gift he'd purchased for Leah. A wedding gift should be personal. There was an uneasiness between them today. As much as he wished he could remedy it, he wasn't even sure what had caused it. And now he worried that the gift he'd gotten her would make matters worse. Even though he'd put a lot of thought and effort into it, perhaps she would think his gift was inappropriate.

There were gaily decorated packages of all sizes stacked under the same enormous awning that protected the food and drinks from the sun. Aunt Mae settled the bride and groom on wooden folding chairs and instructed young fellows to carry gifts a couple at a time. There were tablecloths and candlesticks, parlor lamps and linens, trinket boxes and a coffee grinder.

It took two strapping boys to carry the crate Daniel had brought for her. Perhaps this hadn't been the place. Maybe he should have left it at the house and given it to her later. It was too late now.

He had already pried off the top and examined the contents to make sure they'd arrived in perfect condition, so now he removed the lid and gestured for her to move the straw packing aside.

She glanced at him. "From you?"

He nodded.

Her gaze moved over his face. "All right."

She dug through the straw until she uncovered the plate he'd strategically left at the top and lifted it out. Her expression first showed curiosity and then dawning awareness as she looked at the pattern on the plate. In green and white, lilies of the valley formed a circle around the lip of the plate while the scalloped edges were intricately painted with gold.

"There are twelve of each size plate," he told her. "Plus cups and bowls and accessories."

Around them the bystanders murmured their appreciation.

Leah finally removed her gaze from the plate she cradled so carefully to search his face. Her expression was incredulous. "How—? You remembered these?"

"Yes."

"It's just like my mother's china. She got it as a wedding gift. The dishes were in our house when it burned."

Something he hadn't known until now. Maybe this had been too much—too personal. Maybe there were overwhelmingly painful memories associated. "I didn't know they were a wedding gift, but I remember eating from them on Sundays."

"How did you find a set just like them?"

"I found a fellow in New York who deals in antiquities. They're not terribly old, but he was able to trace the pattern from a drawing I sent him and located an entire set in Boston."

"Daniel, this was an amazing effort. Sentimental and thoughtful."

Her words dismissed his apprehension. "I was concerned you wouldn't like them." The thickness in his voice supported his words.

"Why would I not?" She opened her mouth to speak, but then closed it and her lower lip trembled. She pursed her mouth in a straight line to compose herself. Her lashes fell across her cheeks and cast a becoming shadow. When she looked up, her eyes were bright with unshed tears. "They will remind me of home."

Just as he'd hoped.

She carefully returned the plate to the crate and leaned toward him. "Thank you."

Their neighbors made appreciative sounds and comments, and Aunt Mae blew her nose into a hankie.

"Top that wedding gift for your bride, Will Canfield." Richard Mosely spoke the challenge in fun, and Will shrugged good-naturedly. Dora gave Will an expectant smile and nudged his shoulder. He shook his head and grinned.

"I'm afraid my gift for you isn't nearly as inspired," Leah told her new husband.

"I'm sure I'll love it."

"It's in my trunk."

"I'll see it later."

Cake was served, and the hour grew late. Members of the congregation cleaned up, put away tables and chairs and took down the tent.

Daniel and Leah said their goodbyes and he ushered her into the rented buggy.

He was a man of many accomplishments, a man who executed a lot of plans and saw them through. While a lot depended on his preparation and organization, nothing had ever seemed as important as this. Each day he'd seen the house coming together as furniture, rugs and household necessities had been delivered. Each night he'd gone to bed with expectations about the wedding and their marriage. The past week or so had been hectic, culminating in today's ceremony. It had happened. They were married. Leah was coming home with him.

"Are you feeling well?" he asked.

"Tired. It was a full day."

"And an even fuller week," he said as the horses drew them toward Lincoln Boulevard. "I guess I have a lot to learn about being a husband."

"You accomplish everything you set your mind to," she replied. "This will be no different."

"I should think it will be very different. A wife isn't a horse to train or a plot of land to build upon." Her soft laughter pleased him. "Perhaps I shall concentrate on amusing you."

She offered him a playful smile. "As I recall, you were always entertaining."

"I admit I feel more like my old self now that you're here."

She was silent a moment. "I've been alone."

"You're not alone anymore, Leah. You never have to be alone again."

Not wanting to dampen the lighthearted mood, she fortified her smile.

They reached the house, and Daniel reined in the horse. "Walter Frye will come get the buggy shortly. The ladies left us supper in the kitchen." They entered the house. "Do you need any help?"

She glanced at her dress. "I'm going to change, and then I believe I will be hungry. There was so much excitement this afternoon, I barely ate anything."

"I'll make us plates and we can sit in the library. How does that sound?"

"Perfect."

When Daniel saw her again, she'd loosened her shimmering gold hair and wore it in a braid down her back. Her simple blue cotton dress and satin house slippers looked comfortable. He'd set a side table with a casserole and a basket of sliced bread and cheese.

"You'll spoil me," she said, accepting the plate he handed her.

"Somehow I doubt that."

He found her presence in the home he'd built startling and wonderful. "Do you remember being at our house in Mount Joy on a Sunday evening?" he asked. "Mother used to set out the remains of the noon meal with bread and cheese in my father's study. They drank wine with the meal, of course."

"I do remember," she answered. "I always enjoyed your mother's cooking, and the way she made everyone feel at home. My mother entertained more formally, and we always dressed for supper."

"But when we were all together—Will's parents, too—I never noticed the differences. Only how it felt like family."

Leah rested her fingertips over her heart. "We can't have those years back."

"I'm glad we experienced those young and innocent years together." His eyes revealed wistful sincerity. "I hope we enjoyed those times to the fullest while we were living in them. It's a good reminder not to take days like this for granted."

Leah set her plate aside. Her gaze lifted to his. "I want that for this child, Daniel. I want this child to feel safe and loved like we did. I want him to believe the future holds goodness and promise."

Daniel set down his plate and moved to sit beside her

on the divan. He took her hand. "I'll do everything in my power to make that happen. He—or she—will be loved and cherished and have every opportunity within my power to give him."

"I believe you," she said with a nod. "What are the chances that I would travel all this way and find you? I have to believe God had a hand in leading me here, that He heard my prayers."

"I believe that, too."

"And I don't want to let you down," she admitted, a slight hitch in her voice.

"I'm not asking you for anything, Leah."

"You *should* ask."

He lifted a brow and leaned in a little closer. "What should I ask?"

"For my loyalty. My devotion."

"I trust you to be loyal and devoted to the arrangement we made."

Something flickered behind her eyes. Pain? Disappointment? "I shall be."

He patted the back of her hand and released it. "Let's not be melancholy this night. We have a lot to celebrate and be thankful for. We are the first couple to be married in Cowboy Creek." He thought a moment. "I believe we should have a photograph. I'll send for a photographer."

"Do it quickly, before I outgrow my wedding dress."

He looked at her with amusement and got up to pour a cup of coffee. "Yes, indeed. There's wedding cake in the kitchen. Would you like a slice?"

She deliberated on his offer for only seconds. "Perhaps for breakfast."

He chuckled and inclined his head in acceptance. "If

you outgrow the wedding dress we'll have it altered. I'll clean up. You rest."

"If you don't mind, I think I'll go up and lie down."

"Of course. I'll bring you water. Do you have everything else you need in your room?"

"Yes, thank you. And thank you, Daniel, for the meal. I think an occasional supper in the library should be our first tradition. Sunday evenings, as your mother did in your father's study."

He appreciated the idea of them creating their own tradition. Leah seemed content and hopeful. "I'd like that, too."

After dipping water and carrying it to her room, Daniel wished her a goodnight, returned to light another lamp and attempted to concentrate on a book. He'd done a sensible thing, marrying her. He'd done the only thing his conscience—and his heart—would allow him to do. He knew where she was and was assured she was safe. He was the best man to become her husband. Practical marriages had been around since Biblical times.

He remembered what she'd said when she'd accepted his proposal. She'd laid out the guidelines. Their marriage would be a practical union. He had no false expectations. For now their main concern was to look after her health and that of the baby. Once the child arrived, they could ease into a more intimate relationship. Eventually they would have more children. He liked the idea of filling this house with children. *A family.*

Perhaps he hadn't been her first choice, but he could be her best choice—and her last. She might never love him, but he would do his best to make sure she never regretted marrying him.

* * *

Dressed for bed, Leah turned down the wick, but left the lamp burning on the bureau. She knew better than to waste oil, but this was another new room, and an unfamiliar house. She wasn't prepared for the pitch black of night or the hours that stretched ahead. The new sheets were crisp and clean, but the night was cool and she needed the added warmth of the blanket, as well. She lay on her back and stared at the shadows on the ceiling.

There were moments now and then when she forgot there'd been a war. Her thoughts would carry her away for a few moments or she'd fall asleep and have a rare dream that didn't involve death or dying. Then she'd awaken to the promise of a new day. As soon as she came fully alert, the present and past crashed down around her.

Unconsciously she rested her hands on her belly. Here she was, married to Daniel Gardner and living in his beautiful new home. The overwhelming desire to write her mother and let her know she was going to be all right took her by surprise. That would have been the most natural thing in the world, but she no longer had anyone with whom to share things, no family who cared if she fared well or if she fell off the face of the earth.

Images of those days and nights back in Pennsylvania rose to haunt her as they always did. With her family home stripped of nearly everything they could sell for food, she and her mother and her cousin Hattie had survived most of a winter huddled around the fireplace in her father's study. It had been the last room with comfortable furnishings, and they'd been able to pull the heavy oak doors shut and hold the meager heat inside.

In the deepest cold of winter they had slowly sacrificed her father's books to the miserly flames.

Her mother had kept up their spirits with tales of her youth, of her siblings and of Leah's father—until she'd taken ill and coughed too violently to speak more than a few words at a time. It had been a bitterly cold morning when a half dozen rebels, cold and hungry themselves, had approached the house, attracted by the thin line of smoke from the chimney. The clambering of boots on the porch had awakened the women. The three of them, already dressed in warm clothing, shoes and wrapped in shawls and quilts for warmth, had grabbed only a few items at hand and run out the back to the frigid springhouse.

Their breath was white in the dim interior, the spring having been frozen for months. The rebels must have found their cache of food and it hadn't taken them long to devour it and search the already-diminished house. The women observed the house through the cracks between the boards where the chinking was gone, seeing the first tongues of fire that darted from the windows of the kitchen, and then the upstairs bedrooms. By the time flames leaped toward the sky, the men in ragged gray uniforms were making a search of the property.

"We have to go." Leah's whisper had been frantic.

"We'll freeze to death in the woods," Hattie had said, her teeth chattering, her nose red.

"We have to," Leah insisted. "If they find us here, our fate will be worse than freezing to death."

Her mother stifled a cough and fear shot through Leah at the ragged sound. The men outside would hear. Her mother knew her fear and her actions showed she shared it. "Go. If I fall behind, you keep going," she insisted. "We'll meet by the big rock that hangs out over the creek."

Leah and Hattie had nodded. They knew the spot well. Their families had picnicked there every summer of the girls' childhoods.

"Don't wait long," her mother said. "Hide nearby and if one or more of us are split up and don't make it, get away."

"Where will we go, Mama?"

"Trust God to help you with that," she replied and buried a cough in her shawl.

Her mother had been too weak to keep up. Leah had tried to help her, but unable to breathe, her mother had clutched her chest and gestured for them to go on. Eyes wide, she'd stumbled about for something and came up with a rock she could barely lift. "Go. I'll stop at least one of the rebels."

"No, Mama," Leah had cried in a hoarse whisper. "I'm not leaving you."

The sounds of men's voices nearby reached them.

Her mother's lips were blue. "If you stay we will all die. If you leave me, you can make it. Now go."

"Come on, Leah." Hattie tugged at her arm. "We have to go now."

"Mama," Leah said on a moan.

"Make it for me," her mother ordered. "Don't look back, and live."

Hattie yanked her away.

Blinded by tears, Leah stumbled away. "We can't leave her. We can't! I have to go back."

"She's giving us a chance to get to safety," Hattie told her fiercely. "Don't waste it."

Frozen branches scratched and scraped as they stumbled along a streambed.

Gunfire sounded behind them.

Leah stopped in her tracks, her head roaring with fear and panic.

"Come on!" Hattie insisted.

Leah stared at her cousin whose face was scratched, her once silky fair hair a tangle of knots with twigs caught in the ends. Her cheeks were hollow, her eyes dull with remorse.

Lying in Daniel Gardner's home, on this new bed, ashes collapsing with soft sighs in the fireplace, Leah wiped tears from her temples and her hair. She had no one with whom to share the current state of her life. Her mother had died that day. They'd waited an entire day hidden near the stone that jutted over the creek. By the time they moved on, Hattie had taken a fever. They'd had to avoid the roads in case other marauders were in the area, and by the time they'd made it to the city, her cousin hadn't had the strength or the will to recover.

Daniel had assured her she never had to be alone again. Yet she felt quite alone. He'd made promises. Her child would be loved and well provided for. She couldn't live in the past. In the dim light of the lantern that spat and guttered, she found her Bible on the table beside her bed and held it to her side, grasping to remember something to help her move on. *Something about not remembering former things.*

Remember not the former things, nor consider the things of old. Behold, I am doing a new thing; now it springs forth, do you not perceive it? I will make a way in the wilderness and rivers in the desert.

She had no idea how to forget those things, so instead she worked diligently to keep hold of the good memories. And look forward to new ones here with Daniel in her new home.

Chapter Nine

True to his word, Daniel had provided help for Leah, and Valentine Ewing showed up midweek. She had come to Cowboy Creek at the bidding of her younger brother Owen, the undertaker and cabinet maker. She'd worked as a bookkeeper at their father's lumber mill in New Brunswick for years, and had been living with a nephew and his family since their father died and Owen came west. She spoke with an accent she declared was Scottish, but sounded more French to Leah, not that she would know.

Valentine Ewing was a small woman, with streaks of gray shot through her black hair. Though she had a serene countenance and a calm manner of speech, she moved with efficiency and purpose. Once she'd been introduced to Leah and shown the house, and her duties had been explained, she set right to work and spoiled Leah to no end. She brought a breakfast tray to her room, then gathered laundry and stowed her shoes and jewelry all while Leah ate.

"If it suits you, Mrs. Gardner, I've had Mr. Gardner fetch a rocker for the kitchen. You can rest there and sort your new kitchen items and china. I will wash them and you can direct me how to put them away."

Leah was arrested by the new form of address, and worked it over in her mind. "Please, won't you call me Leah?"

Valentine seemed to think it over. "Very well."

"Thank you. And rest assured I am not an invalid. I am simply using extreme caution during my pregnancy and avoiding exertion."

"Yes, ma'am."

"I'm thankful you agreed to come and help out. And that you were available."

"My brother's home is already clean and organized. There are only the two of us and he refuses to allow me into his work area, so I have little to keep me busy." She shrugged. "I was used to working with my father, and I don't much care for being idle. Mr. Gardner's offer is a good opportunity for me to stay busy."

"I hope we'll be friends."

Valentine paused, folding a clean handkerchief and gave Leah an appreciative smile. "I hope so, too."

Leah returned her smile. "Your suggestion sounds perfect. We can put the kitchen to order."

Valentine had brought cleaning supplies, white huck toweling and sweet rolls she had baked already that morning. The crate of wedding china had been carried in and opened. Leah set to work carefully unpacking the dishes.

"Those are lovely," Valentine said, admiring the growing stack on the table.

"They're my wedding gift from Daniel," she told the other woman. "He remembered my mother had a set like them and located these."

"The day he announced your engagement I heard him say that you'd known each other for many years."

Leah nodded, and as the women worked she shared bits and pieces of her youth and her friendship with Daniel and Will. At first, she was hesitant to share that she'd been engaged to Will at one time because her past behavior now seemed childish and shallow. Valentine didn't seem judgmental or critical, however, so she took a fortifying breath and shared the story.

The older woman reverently washed and dried the set of china. "Things don't always turn out the way we plan when we're young and idealistic. Even foolishly naïve, I suppose."

"No, they don't."

"I was once engaged to a dashing young man."

Leah set aside the towel she was holding. "You were?"

Valentine nodded. "He was a British sea captain."

"What happened?" She caught herself being too inquisitive. "I'm sorry. You don't have to tell me if you'd rather not."

"His name was Stephen. He was kind and intelligent. He had a smile that could clear up a rainy day." She paused at the sink, her fingers dripping suds, seemingly lost in those memories. After a lengthy moment, she straightened and went back to her task. "We were to be married, but he was lost at sea."

The words were far more matter-of-fact than the emotions clearly behind them, even after all these years.

Her heart went out to the woman. Leah wasn't the only one who had suffered loss. But Valentine had bravely gone on with her life, working, sharing her talents with others, and Leah admired her for that. "I'm so sorry."

Valentine nodded. "It was a long time ago. The pain has dimmed. Your loss is much more recent."

"You never married another."

The woman shook her head. "I didn't let myself get close to anyone for a long time, and after that, well, it just never happened."

"There are a lot of men in Cowboy Creek. God might still have one for you."

Valentine laughed at that. "Bless your heart, Leah Gardner. You're an optimist."

She grinned. "Perhaps."

Daniel returned early that evening, with time to sit in the library, while Valentine set the table. "How was your day?"

"It was nice. Valentine is a blessing. I can't thank you enough. She is going to spoil me, however."

"I doubt that."

"The china is all washed and put away in the cabinet. I must have stared at it for an hour."

He grinned. "I was thinking about something today. We planned a wedding quickly, and right now you need a lot of rest, but later, after the baby comes, we will do something special. Take a trip."

Thoughts of leaving her baby behind left her uneasy. "Like a—a honeymoon?"

"Well." He appeared to think about it. "If you can call a trip with a new baby a honeymoon."

"With the baby?"

"Of course."

"All right. Yes, then, a trip." She gave him a broad smile.

Her smiles would be Daniel's demise. He enjoyed seeing them so much he might be tempted to behave foolishly to coax one. When she smiled at him years fell away, and he saw only the beauty of the moment. Her presence brought a queer warmth to his chest, and arrested his thoughts. He'd thought of little today, save returning to the house to see her. It would be wise to use caution when emotions were at risk, he reminded himself, but defenses where useless where she was concerned. "Consider where you'd like to go," he said.

"I'll do that."

Valentine appeared in the doorway. "Pardon me, but supper is on the table."

"Will you be eating with us?" Daniel asked. "You're welcome any time."

"Thank you, but I have a basket of food for Owen and I'll be heading home to have supper with him. Leave the dishes. I'll do them tomorrow."

"Perhaps some evening your brother can come join us," Leah suggested.

Valentine nodded. "I'm sure he'd like that. Good night. I'll be here early tomorrow."

"You don't have to take my breakfast upstairs," Leah replied. "I can eat in the kitchen with Daniel before he leaves."

Miss Ewing was a good cook. She'd prepared a hearty meal of roast and potatoes, with slaw and warm rolls. They'd nearly finished when the unmistakable sound of gunfire startled them. Daniel met the surprised look in Leah's eyes.

"Is that usual?" she asked. "Isn't there a no-gun ordinance?"

"There's definitely a law against guns in town. I'll be back after I check it out. Stay inside."

Daniel got his rifle from the trunk in the library, checked it for ammunition and grabbed his hat before heading out. A block from home he reached the corner where the boardinghouse sat and emerged onto Eden Street. From farther south toward Drover's Place and the railroad station came the sound of shots. Whenever there'd been a commotion, it had come from across the track, on the south side of town, where the cowboys sometimes did too much celebrating. This disturbance, however, was closer to the main center of town. Another shot sounded and glass shattered.

Sheriff Quincy Davis was already ahead of Daniel, and Will had emerged from the hotel. Several other men stood in the recessed shadows of the doorways, observing the rowdy men on restless horses. Light from the windows at Drover's Place delineated the mounts, a black and a gray among them. Five in total.

"No guns in town!" Quincy shouted.

"Come get 'em, Sheriff!" came the reply, followed by a shot that took out the window in the land office. Glass showered onto the boardwalk. Laughter followed.

"We don't want trouble," Quincy called out. "Head out the way you came."

"The whole bunch of 'em ate and didn't pay." Floyd Yates ran Drover's Place. "When I asked them to pay up, they drew their guns and robbed the other men in the place."

"That's Zen and Xavier Murdoch," D.B. said from behind Daniel. "Had trouble with them and their gang back in Harper." D.B. spoke of the town eighty miles away. "There's more of 'em than what's here," the newsman warned.

If more of the gang might be looking on, they couldn't afford to bring this disturbance to a head.

Daniel walked out into the street and strode toward the troublemakers.

"Drop what you stole and head out," he demanded.

"Or what?" came the reply.

"We don't want trouble." Quincy and Will walked up and stood on either side of him. In the moonlight Daniel made out a couple of tall narrow men with beards. He'd never seen them before.

Three shots pierced the wooden sign hanging over the land office, and the sign swung haphazardly on its one remaining chain.

The riders dug their heels into their horses' sides, and the animals' hooves kicked up dirt as the men retreated. Bullets resounded off the metal side of a railcar and the sound of galloping hoofbeats resided.

Will turned to the men gathered in the street. "We haven't seen the last of them."

"I'm fearin' you're right," Quincy said.

"They brought trouble to Harper regularly," D.B. offered.

"What did your sheriff do?" Quincy asked.

"Shot back."

"Last thing we want is a bunch of killin'." Old Horace had been roused and now stood dressed in his union suit and trousers.

James Johnson had joined the gathering, as well. Without his hat, his black curly hair fell into his eyes. "Ain't no reasoning with fellas like that. They don't have no sense of propriety. If you want to protect the town from 'em, you'll need sentries."

The thought made Daniel feel sick. He'd seen enough fighting and killing to last a lifetime. Just the sound of the shots made his stomach lurch. But the drover had a good point. "We need to have a town meeting and decide how far we're willing to go to keep them out of Cowboy Creek."

His suggestion was sobering, and the men exchanged glances.

"Any one of those shots could have ricocheted and hit someone." Amos Godwin had been roused from the rooms he shared with his wife over his boot shop. "What if they come back during the day when there's women on the street?"

"Let's meet tomorrow at the Cattleman Hotel." Will said.

A couple of men helped sweep up glass and board up the window opening at the land office. Others cleaned up broken glass from the bakery's window.

James Johnson approached Daniel, Will and Quincy. "I'll keep watch down by the station tonight if you want. I don't have nowhere to be in the mornin'."

"Thanks, James. That's much appreciated," Quincy said. "I'll have Buck station himself at the north end of town."

The men dispersed and Daniel hurried home.

Leah had washed dishes and tidied the kitchen. She dropped the towel she held and hurried toward him when he came through the front door. Her concerned blue gaze swept over him. "That was a lot of shooting. What happened?"

He filled her in on what had gone on.

"Sit down. I'll pour you some coffee."

He didn't sit, but stood and shifted his weight from one foot to the other. "We can make plans and laws, but that doesn't stop men like those. You'd think after all this country has been through, men would be looking for peace now, be happy to go about their lives and not stir up trouble."

She set a full cup on the table. "I understand your concern, but don't be discouraged. You've worked too hard to let these men undermine what you've done—what you and Will and Noah have done together. We'll pray. You'll think of something."

She was still the prettiest woman he'd ever laid eyes on, her gold upswept hair shiny in the lamplight. Her cheeks were pink against her fair skin, and her eyes wide with sincerity. He released a ragged breath and took her words to heart. "Yes."

A few months ago he'd been living in an empty house, devoted to the development of this town, never letting himself get ahead in his thinking to actually hope or plan for a wife. Whenever he thought of it, he imagined he'd eventually take a bride and make the best of a convenient arrangement.

Marrying Leah might have been a convenient arrangement, but he certainly hadn't settled for second best. He wasn't her first choice, but she had always been the woman of his dreams, the wife he'd have chosen had he been given the opportunity. He prayed she wasn't resentful of her situation or that she didn't feel forced into a marriage she didn't want.

Her encouragement meant everything to him.

She smiled and moved forward to hug him, nestling her hand on his shoulder and her head under his chin. Her hair smelled of citrus and she felt small and soft in his arms. The years fell away, and they were friends again, sharing, supporting. He spread his hand on the small of her back. *My wife now.* Even with the state of conflict in town, he experienced a satisfying sense of optimism. He couldn't fool himself that she suddenly felt more than friendship or appreciation, but he could hope for more.

She pulled back and offered him a smile. "Sit now. Drink your coffee while it's hot."

"Miss Ewing would have done the dishes in the morning."

"I'm perfectly capable of washing a few dishes, Daniel. I rested with my feet up most of the day."

His lips quirked, but he sat without further comment. She seated herself across from him, folding a stack of embroidered towels they'd received as a wedding gift into perfect squares. He thought about how he'd taken her in his arms and kissed her after Reverend Taggart had pronounced them man and wife, and then he thought about kissing her again, with no one watching.

It had been a long time since he'd spent time in the company of a woman, and he enjoyed watching her movements. Her shoulders were so narrow he could wrap his arms twice around her. Her hands were small, her fingers long and delicate. She smoothed and folded the towels with impressive precision. She glanced up and found him watching her.

"We'll be having a town meeting tomorrow to discuss what happened tonight and figure out if there's anything we can do," he said to break the silence.

"Will there be women there?"

"You're welcome to join us. The more heads the better." He finished his coffee and banked the fire in the stove. He found a pail and dipped water from the reservoir. "I'll carry water up."

She stored her towels and disappeared.

* * *

Daniel woke during the night. His room was still dark, the house silent. A sound met his ears and he realized the soft cry was what had awakened him. He stood and pulled on his trousers before padding across the hall to Leah's door. The muffled sounds of distress and a piteous cry were alarming. He pushed open the door, not knowing what he'd find.

A surprisingly serene sight met his eyes. Through a slit in the curtains, moonbeams danced across the coverlet, outlining the slender figure beneath. He didn't know what he'd anticipated finding, but it hadn't been Leah sleeping soundly. What of the sounds he'd heard? But then her unmistakable cries came again.

Her sobs tightened a cinch around his chest. He moved forward, so close he could smell the scent of her hair. "Leah," he said softly. When she didn't respond he touched her shoulder. Beneath his hand, her body trembled. "Leah?"

"No, I'm not leaving Mama," she said on a sob. "I won't leave her."

"Wake up. You're dreaming."

"Mama! Come on, you can make it."

"Leah, wake up," he said more sternly.

She twisted and sat straight up with a start, her tangled hair a silver mass of curls in the moonlight. Tears streaked her cheeks, and her entire body shuddered violently.

He'd seen similar behavior among the soldiers. Men reliving battles and death in vividly cruel nightmares. Even Noah jumped in wild-eyed panic at the sound of unexpected gunfire. No doubt that was why his friend preferred isolation and stayed so far from town, the saloons and all the careless revelers. Daniel had suffered his own repercussions after the war, and then it dawned on him that Leah must have experienced terrible things as well.

She raised an unsteady hand to rake her hair away from her face. "I—I'm sorry I woke you."

"Shh...it's no bother." He found a match and lit the lamp on the bureau. "Want to talk about it?"

She blinked. In the lantern light her flushed face and neck took on an apricot glow. "I was just having a dream."

He took her hand and felt her body quivering. "Must've been a frightening one. You're shaking."

"I'll be all right."

"Can I hold you?" he asked.

She paused only a moment, and then scooted aside so he could sit and wrap his arms around her shoulders. She rested her head against him and released a quivering sigh. "I feel foolish."

"No need to feel foolish." He rubbed her back in a soothing circular motion. Her hair was soft against his chin, her arms warm through the cotton gown. She smelled like lemon and almond. Even someone as lovely and delicate as this woman carried the scars of war, and Daniel knew all about terrors in the night. "I've been in this house for months and I've only started to sleep on my bed," he admitted. "I couldn't get any rest until I put the blankets and quilt on the floor and laid there."

"Why?"

"The bed was too soft, the stillness of the house too quiet and disturbing. It's impossible to ignore the thoughts—and the losses at night. I slept on the floor at the hotel, too."

Sometimes when he woke it took him a minute to remember he wasn't in a tent with a dozen dirty, hungry men, and it wasn't until then that the constriction in his chest eased. Mornings were still a surprise. Each new day meant he didn't have to put on wet socks or stiff boots and march or burn fields or homes or kill anyone. He could lie in bed all day if it suited him. But instead he got up and worked to change things for the better.

Perhaps eventually she would tell him about the memories that woke her and left her trembling. But she didn't have to. "I understand, Leah."

She raised her head and released him, studying his face in the dim light. What did she see when she looked at him? Someone who reminded her of home? Someone who made the tragedy more real? A friend, perhaps. Common sense told him this arrangement was based on convenience prompted by his desire to protect his friend, but his heart didn't seem to understand that logic because it beat a rapid tattoo under his shirt. Yes, he wanted to keep her safe, protect her from the world, erase the hurt and loss, but he wanted to take her in his arms and kiss her as well.

Leah was still a beautiful woman, still the girl he'd secretly longed for and still just beyond his reach. She'd lost two babies, her parents and brother, her husband. She had a lot of misery on her plate and she didn't need him confusing her with his selfish desires. It pained him to stand and take a step away, but he did it. He gestured to the nearby chair. "I could sit here a while if you like."

"No, you go sleep."

He backed away a few steps. "I'll have my door open. If you need me, call out."

"Thank you."

He left, closing her door to give her privacy. In his room he stood in the dark for several minutes, studying the walnut four-poster bed with its thick mattress. Finally he yanked the covers from the bed and folded them in half on the floor, dropped pillows, then lay down and stacked his hands under his head. He racked his memory for a verse to help him relax and sleep, and finally a snip of a Psalm came to him. *I will both lay me down in peace and sleep, for thou, Lord, only makest me dwell in safety.*

"I am lying down in peace, Lord," he said under his breath. "And Leah as well."

Chapter Ten

The following day men and a few women gathered in a private dining room in the Cattleman Hotel, where chairs had been lined up and a table placed at the front for Sheriff Davis, Daniel, Will, Noah and D.B. Leah took a chair at the side of the room where Hannah, Prudence, Dora, Pippa and Opal Godwin sat.

"By now everyone is aware of the incident in town last night," Will began in a calm, authoritative voice. "We're here to talk about solutions for the safety of our residents."

"D.B. recognized a couple of them as Zen and Xavier Murdoch," Daniel said. "They're part of an outlaw gang."

"They caused trouble in Harper, too," D.B. explained.

"Eight of 'em in total from what I learnt," Quincy added. "They're holed up somewhere outside town."

"Are the ranchers safe?" Walter Frye, the liveryman, asked. "Maybe we need men riding out to alert them so they can be on the lookout."

"That's a wise idea," Noah said. "I'll let the families on either side of me know. We'll need a few more volunteers."

A few men raised their hands and Will took note of which ranches they would travel to.

"Meanwhile we've got the town to look out for," Amos Godwin said. "We can't have our windows shot out. Nearly the whole south end of Eden Street is boarded over today."

"Business owners, you keep guns in your establishments?" Will asked.

Floyd Yates, Amos, Walter and others nodded.

"Maybe we need to lift the no-gun policy until this is settled," D.B. suggested.

Several voices interrupted each other all at once.

"We have that law for a reason," Noah objected. "We're promoting Cowboy Creek as the safest little town in Webster County. We're bringing in women-folk. There will be more children soon."

"The school will be opening," Daniel added.

"We have to keep our women safe," Owen Ewing agreed. He glanced at his older sister, Valentine, sitting beside him. She held her lips pursed in a line of displeasure.

More arguments of dissension went back and forth before Will raised a hand.

"All right. All right," Will said, directing attention to himself. "Lifting the no-gun ordinance is the last resort. Until we resort to that, we will be vigilant."

"We need sentries with guns," James Johnson chimed in.

"Yes," Will agreed and Daniel nodded.

"There are plenty of drovers in town," James added.

"I'm willing to take turns, and others will be, too. We're used to sitting under the stars at night."

"I'll make a schedule," Will offered. "Anyone who is willing to take a turn, sign up."

"Meanwhile," Noah said, turning to Quincy. "You and your deputies see if you can find where these fellas are hiding out. According to the papers on them, they're mostly all wanted for a crime worthy of jail time. The sooner we can lock 'em up, the better. Are we all agreed on this plan for now?"

The men congregated near the front of the room and continued to speak in low voices. Pippa turned to the group of women. "Ladies. I'm glad we have this chance to talk because I have something to ask you. Supplies were replaced and work has begun on the construction of the opera house. This will be a splendid opportunity to bring the arts to our little community."

The ladies murmured appropriate responses.

"I've been asked to be the director, isn't that positively thrilling?"

"You are the likely person to handle things," Prudence said with a nod. She was never without her cameo brooch at her throat.

"It will be a very small operation at first, of course," Pippa continued. "And securing performers who are touring may be difficult until we've established ourselves, but I do have contacts." Today she was wearing one of her feathered hats and a jade dress with an impressive bustle. "But until then, we shall incorporate the local talent and form our own troupe to perform and sing. I'm counting on you ladies to volunteer your talents."

Opal rested a hand on her protruding belly. "It will

be months before I'm able to commit to something like that. Not now and certainly not with a new baby."

Valentine had joined the gathering. "I sing a little, dear."

"Wonderful, Miss Ewing." Pippa beamed with pleasure.

Prudence lifted her chin. "You won't get me on a stage."

"I will try my hand at acting and singing," Dora told Pippa. "I'm good at memorizing poetry and Bible verses, so you can assign me a lead role."

"Excellent," Pippa said with a smile.

Aunt Mae joined them then, and Pippa shared her plans.

"Well, you don't want to hear me sing anything," she said with a good-natured laugh. "But you know, some of those cowboys can carry a tune and play fiddles."

Leah left the women discussing the troupe for the opera house and sought out Opal, who had found a seat near the door. "How are you feeling?"

"Exhausted, actually. I'm having trouble sleeping."

"A lot of mothers complain of that. Keep up your strengths and eat even when you're not hungry. I'll ask Valentine if she'll make a pot of broth for you. Drink plenty of water."

Opal rolled her eyes.

"I know, I know." She sat beside her. "You're already up during the night, but it's good for you. Rest with your feet up as much as you can. Amos is getting by without you at the store."

"I feel like I'm letting him down. I am so unprepared for this."

"It's normal to feel this way," Leah said to soothe her.

"Your body is going through a lot of changes, and that baby is determining your moods right now."

"How did you learn so much about having babies?"

"I had a close friend who was a midwife. I learned from her." She didn't want to add to Opal's concerns, so she didn't tell her she'd been expecting her own child at the time. The anxious young woman didn't need to hear those stories right now.

"I'm so glad you're here."

"So am I."

Opal reached for her hand. "I don't know your story, and it's none of my business, but I have a feeling you and Daniel are going to be good for each other."

"I hope you're right."

"The way he looks at you does my heart good."

Leah looked at her with surprise. "What way is that?"

"Like you're an exotic flower. His face relaxes and his eyes drink you in."

A touch of embarrassment brought a flush to Leah's cheeks. "You must be mistaken."

"I might be." She glanced at the gathering of men, where Daniel was already watching them. "If I am, I'll do a tap dance on Pippa's opera house stage."

Leah chuckled and met Daniel's eyes across the room. He stood tall and handsome, his shiny chestnut hair combed neatly back, and she caught her breath at the sight of him. Her thoughts immediately went to the night before when he'd come to her room, held her in his strong arms and comforted her. Hannah mentioned she'd cried out in her sleep a time or two on their trip. Even in uncomfortable sleeping arrangements, getting only intermittent sleep, she'd had the nightmares. She'd hoped to not bother Daniel, not let him learn of her private suffering. She had to put the past behind her. During the day she kept those thoughts under control, but sleep made her vulnerable.

"You didn't mention when your baby is due," Opal pointed out.

"September."

"And you're feeling well yourself?"

Leah nodded. "Very well, thank you.

"Good for you." She put her arm around Leah's shoulders, giving her a brief hug. "Our babies will go to school together when they're older."

"I guess they will."

The women smiled at each other.

Valentine joined them then. "Valentine, I thought we might shop for some beef to make Opal a pot of broth."

"Why don't you both skedaddle and I'll do the shopping?"

"If you're sure. Thank you." She bid Daniel and the other ladies goodbye before seeing Opal to her door. She then headed for Daniel's home. *Her* home now, she reminded herself. The sky was a brilliant blue, with a few clouds skittering across the sky. The wind caught her skirts, and she held on to her hat. It was a beautiful day in Kansas. In the distance a train whistle sounded a long mournful cry. The sound signaled prosperity. Cattle and new residents were arriving. Lumber, glass and all manner of items for homes and new businesses were being delivered.

The steady beat of a hammer echoed across the lot as she passed the schoolhouse where the roof was going on the building. Further down Lincoln Boulevard another new home was in the beginning stages of construction, and she imagined it was one of Daniel's projects.

The way he looks at you does my heart good.

What way is that?

Like you're an exotic flower. His face relaxes and his eyes drink you in.

She didn't have any business misleading herself about Daniel's true feelings toward her. He was dear and familiar, as he'd always been. A good friend. And she wouldn't spoil what they shared now with foolish expectations. She'd done that once. She'd chosen Charles because he had a good family and ambition. She'd believed her security depended on marrying a successful man, but she'd also believed that man when he'd taken his vows to love and cherish her. She'd let herself have fanciful ideas about marriage.

With Daniel she knew where she stood. He was a good, trustworthy, hardworking man. His self-made success did mean security, but security of possessions meant nothing without the assurance of his steadfast kindness and integrity. No matter what happened, Daniel was an honest, dependable man, and he would be here for her and her child. They had an arrangement.

Daniel hadn't made any false promises or pledged his love. Opal had simply seen concern in his expression. And Leah was satisfied with that.

Assured that Leah was good to walk home, Daniel tarried at the hotel. Several of the ranchers and homesteaders had shown up for the meeting and they wanted to discuss problems with their cattle.

"I had ten cows die day before yesterday," Judd Ernst said. "At that rate I'll be broke b'fore I can ship 'em out."

His announcement created a ruckus among the cattlemen.

"This never happened b'fore the Texas cows were loading here."

"Somebody needs to pay for the cows lost."

"Cain't afford to lose our own stock."

"Gentlemen, we don't know this is splenic fever," Will said, hands upraised to silence the chaos.

"It's Texas fever all right," Billy Simms argued. "None of the Texas cows are sick and ours are droppin' dead like flies. We need to move the drives west. Some of them are trampling farmland."

"It does sound like Texas fever," D.B. said with an apologetic glance at Daniel.

Daniel felt half sick at the speculation. He'd made a huge financial commitment to this town. He and Will had encouraged families and businesses to travel here and invest all they had. Those people would go broke if the cattlemen took their business farther west. This would be another ghost town like Harper.

"Having the railroad here is what brings the cattlemen," Will argued. "We wouldn't have a town if not for the longhorns."

"We were here runnin' stock before the railroad," Judd pointed out. "Their infected cows kill all of ours, and then where will we be?"

"Why don't we send for the veterinarian in Salina to come over and look at the stock?" Daniel suggested. "In the meantime, we'll do all we can to keep the Texas herds confined. There isn't a drive scheduled to arrive until next week now, and the last of Theo Pierce's cows just shipped out."

"Good riddance," Billy mumbled.

Noah hadn't said anything during the heated discussion. He was part of bringing the Texas cows through, but he ran his own shorthorn stock, as well. So far none of his herd had been affected. "Make sure your stock has clean fresh water," he told the other ranchers. "And we'll wait for the Salina horse doc before making any decisions."

"Make it fast," Billy said.

Daniel nodded. "We will, Billy. No one wants any more cows to die."

He and Will exchanged a concerned glance. The sooner they figured this out the better.

The following morning Valentine prepared them a breakfast of sausage, eggs and biscuits and set a small table in the shade of the overhang outside the back door.

"I think I should build us a porch," Daniel suggested. "For mornings like this. And for evenings. I don't know why I didn't think of it before."

"You had a lot on your mind I'm sure." Leah glanced across the side yard and spotted the horse and plow. "Daniel, what is the horse doing out there?"

"Why, waiting to turn up the earth, of course. I'm going to plant you a kitchen garden."

"A garden!" She looked at him in surprise. "Why that's a lovely idea. And you're doing it yourself?"

He lowered one brow and offered her a twisted grin. "You don't think I'm getting soft, do you? I still work horses and get my hands dirty. I haven't turned into a dandy simply because I operate a few businesses."

She laughed. "I don't think you're getting soft. I simply thought you might have business to attend to."

"This is my business today."

"There's an advantage to being the boss," she supplied.

He grinned. "And having a good pair of boots."

She moved aside the draping tablecloth to examine his footwear. "Did Amos make those?"

"He did. I own four pair."

She raised an eyebrow.

"I was his first customer, and he gave me a free pair for each pair I bought."

"Still, four pair seems excessive."

"I marched hundreds of miles in winter and summer, in snow and rain, wearing boots that were ill-fitting with holes worn in the soles. My feet were swollen, blistered, bandaged and wet. Just the memory of it now makes my feet ache to the bone." He took a breath, let it out slowly. "I swore if I lived through the war and made it out in one piece I'd own the finest boots money could buy. Godwin's boots are the finest I know."

Leah studied him now, so at ease in this setting—his hair mussed, his skin golden, a man of his own making—and imagined the years of hardship that had taken a toll. Her chest ached at the thought of so many men living and fighting under those conditions, so many who'd had the same dreams, but who hadn't lived to make them come true. Her father and brother had been among those who'd experienced the same adversity, far from home, missing their families. Her eyes burned with tears and she blinked them back.

"I'm sorry, Leah. I shouldn't have brought up the war."

She reached immediately for his hand and grasped it until her knuckles turned white. "No, Daniel, I believe you should. I want to hear where you were and what you did, as painful as it may be." A lump rose to her throat, but she forced herself to meet his eyes. "I thought all I wanted to do was forget, but we can never forget. We have to remember what we fought for. What we lost and what was gained. It's the only way to move forward and the only way to never let it happen again."

He turned his hand over and placed his other one on top of hers. His hands were strong and warm, the skin at the base of his fingers lightly callused. Something passed between them in that moment. Something as radiant and warm as the morning sun. Something that bound them by experience and their shared humanity. Something hopeful and honest and right.

Daniel leaned toward Leah and touched his firm warm lips to hers. "Thank you for marrying me."

She blinked in surprise. "You're welcome."

"Finish your breakfast," he said, and they ate and sipped coffee to the sounds of Valentine washing pans and lids in the kitchen.

After breakfast Daniel supplied her with a comfortable canvas chair and the same awning he'd set up for their picnic.

"I'm undoubtedly the most spoiled woman in Kansas."

"Probably. All your hard work is coming after the baby arrives, so enjoy your time now."

"I shall." But she knew motherhood would not be a hardship. She wanted children and couldn't wait for this one.

He hitched the plow to the horse and plowed a sizable plot of land for the garden. He finished and unharnessed the animal and rubbed his nose.

"Is that your horse?" she called.

"No, he belongs to Walter Frye. Mine has never

pulled a plow and the job would have taken three times as long."

"Now you plant the seeds Noah gave us?"

"Now I do a lot of raking to break up these big clods. Then I plant the seeds."

Leah went inside and carried out a tray with a pitcher and glasses. She poured Daniel lemonade. He joined her under the canopy, tossing down his hat and displaying hair wet from exertion and a smudge of dirt on his nose. He sat on the grass, strong, corded forearms over his bent knees and drank three glasses of the refreshing sweet liquid.

"What about Noah?" she asked.

He glanced up at her. "What about him?"

"Why doesn't he have a wife? He doesn't show any interest in the other brides. Has he lost a wife perhaps?"

"No. He stays to himself. He wanted no part of the new brides."

"Is it because he's self-conscious?"

Daniel nodded. "And in more pain than he lets on. The burns aren't only on his face. His chest and arm are scarred as well."

"What happened to him?"

"In the summer of '63 we joined the regiments at Gettysburg. Despite his struggle about fighting his fellow Virginians, he was a good leader. He's brave, honorable. I think he always thought he had to do more, fight harder because he's a southerner. We were fighting at Little Round Top and Brigadier General Weed was killed by a sniper. The rest of us were stunned. Noah, though, he ran forward to take the general's place. His gun backfired and he was burned."

"That's awful."

Daniel nodded.

"I suppose his recuperation took a long time."

"And once he was released he came here, staked a claim," he said. "Will and I found him after the war."

"And you started the town?"

"Honestly we just relished the peace and quiet for a time. Bought up the land with our army pay. Raised some horses. There was a stage station, a few buildings. Then the Union Pacific came through." He took a long sip of lemonade, then went on. "Land value went up and so we sold sections of our land for outrageous amounts. Once the rails were here, the Texans flooded north looking to ship their longhorns east. Will brought in business owners. I built the stockyards."

"And houses."

He nodded. "Need homes for wives and families. Need families for schools and churches. It took less than a year for Cowboy Creek to become an honest-to-goodness town. Seemed like the homesteaders, farmers, businessmen arrived every day. Drovers came through, bringing their cattle, and the cowboys spent their money in town."

"But no women."

"Very few. We decided something had to be done about that." He handed her his glass. "As enjoyable as this is, I'm not going to get the ground ready if I sit here talking all day."

"I guess I'm a bad influence."

He stood. "You're a good listener."

She crooked a finger. "Come here."

"What?"

"Bend down here."

He took a step to stand in front her and leaned down until their faces were inches apart.

She reached up with the pristine white napkin she held and wiped the spot of dirt from the side of his nose.

Their eyes met and held. A dozen questions stirred in the depths of his green eyes. His gaze lowered to her lips.

Leah's heart fluttered. She remembered the kiss he'd given her after they'd said their marriage vows. And the kiss he'd offered only a few hours ago after breakfast. She liked that they were still friends, friends who shared things. This element had been missing from her relationship with her husband. He'd never seemed to have time for her—or interest in her or her feelings or her experiences. She'd never felt important, wanted or needed. She suspected he'd married her because she was reasonably attractive and made a nice picture on his arm at officer's functions. He'd certainly never looked at her the way Daniel was looking at her now.

"That's better," she said a bit breathlessly. "Back to work with you now."

His lips widened into a grin that made her heart skip a beat. "Yes, ma'am. There's more here to do, you know. Besides your kitchen garden."

"What do you mean?"

"I'm planting all the vegetables out here, but Noah also gave us bushes and flowers I've been keeping watered. We need to plant a few trees and get a proper flower garden started."

Daniel went back to his task. The sun felt good. The day was bright and beautiful, and after all this time he had someone to talk to. Will and Noah were good friends of course, but men held their feelings close and avoided uncomfortable subjects. He felt as if he could share anything with Leah. Although he hoped he wasn't being foolish, setting himself up for more disappointment, deep down he sensed she seemed to truly care and was interested in what he had to say. If not for the problems going on with the sick cows and the Murdoch gang, he'd be a happy man.

Now more than ever, the success of Cowboy Creek was imperative.

Chapter Eleven

The following day Daniel got word that the veterinarian from Salina had arrived. He met him at the Cattleman Hotel, where the council had reserved a room for him. They rode out to survey the stockyards and check with nearby ranchers.

"It just don't look like Texas fever," Henry Lowell told him after they'd inspected sick cows on yet another ranch. "They're mighty sick, no doubt about that, but these cows we saw today are getting skinny, their coats are patchy. They stumble." He took off his hat and scratched his head. "True, Texas fever makes 'em stumble, but splenic fever always produces fever and bloody urine."

"I thought the same," Daniel acknowledged. "This looks more like something they ate. I've seen oats get contaminated with pigweed or sorghum with Russian thistle, but not all the ranchers get their feed from the same place. Most of these ranchers grow their own feed, and the same symptoms exist in cows fed differently. It doesn't make any sense if the problem isn't something contagious."

"No, it don't." Henry settled his hat back on his head.

Daniel didn't like where his thoughts were taking him. He glanced around the pasture where they stood. "Let's check their water source."

They found a creek fed by the Smokey Hill River and rode along the bank. Daniel dismounted and walked along a rocky edge, where the water below was deep. After standing still for several minutes, a carp opened its mouth above the water. Farther out he spotted a large bass. Henry had gotten off his horse and investigated upstream. They walked toward each other.

"Nothing wrong with this water," Daniel said.

They rode the fence line, looking at the grass. There were no harmful weeds in sight.

They found Judd Ernst cleaning a horse's hoof outside his barn.

"These cows have any other source of water?" Henry asked.

Judd pointed to the windmill in the nearest pasture. "Well out there a ways."

Daniel and the vet rode out to the well and examined the stock tank. Henry smelled the water. Daniel rode in increasingly wider circles around the area. Spotting a dead snipe, he recalled a magpie he'd seen on the ground earlier. He took a pair of leather gloves from his saddlebag, picked up the bird and went back for the other.

Birds in hand, he headed back to the barn.

"It's possible someone poisoned your stock tank," he told Judd. "Birds probably drank from it."

Judd smacked his hat across his thigh in anger. "I picked up three or four swallows the other day. The missus' cat is missing. Doesn't that beat all? Who'd poison a man's stock?"

Henry joined them and Daniel showed him the birds before finding a shovel in the barn and burying them.

"Well, it ain't splenic fever," Henry confirmed. "Which means the Texas cows didn't bring it here."

"But someone is poisoning our cattle," Judd said with a scowl. "Don't know who. Don't know why."

The fact that the cattle hadn't died from the fever was a relief, but the thought that someone—or more than one person—was out there causing harm was disturbing. Could it have something to do with the Murdoch gang? What possible reason would they have to kill cattle?

"Empty and scrub that tank good," Henry told Judd. "Set a watch or get a dog out there. You got a dog?"

"Dog ran off a year or so ago."

"I'll bet Wolf is the reason no one was able to poison Noah's stock," Daniel said, thinking aloud.

"I'll get a dog. Until then me and my boys can take turn keeping watch."

"Be careful," Daniel warned him. "Whoever this is doesn't have a conscience."

He and Henry headed back to Cowboy Creek. He would alert Quincy and ask for help spreading the word to the homesteaders and outlying ranches. He needed to come up with a plan to safeguard the tanks at the stockyards. At least he was aware of the problem now.

"Enjoy a night at the hotel," he told Henry. "I let them know you'd put your meals on my tab tonight and in the morning. I appreciate you coming all this way to help us figure this out. I knew something was fishy."

"Glad to be of help." They pulled up their horses in

front of the hotel just as Mrs. Foster, the housekeeper, was making her way toward the door with a parcel.

Henry slid from his horse and dashed to take the package from her. She looked surprised, but after a glance over his shoulder at Daniel, she gave the vet a smile and he accompanied her inside.

Daniel headed for the sheriff's office. He had to get to the bottom of these dead cows and safeguard the rest of the cattle. The future of Cowboy Creek was at stake.

"Thank goodness there's an abundance of men in this town," Pippa said to the ladies who gathered in the churchyard the following morning. "From what I hear there are guards posted everywhere—at all the major entrances to town, at all the ranches. This outlaw gang has caused everyone trouble."

"Are they the ones poisoning the cattle?" Opal asked.

"Poisoned?" Dora asked. "It's not Texas fever then?"

"Daniel and the veterinarian investigated yesterday and they determined that the cattle have been poisoned." Leah explained their findings.

"So they think the Murdochs did it?" Pippa asked. "They're robbers. What is the benefit to killing cows?"

Leah shrugged and Valentine shook her head. Everyone was puzzled.

"Let's pray," Hannah suggested. "For the men responsible to be exposed and caught and for the safety of all the men. Even the drovers who are still in town are taking watches and putting themselves in danger."

The congregation was gathered that Saturday for the spring cleaning of the churchyard. There weren't that many graves yet, but it was a tradition many of them had carried from their previous homes, and it gave them peace of mind at a time when so many situations were outside their control. Once the ground was raked and the markers cleaned, the men would work on building a fence, and the women would plant flowers. Valentine and Owen had dug three elm saplings from along Mud Creek to plant.

Leah and Opal had stern instructions from their husbands to rest on the blanket Daniel had spread. By now news had spread that Leah was expecting a baby, so she accepted good wishes from their neighbors. All the women gathered near the blanket, and Opal motioned for a woman Leah had never seen to join them.

"This is Aideen O'Neill. She and her family just arrived and are homesteading to the east."

The women welcomed her.

"A pleasure, i'tis to meet you," Aideen said, in a thick Irish brogue. She wore a plain homespun dress and a clean white apron.

"Aideen has two children," Opal explained.

"Aye, my Owen and little Janet there."

The children she spoke of stood beside a burly red-headed man in work clothes, where he stood speaking to the reverend.

Hannah led a prayer for the town's safety. Others joined in, and their soft voices petitioning the Lord for the safety of their friends and this fledgling town touched Leah.

Afterward, the ladies gathered their tools and set about their tasks. Valentine offered to help Aideen introduce her children to the others, and Leah and Opal settled themselves on the blanket. Hannah joined them, sitting in the center of her riotously ruffled dress. She'd done such beautiful work on Leah's wedding dress, and

Leah had seen a few of her other projects. All were elegant and lovely, yet she dressed herself in almost outlandish dark-colored frills and ruffles, with drapes and enormous collars. She wasn't a tiny woman to start with, plainspoken and unassuming, so her choice of clothing seemed at odds with everything else Leah knew about her.

"Are you feeling any better?" Leah asked.

"Not really. I'm drinking fluids like you suggested, but I'm tired and achy."

"Well, you just rest, dear," Opal said. "We're happy for your companionship. Goodness knows I'm tired of my own company. I've never rested so much in my life."

"It's going to be worth it when you have a healthy baby," Leah said with a smile.

"Amos is such a worrywart," Opal lamented. "He fusses about and refuses to let me even look at the books. He's doing all the work I used to do."

"You're both fortunate to have husbands who are concerned for your welfare," Hannah reminded her.

She was so right. Leah counted her blessings every day. Daniel was kind and thoughtful, always putting her well-being first. "You'll have a husband soon, too," Leah told her. "Has anyone caught your eye? I'm sure you're dodging offers daily."

Hannah blushed. "I've had a few invitations, but I truly haven't felt up to the courting rituals just yet. Perhaps very soon."

"Have you visited Doc Fletcher?" Opal asked.

Hannah glanced away. "Yes. I'm fine, really."

Leah and Opal exchanged a worried glance.

Opal nodded toward a small gathering of men and one short curvy woman, all tidying the same grave.

"The Widow Haywood is certainly enjoying her popularity."

"Yes," Leah said. "Prudence is not lacking in admirers." The young woman wore an apron over a dark blue dress, and even from here Leah made out the cameo brooch on her collar.

"It's encouraging to see the children, isn't it?" Opal remarked. Two of the nearby homesteaders had come for the morning's work, and several children were busily helping their parents rake and pull weeds.

"And soon they'll have a school. Daniel oversees the progress every day, and the roof just went on. I can see it from our porch and from all the south-facing windows."

"Our children will get a good education," Opal said.

Leah gave a satisfied nod. "Yes, they will."

"You will both be wonderful mothers," Hannah said. "Your children are blessed to have you. My mother was beautiful and kind, as well. I miss her every day."

Leah offered the preacher's daughter a gentle smile. "Thank you, Hannah." She gazed across the cemetery. "I miss my mama, too."

"Cowboy Creek is a new beginning for all of us, isn't it?" Opal said. "Our nation is rebuilding and recovering, and here we are in a brand new town with fresh starts."

"It's important we remember that," Hannah added. "The Bible tells us there will be tribulation in this world, and we've seen that aplenty. Even here, with these threats to the cattle and all the schemes those outlaws are coming up with. But Jesus said He came that He might overcome the world. We have to trust Him."

She turned her gray eyes from the landscape to implore Opal and Leah.

"You're right, of course," Leah agreed. "We'll keep praying."

She was thankful to the young girl for her encouragement. She'd been caught up in her concern for this marriage, for her child, for the turmoil and danger threatening this town, but it was always helpful to step back and remember she wasn't alone. She could face what lay ahead, because none of it could be as bad as what was behind.

This was a new day. Tomorrow was another new day. Her future was filled with new days. And she had a lot to make up for and much to appreciate and to be thankful for.

The following morning, Daniel sat beside his new bride as Richard Mosely played the organ and Reverend Taggart led the congregation in a few songs. Thank goodness the reverend sang in a deep, pleasant baritone. Not all ministers had the gift of preaching and the gift of song, so he figured they were doubly fortunate.

He glanced at Leah beside him, and she gave him a becoming smile that made his morning even brighter. She looked so young and pretty in a blue dress, her pale gold hair swept up with a few errant curls on her neck and at her temples. After they'd seated themselves, and while the reverend spoke, Daniel wanted to reach over a scant few inches and grasp the hand she'd rested on the open page of her Bible. Her shiny gold wedding band drew his attention. The warm sun coming through the windows matched his mood, creating a golden moment in time he wanted to remember forever, clear and poignant. This felt so good, so right, so normal. He'd prayed often for a moment like this.

Reverend Taggart finished his message to the hearty amens of the congregation, and the offering baskets were passed. The baskets reached the rear row just as a commotion sounded outside, and the doors to the church were flung open so hard they stretched to the limits of their hinges and sprang back a ways.

All heads turned to see who had caused the ruckus.

Revolvers drawn, two dusty, whiskered men in hats stepped inside the building, their boots and spurs loud on the wood floor. Another clamber alerted them to another two men who had entered from the back entrance and now stood behind Reverend Taggart. The tallest one trained his gun on the crowd, and the other pointed his weapon directly at the reverend's back.

Daniel's blood surged and his heart hammered in his chest. He got to his feet, as did several others, including Will, Owen and Walter Frye. Men on horseback had somehow escaped the notice of the sentries and gotten all the way to the church unnoticed? Nearly every local man, woman and child was gathered in this building, each one vulnerable to whatever the Murdochs had planned. He did a quick calculation of who wasn't present. Neither Quincy or Tim Watson. Only a couple of the drovers ever attended services. He thought he'd seen Buck when he'd come in.

The two tall, thin young men with dirty blond hair and unkempt beards met the descriptions of Zeb and Xavier Murdoch. Four of the gang were accounted for right here, meaning there could be more outside, with the horses most likely.

"How can I help you? What did you gentlemen come seeking?" Reverend Taggart asked.

The one who appeared the older of the two Murdoch

brothers gave a barking laugh and swung the barrel of his revolver in an arc that encompassed half the room. "Why, we came seekin' fame and fortune, don't you know? This here's a pretty little town. Appears the town folk are flush, don't it? Thought maybe we'd drop in and avail ourselves to some of your Christian charity."

"Why don't we go outside, away from the women and children and see what we can do," Will said calmly, taking a step into the aisle.

A shot rang out, provoking a shrill scream and several exclamations of surprise. "Stay right where you are, Mr. Fancypants."

"Shoot 'im, Zeb," the shorter of the brothers said.

"Let's all just stay calm." Daniel raised his hands and turned to fully face the leader, inching his way into the aisle. "Nobody wants to see anyone get hurt."

"I don't much care who gets hurt," Zeb scoffed. "Who are you?"

"Daniel Gardner. That's Will Canfield."

"Enough talk, Gardner. I want that pretty little lady right there…" With the barrel of his revolver, he indicated Pippa, who'd been seated in the front row on the aisle. "To come get these here money baskets and put all the money in here." He took a canvas sack from his waistband and tossed it on the floor.

Chapter Twelve

Daniel met Will's dark, somber eyes for a mere second. Perhaps he could convince the outlaw to let one of them collect the money instead. Will nodded as though interpreting Daniel's look. Pippa Neely was pretty and young, and he had a bad feeling about Zeb Murdoch singling her out. Before anything else could happen, Pippa popped up from her seat and sashayed toward those men as though she dealt with thieves and crooks every day of her life and they didn't trouble her a whit. She snapped up the bag.

"Why you can't just collect your own ill-gotten plunder is the questionable factor here." Her voice was a squeaky octave higher than she'd ever spoken, and she darted forward so quickly the seemingly undauntable Zeb Murdoch started and took a step to the side to avoid her, clumsily bumping into his brother. "Land sakes, you'd think you'd all been raised in a barn, the way you come tromping into the Lord's house with dirt on your boots and your hats on! Is this the way your mama raised you?" She tsked. "I'd be willing to bet that if your mama could see you now she'd box your filthy ears and thrash you a good one. Shamin' your mama, that's what you're doin'."

Daniel couldn't believe his ears or his eyes. Pippa had claimed all along to be an actress, but this brash performance beat everything.

Yapping all the while, the spunky young lady took both offering baskets and dumped their contents into the bag, then shoved them at Zeb and stepped back, fists on hips. "You boys should be ashamed of yourselves, that's what. There's enough pain and heartache in this world to go around. What you should be doing is contributing something positive, instead of robbing and bullying people."

"Enough, woman!" Xavier surprised them all by stepping forward. His brother might have been intimidated by the tiny little spitfire, but he'd apparently had enough. He extended his arm and beckoned for Zeb to give him the bag. "Put those earrings in here and shut your trap."

Pippa gave a sharp laugh and reached for the bobs dangling from her ears. "These are paste. You won't get enough for a penny candy. 'Let him that stole steal no more: but rather let him labor, working with his hands the thing which is good, that he may have to give to him that needeth.'"

Xavier turned to his brother with an evil sneer. "What did she say? Is she actually preaching at us?"

"It means get honest work." She arched an eyebrow, and even though she was probably a foot and a half shorter and a hundred pounds lighter, she managed to look down her nose at the pair of them.

"Pass all your jewelry to the aisle and toss it out here," Xavier barked at the parishioners.

Leah grabbed the back of Daniel's jacket. He turned, grasping her hand, and looked down into her frightened face. He raised his gaze to all the citizens looking to him and to Will. His gaze passed over Amos and Valentine, noted the frightened looks on the faces of their new German neighbors. What an impression this was for their first Sunday morning church service. He clenched his jaw in helpless anger. A movement caught his eye, and he distractedly noticed Miss Haywood with her fingers over the brooch at her throat. Nothing was worth risking these people's lives. He gave a nod. "Pass your jewelry to the person on the aisle. Saving it is not worth someone getting hurt."

Clothing rustled as people removed their rings and necklaces. A couple of the women sniffed. Leah stared at the gold ring on her left hand, the one he'd admired only minutes ago. "It's okay," he said softly.

She slid it from her finger and handed it to him, along with the watches and earrings being passed to her. As others were doing, he made a pile on the polished wood floor.

"Gather 'em up," Xavier ordered Pippa.

Without meeting anyone's eyes she made quick work of sliding all the jewelry into the bag and stuffed it into Zeb's face. He snatched it and took a step back, putting distance between himself and the intrepid little gal.

Zeb's spurs jangled as he walked backward, gesturing behind him for his accomplices to back out the open doors. "If anyone opens these doors before we're out of town—or the rear door—they'll be shot. Don't do anything stupid."

No one said a word as the thieves backed out and banged the doors shut. As soon as the doors were closed, people murmured. Daniel, Will, Owen and a few other men gathered at the rear near the doors.

"We should have guns," Old Horace said.

"So there coulda been a shootout in the middle of the church?" Gus groused and poked Old Horace in the chest with a long finger. "You old fool."

The only lawman present was Buck Hanley, and he was dressed like all the others that morning, his badge hidden beneath his Sunday suit jacket. "I got a good look at all of 'em," Buck said. "It's the Murdoch brothers for sure. We don't know how many more are out there."

Remmy Hagermann had recently started another mercantile on First and Lincoln. "What do you think we should do?"

"Wait until they've cleared town," Buck answered. "Then I'll go fetch Sheriff Davis. He'll likely want to form more than one posse to figure out where they've gone."

"We have fresh tracks now," Will said.

"And someone out there saw them leaving and knows which way they headed," Daniel added.

"Those thieves got my father's watch," Abram Booker said indignantly. "They need to be caught!"

"Prudence's brooch is gone," Dora nearly shouted, bringing attention to the face of the young woman standing on the edge of the crowd. Dora urged her forward. "She's never without that. Was it your mother's, dear?"

Prudence touched her collar nervously and nodded. She didn't lift her gaze.

Leah put her arm around Prudence's shoulders. "I'm sorry. Hopefully you'll get your brooch back, but the important thing is no one was hurt."

The young woman said nothing, but she glanced at D.B. The newspaperman had nothing to say for once. He just shook his head.

Aunt Mae nodded toward Pippa. "Miss Neely's quick thinking confounded them, that's for certain. I don't think they could wait to get out of here."

Opal laughed at that and others joined her.

"I was concerned for you when Zeb singled you out," Daniel admitted to Pippa. "But you proved your worth as an actress today."

"Nobody likes a harpy," she said with a grin. "I figured if I bullied them with my sharp tongue they'd be glad to be rid of me."

Aunt Mae pulled Pippa into her cushioned embrace and the diminutive woman nearly disappeared.

Gus cackled. "I bet they think twice about comin' back."

"I don't know," Amos said. "They got a pretty good haul today, considering the offering—watches, wedding rings and Miss Haywood's brooch."

"My earrings *are* rubies," Pippa regretfully admitted, extracting herself from Aunt Mae. "I lied, hoping to discourage them."

The gathering sobered. The thieves had intimidated them and stolen quite a lot.

Daniel glanced at Leah, keeping a calm demeanor when she was probably shaken. "These things can be replaced," he said. "Everyone is safe."

"Prudence's brooch can't be replaced." D.B. spoke up finally, not bothering to hide his displeasure. "None of us came to Cowboy Creek to get robbed." He made his way through the milling congregation to stand at the door. "May I leave now? Of course we have no way of knowing how much time has passed."

Daniel conferred with Will and Buck. The deputy reached for the door handles. "Go home and get your guns, men. We'll meet in front of the marshal's office in fifteen minutes. Quincy will direct us from there."

Just as the doors pushed open, the sound of gunfire erupted. Shots volleyed from the west, rather than from the center of town, which meant the Murdochs had headed that direction and run into either opposition or victims.

"Get back inside!" Buck motioned for everyone to hurry back in, and the women complied.

Hoofbeats sounded and James Johnson galloped toward the gathering of men in front of the church. "Is everyone all right?"

"Yes. What's happening?" Daniel asked.

"One of the sentries was knocked out. Another rode in and let Quincy know the Murdochs were headed for town. We caught up to them before they could get out of town, but we couldn't outrun them. I think one of them is shot. Go home and get your guns. We're going after them."

"We need to get the women to their homes safely and quickly." Will opened the door and barked instructions. "Everyone go home as quickly as possible. Stay inside."

Leah grabbed on to Daniel's hand and people hurried past them. They were some of the last to leave the church building. They had walked that morning. "Are you feeling well enough to walk home?"

They headed for Eden Street. "Yes, I'm good."

"I'll buy you a new ring," he promised.

"I know."

He took her hand like he'd wanted to in church and raised her fingers to his lips, kissing them as they walked. He didn't want to hurry her, but she kept a good pace. They arrived home and he made a quick change of clothes, strapping on his holster and loading his rifle. Leah filled his canteen and handed it to him as they stood on the front walk. Worry lines etched her brow. He took her upper arms and leaned down to kiss her forehead. Standing straight, he gazed into her eyes and read her concern.

"Daniel." Her voice trembled.

"It's going to be all right, Leah."

Swallowing hard, she whispered, "Please be safe."

"I will."

"Promise me."

"I promise I will be cautious." He released her shoulders and she pressed her clasped fingers to her mouth in a prayerful manner. "Please don't worry, Leah." His admonition was spoken in a thick voice, betraying his own concern. "It's not good for you."

She shook her head as if to agree she wouldn't worry, but she didn't allow herself to speak. Her eyes said it all. Large and blue and luminous, they petitioned him to come back. She'd lost her family, lived through nightmares equal to his, survived by sheer grit and the grace of God, and had finally found this oasis of safety.

"Nothing is going to happen to me, Leah," he assured her, and then decided she needed to know something so she didn't live in constant fear of displacement. "If anything ever did happen to me—no, I just have to say this to set your mind at ease—everything is yours. The house, money, property. You're taken care of."

Nostrils flaring, she narrowed her eyes. "Daniel Gardner, don't you even speak of it!"

"I should have told you a couple of weeks ago when I had the legal papers drawn up. This wasn't the best time, but you needed to know."

She looked away, her gaze traveling toward the nearly completed school, and she sighed. "All right then."

"Get some rest." He backed away, grabbed his hat and settled it on his head. After he picked up his rifle, he turned and loped toward the livery.

Leah watched him go, her breath catching in her throat, her heart an ache in her chest. She was angry with him for telling her he'd left everything to her, as though there may be a chance he wouldn't return, but she was grateful he wanted to set her mind at ease as a precautionary measure. That's why he'd told her, of course. He had a heart as big as the wide-open state of Kansas.

Thirty minutes passed, and in that time all she saw was the revealing expression on his beloved face when he'd looked at her before he left. He didn't know all of her circumstances, didn't know who she was inside. She was weak and selfish, and he was strength and warmth and goodness. Daniel's honesty scared her. She was so fragile, she would break if he knew who she really was. She wanted to cry when he looked at her the way he had, because she was so hungry for his concern and compassion. She could not wait here alone, so she closed up the house and walked to the Godwin's, where she climbed the outside stairs and knocked on the door. A moment later, Opal opened it. They spoke at the same time.

"I couldn't sit at home."

"I'm so glad you're here."

Opal smiled. "Come in. I'll make tea."

The Godwins had comfortably furnished the rooms over their boot shop. "This is so nice," Leah said, looking around the kitchen.

"We have a sitting room, two bedrooms, plus storage under the eaves. The stairs are getting to be a bit much, however."

"Does the climb cause you any pain?"

Opal shook her head. "Not pain, no. I just feel so tired and my body aches."

"Are you sleeping?"

"I can't seem to find a comfortable position, but I sleep a few hours at a time."

"Most of the things you describe are fairly common," Leah explained, "but you haven't gained weight, which concerns me. Rest, eat and drink water is my advice."

"So you've said."

"I have. And I'm following my own advice." Leah smiled. "I will make the tea," she offered. "You sit." She boiled water and poured it over the tea in Opal's china pot, then seated herself.

"I'm so thankful you're here." Opal looked up from her cup. "Not just right now, though I am thankful you came, but that you came to Cowboy Creek. Having you here has made a big difference. Amos is more assured about leaving me during the day because you set his mind at ease, and I feel better knowing I could call on you if I needed you."

"Yes, any time."

"Well. Thank you."

"Don't thank me. I came because I was desperate for

a fresh start and needed a home for my baby. Thank the men who sent for the bride train."

"That must have been terrifying for you, to lose your husband knowing you were going to have a baby and having nowhere to go."

"My family home is gone," Leah agreed. Along with the homes of a lot of others. She'd never felt safe or secure with her first husband. When she'd learned she was pregnant the second time after losing a baby while living on an outpost, she'd insisted she go back to Pennsylvania. That hadn't worked out well either, because their desperate escape from the rebels had taken its toll on her body, and she'd lost that baby soon after her mother and cousin died. She'd eventually had no choice but to make her way back to Charles. He'd been no comfort. She couldn't tell Opal about the other babies. Perhaps one day she would, after Opal's baby was born strong and healthy.

She sipped her tea. "How bold was it of those outlaws to come right up to the church and disrupt the service?"

"No doubt they knew the men would be unarmed. It was a heartless deed, taking our wedding rings besides the cash." Opal looked at her hand with its bare ring finger.

Leah absently curled the fingers of her left hand and rested the other hand over it. "It's not easy to tell ourselves not to set up our treasures on earth when those treasures are symbols of wedding vows."

"And love," Opal added, her tone wistful, and then looked at Leah apologetically. "I'm sorry, I didn't mean—"

"No offense taken. Daniel and I have a partnership. You and I may have different circumstances, but each of us had something important taken from us, and now our husbands are out there risking their lives to hunt down those thieves."

Leah had a thought and glanced around. They must do everything in their power. She prayed for Daniel's safety, but there was power in numbers and the men needed all the prayers they could offer. "How many people do you think we could sit in here?"

"I don't know. A dozen maybe? Why?"

"I don't want you traveling those stairs again, but what if I go find a messenger and send him to gather the other ladies and bring them here for an impromptu prayer meeting?"

"I doubt anyone has eaten yet," Opal answered.

"I'll let the messenger know the women can bring along something to share for a meal."

Opal smiled. "Let's do it."

Thunder rumbled, and the first fat drops of rain spattered on Daniel's shirt. The late afternoon had grown increasingly dark, and black clouds rolled across the Kansas sky. He took his slicker from his saddlebag and pulled it over his head, covering the holster that held his rifle and noting Will and Buck had done the same. The tracks had split hours ago, and they'd been following what seemed to be a wild goose chase ever since. The men they were chasing were crafty and had plenty of experience outsmarting posses.

"No chance of finding their trail now," Will said as rain pelted the ground.

"Might as well head back to where we split up," Buck agreed. "I have a feeling they're long gone."

By the time they met up with the others, the ground

was becoming soft. Rain drizzled from the brim of Daniel's hat. A blinding flash of light and a resounding clash startled the horses. Walter Frye's horse reared up and Walter slid from the saddle, landing on the ground with a hard thud. Daniel rode up close and leaned out to grab the bay's reins and lead it away from the man on the ground. Walter wasn't getting up.

Will and Amos jumped to the ground and ran to kneel beside him.

"You all right?" Will asked.

"My arm's busted," Walter gritted out between clenched teeth. He sat upright and Amos gingerly helped him to his feet. He released a shout of anger. "I didn't need this! I got a business t' run."

"We'll get you fixed up," Remmy said.

Buck grabbed what looked like a shirt from his saddlebag, lifted Walter's slicker, and firmly tied the fabric so it secured his arm against his body. Walter sucked in air through his teeth and blew it out in a curse. Buck held the stirrup while Daniel kept the rein in hand and the horse still so Walter could get back onto the saddle one-handed. Daniel gave him the reins.

A couple of hours later, night had fallen, rain still pelting the streets, and Walter sat in Doc Fletcher's office, letting a plaster cast dry. "Will and I will take care of the livery tonight," Daniel told him. "You should probably stay here and let that cast harden. Get some rest. I'll bring you clothes in the morning."

"You'll get a fine breakfast," Doc said. "Aunt Mae always sends over meals for my patients when she knows they're here. Almost worth a busted arm, it is."

"I doubt that, but looks like I don't have no choice. Thank you, Daniel."

"Least I can do."

"The drovers' horses are stabled, besides the regulars. Theo's and Johnson's. They'll need let out into the corral in the morning if the rain lets up."

"I've got it, Walter."

He found Will across the street at the sheriff's office, along with half a dozen other men.

"We need to lift the gun ban until this is figured out." D.B. Burrows sat on one of the two chairs, his feet on the desk, fingers laced over his belly.

"It's a law for a reason," Will disagreed. "We go changing the law, we lose control. Our goal is peace and quiet."

"We've got no control," D.B. argued. "We're sitting ducks here. It'll be real quiet once half the town is either shot or packs up and moves out."

Daniel raked a hand through his hair and stretched his neck and shoulders hoping to release kinks of tension. "Quincy shot one of them. They found out they can't just ride in to make trouble and get away without a fight."

"The sentries worked," Will said. "They alerted the sheriff."

"Those men could've barged into the church shooting." D.B. lowered his feet and stood. "I don't call that protection."

"We'll double the sentries," Will insisted.

D.B. headed for the door. "Have Owen build some coffins. You're gonna need 'em." He exited and slammed the door behind him.

Chapter Thirteen

Daniel entered the foyer, and Leah met him before he reached the doorway to the sitting room. "Daniel!"

He caught her as she threw herself into his arms. "I'm wet and muddy."

"I don't care," she said, burrowing her face against his shirt. "You're safe."

"I'm sorry you had to wait so long."

She leaned back and looked at him. "Did you catch them?"

"No, they're long gone. They had their escape planned."

"Do you think they'll be back?"

"Hard to say. This didn't turn out as well as they'd hoped, so they may be discouraged." He tightened his arms around her and held her close. "One of them was shot. Hopefully they've moved on."

"I went to Opal's and we gathered the women to pray."

He raised an eyebrow. "You were supposed to stay in."

"We were inside when we were at Opal's. I've already heated water," she said, pulling away and gesturing for him to follow her to the kitchen. "If you bring in the tub, I'll fill it."

"I'll fill it. You'll watch."

"Very well." She sat on a kitchen chair and observed as he carried in the copper tub and used all the kettles of water she'd kept warm on the stove to fill it half full. She'd set out towels, soap and clean clothing. "I knew you'd be wet and tired."

"That's thoughtful of you, Leah."

She stood and headed toward the hall. "I kept something warm for you to eat, as well. It was a long day. Let me know when you've finished."

He washed in the warm water. Only a few months ago he'd had no one to come home to. This was an entirely different life coming home to someone who'd been waiting for him. Someone who cared about his welfare. Leah did care, he was sure. They had entered this arrangement as a convenience, but he admitted to himself he'd hoped for more all along. He was all she had, he reminded himself. She might care, but he wasn't the one she'd fallen in love with or the one she'd chosen to marry.

A short time later, after he'd eaten the casserole she'd kept hot, she served him a slice of apple pie and poured coffee. "You cooked, too?"

"No, the ladies shared a meal at Opal's, and I brought home a plate for you. Apparently this is Aunt Mae's award-winning pie. Seems she enters it in the county fair and has won every year."

"Not to take away from Aunt Mae's accomplishment, but we've only had two fairs so far and there aren't that many women to enter pies," he said with a grin. He ate a few bites of the pie and drank the coffee. "This is all new for me, Leah."

"What's that?" She'd seated herself in the nearest chair.

"Someone waiting at home. Someone concerned."

She folded her hands on top of the table. Her gentle gaze moved over his features. What did she see when she looked at him? What went on inside her head and heart that she didn't speak aloud?

"I suppose you've already done more than your share of waiting at home."

"I suppose I have."

He pushed away the plate. "I'm sorry about the way I told you I made a will."

She lifted her chin. "That scared me a little."

He reached and lifted her hand. It felt small and delicate in his, her skin soft and smooth. His own were rough and clumsy. He used one finger to trace the spot on her finger where her ring had been that morning.

She lifted her bright blue gaze. "None of this is your fault."

"I'm responsible for these people. Will and I, we set up this whole town, advertised for shop owners, tradesmen, got the town council to agree to send for brides." A muscle ticked in his jaw. "We promised to bring cattle through, finance businesses, build homes, provide a prosperous community."

"And you have."

"And now we can't protect them," he bit out.

She sat straighter. "Don't count these people short," she told him. "The women got together and prayed. We're all strong. The men are resourceful and determined. The Murdochs couldn't have been expecting to be confronted as soon as they left the church. They've seen that the people here are peace-loving, but that we will defend ourselves. Hopefully, we've seen the last of them."

"I pray you're right."

She turned her hand to grasp his. "I trust the decisions you're making."

He lifted her hand to his lips and kissed her soft skin. "Thank you, Leah."

She got up and moved to hold his head against her midriff. He wrapped his arms around her, and she threaded her fingers through his damp hair. He remembered the baby growing under her apron and leaned back to lay his palm flat against the fabric. Of course there was nothing to feel yet, but he marveled that a life was nestled safely beneath his hand. "I haven't been around many babies," he said hoarsely. "I admit I'm a little intimidated by the whole thing. By this. By the fact that a newborn will be with us soon."

"I've helped quite a few women bring their babies into the world," she said. "The babies themselves aren't so frightening. They just need to be held and fed. But to tell you the truth, all I've ever felt for myself is inadequacy. And fear."

"Even the first time?"

"Yes. I was stranded on that outpost and I didn't know a thing about what to do or what was going to happen. After the baby didn't make it, I was still alone. And heartbroken."

"Your husband was in the field?"

"Yes."

He looked up at her. "I have so much to be thankful for. We have a good life ahead of us. I understand you've already lost a lot, Leah. Too much. I won't be leaving you."

Cupping his head, she smiled down at him and stroked his cheeks with her thumbs. "We have a lot of living to do," she agreed.

Daniel stood then, taking her into his arms and holding her close. Her heart beat steadily against him. Inching back, he looked into her eyes, recognizing the trust in their luminous blue depths. The touch of her hand on his shoulder was a warmth he welcomed. "You're not inadequate," he assured her. "And you have no reason to be afraid any more. You're healthy and strong. The baby will be healthy and strong. And you're going to make a wonderful mother."

Her lower lip trembled. She swallowed and grasped his shirtfront as if holding on to him made his promises so. With one fingertip he caught a single tear glistening on her lower lash. She attempted to duck her chin, but he caught it with a knuckle and didn't let her hide her emotions from him. He took away the support of his hand and used his knuckles to graze her jaw. She released a trembling breath.

"I was worried about you," she confessed on a shaky note.

"I will always come back to you," he said.

A line furrowed her forehead. "You can't promise that. No one can."

"I promise I will always use caution and not place myself in unnecessary danger." She cared. She'd always cared, but as a friend. She'd come west to find a husband and he'd filled the bill. He wasn't foolish enough to think he was any more special to her than he'd ever been. But he could live with their relationship if he didn't expect more than she was able to give.

She raised herself on tiptoe and bracketed his face with her palms while she bored her cornflower-blue gaze into his. "You'd better not place yourself in danger."

She'd lost everyone. He was her last connection with the good memories of her past. They had each other now.

He only had to move an inch or two to place a gentle kiss on her waiting lips, and she met the kiss. Too gentle, too brief for his liking. She gave him a wondering smile and they kissed again.

Friends didn't share kisses like that one. The kisses confused him and pleased him at the same time. They gave him hope.

Daniel released her. "You need your rest."

She reached for the dishes on the table, but he stopped her hand with his.

"I've got these. You go ahead. I'll carry water up for you."

She backed away and left the kitchen. Daniel stood an entire minute, allowing his heart to find a respectable cadence. Perhaps they were destined to be more than friends after all.

News traveled fast and stories grew larger and better. Pippa was the talk of the town, having taken the Murdoch brothers to task and making a show of being an unappealing victim. The other news that gave them ease came by telegraph. Ruffians had shot up the town of Morgan's Creek, forty miles to the north. Half a dozen horses were shot in a corral and the saloon was robbed at gunpoint. One of the thieves had been wearing a bandage over his left ear and wrapped around his head, and that person's description could easily identify him as one of the Murdoch brothers.

For all intents and purposes, it looked as though the Murdochs had moved on. Perhaps they'd keep going. The town council kept the sentries in place, just as a safeguard, but the atmosphere in town improved.

Leah asked Daniel if they might host a small dinner, inviting his good friends Will and Noah, and he thought it sounded like a fine idea. Noah declined the invitation, and Leah was disappointed. She barely knew the man, though he and her husband were close. Will and Dora arrived on time, however, and Valentine stayed later that evening to serve dinner and clean it up afterward.

"You set a lovely table, and your wedding china is beautiful," Dora told Leah over dessert. "I see you have all the pieces in your china closet."

"Daniel ordered the cabinet, and I look at the china every day," Leah answered. "It reminds me of home. Of long ago, when my family was together and we gathered around the table with friends. Those were the best days of my life. We were carefree and innocent."

"Where did you grow up, Dora?" Daniel asked.

"My grandfather taught at Geneva Medical College in New York. He died when I was very young, and my parents moved us, along with my grandmother, to Ohio. All of us—my father, my two younger brothers and I—worked for my uncle who owned a textile factory. We didn't know many happy-go-lucky days there." She set down her fork and looked directly at Leah. "My grandmother passed away, and a couple of years later the war came and my brothers went off." She glanced at Will and back at her plate. "One of them survived and lives in Ohio. Then my father read about Cowboy Creek and decided it was time to start a new venture, so my parents came here and opened the general store."

Everyone had a story. Dora's was obviously wrought with difficulties, as well. Everything Leah knew about textile factories was unpleasant. She didn't want anyone asking her questions about her experiences once the war had come, so she didn't voice her curiosity.

"At one point I returned to New York and was a part of the Loyal League," Dora told them.

"Collecting signatures to pass the Thirteenth Amendment?" Will asked, and turned to look at her. "You never mentioned that."

Dora shrugged. "My group did a bit of traveling. I rode the train with Elizabeth Stanton and visited northern states. We disbanded a couple of years ago, but it was a good experience. I traveled to Illinois with a friend for a time, but after reading my parents' letters about this new town, I decided to see what it was like. I came and I met Will."

Will gave her a brief smile and sipped his coffee. Leah hadn't seen any affection displayed between the two of them, but she knew little about warmth between men and women, save the kindness Daniel showed her, and that was the mark of friendship.

"Perhaps we could see how progress is coming along on the house," Dora said to Will. She tucked her arm through the crook of his, her unusual square smile revealing her bottom teeth.

Dora had her own little house in town, which seemed surprising since she only occasionally helped out at the store and didn't appear to have another income.

"Have the Murdochs been spotted?" Dora asked. "I've heard nothing."

"They seem to have hightailed it out of our area," Will replied.

"Well, that's good news." Dora patted his arm through his sleeve and turned her attention to her cup of tea.

"Just in time," Daniel replied. "Burrows was pushing to lift the no-gun law. The last thing we need is for the citizens to be walking around armed. Though we came close for safety's sake."

"I feel safer knowing there are sentries out there," Leah confessed.

"That's not changing for the time being," Will added in a reassuring tone. "Until we're sure they've moved on."

"Thank you for dinner," Dora said. "Once Will and I are married and the house is furnished, we'll have you over."

"I'll look forward to it," Leah replied. "I wish Noah would've come."

"Maybe next time," Daniel said.

Valentine appeared silently and removed their plates.

Dora watched the woman's efficient movements, and after she'd returned to the kitchen, she leaned toward Leah. "You must tell me how you located such an efficient woman. I'm going to want help just like her."

"Miss Ewing isn't in our permanent employ," Daniel said. "She's here so Leah doesn't tax herself and is able to rest. Once the baby comes, and both Leah and the baby are doing well, we won't need her, unless Leah wants to keep her on."

"Perhaps she'll be able to work for us then," Dora said excitedly.

"That will be up to her," Leah replied. "I know she likes to keep busy, and I'll feel bad to see her go, but I won't be able to justify the help once I'm on my feet again."

"You don't have to justify anything," Daniel said to her. "If you want her help, it's yours."

Dora glanced from Daniel to her fiancé. "That's so romantic. Isn't it, Will?"

Leah's cheeks warmed. She met Daniel's gaze and let hers dart away. "It's practical and it's extremely generous. Thank you, Daniel."

"Anything to keep you safe and well." She looked back at him, and the warmth in his gaze took her breath away.

Dora drew their attention by setting down her glass with a thunk. Her blue-eyed gaze flicked over her dinner companions, surprising Leah with an undercurrent she couldn't put her finger on. Admiration? Jealousy?

"I suppose it's too dark to see the house tonight?"

"Yes," Will replied. "If you'd like, we can go in the morning."

She leaned into him and rested a hand over the front of his shirt. "Thank you. I'd love to."

Will's stiff expression surprised Leah. Dora certainly seemed to make him uncomfortable, though their interaction was polite and Dora seemed enamored with him. Perhaps her demonstrations in front of Daniel and herself embarrassed him. He'd always been a private person.

After they'd gone, Valentine squared away the kitchen and let herself out. It was late, but Leah joined Daniel in the library. Owen had built a wall of shelves, three-fourths of which were empty. Seeing them reminded her she could purchase him books as gifts.

"Thank you for planning tonight's dinner," he said.

"You're welcome. I'm only sorry Noah didn't accept our invitation."

He tilted his head. "Don't take it personally. He doesn't leave his place often."

"It's a testament to your friendship that he came to our wedding, then, isn't it?" She admired the strong line of his jaw, the breadth of his shoulders.

"I suppose it was."

She let her lips curve up in a saucy smile. "I guess you'll have to take me to visit him then. I want to know the important people in your life."

Daniel crossed to where she stood. He rested his fingertips against her cheek, and she looked up into his eyes. "That's a good idea. There's a good fishing spot near his place. We could go fishing and drop by."

"Fishing?"

Daniel nodded.

"I haven't been fishing…well, probably since the last time I went with you and Will."

"The river is pretty," he mentioned. "I can bring the canopy."

"That's too much work. I'll wear a hat."

"I have a canvas folding chair."

She raised her eyebrows. "That you can bring."

He grinned. "We're going to do just fine together, Leah."

She studied him with contentment, then smiled back. They'd been friends for many years. Daniel was good-natured and kind. She rested her head against his chest, where she heard the steady beating of his heart. He wrapped his arms around her and held her in his warm embrace. He was safe and dependable. She regretted the times she'd looked over him, neglected him in her search for security and a solid marriage. "You're not the same person you were back home, Daniel."

"How do you mean?"

"You frightened me with your talk of ranches and cattle and heading west," she admitted. "You never sat still. You were always planning, working, looking to the future."

"I don't think I've changed at all."

She eased away and looked up at him. "How is that?"

"I still talk about horses and cows, I did come west, and I'm still planning and building and looking to the future."

"I suppose so." She shrugged. "I guess because I didn't want those things, your big talk scared me. I wanted to live in the city and have a safe, comfortable life."

Stiffening, he released her and took a step back. "You will be safe and comfortable here. I'll see to it."

She felt bereft without the solid strength of his arms. She hugged herself and nodded. "Yes. Yes, we'll both be safe and comfortable here."

But she'd said something wrong, because he moved to his desk and seated himself behind it.

Daniel wished Leah a good night after she'd selected a book and told him she was going to her room. It had been a nice evening. She was an excellent hostess and a pleasant companion. It had been thoughtful of her to invite Will and to consider Noah. These past few days he'd been lulled into the pretense that theirs was a normal marriage.

He'd never hoped to fool himself. He shoved a hand through his hair, frowning as he replayed their last conversation. Leah hadn't meant to expose her disappointment in how her life was turning out. She'd wanted to live safely and comfortably in the city. She had never wanted to move to a cow town in Kansas and live within sniffing distance of the stockyards. Life had dealt her a cruel blow, and she was only here because of Cowboy Creek—because *he* was her last resort. Her second choice. Just as he'd always been.

It wasn't that she wasn't gracious or grateful, and it wasn't that she wasn't trying her very best, because she was. The problem was that underneath the average everyday facade of their marriage was the bitter truth.

Leah had settled for being his wife and there was nothing he could do to change that.

At breakfast the following morning, Daniel surprised Leah with an invitation to go fishing.

"Now? Don't you have to go to work?"

"I'm the boss, remember? I haven't taken many days off and it's about time I enjoy myself more."

"In that case I'd love to."

"While you get ready, I'll go get a buggy and buy a lunch at the Cowboy Café. Nels Patterson makes mouthwatering chicken salad. He always sells his sandwiches at the county fair."

She dressed in a cotton dress, comfortable shoes and gathered a wide-brimmed hat. She tucked a book in a small basket as the sound of the horse and buggy drew close. Daniel helped her up to the seat.

"I didn't bring the canopy because there are trees along the bank if you need shade."

"I won't wilt in the sun," she assured him with a smile.

He did carry the canvas folding chair and settled her comfortably where she could watch the sun sparkling on the water and hear the sounds of the frogs and birds. He squinted at her from beneath the brim of his hat. "I brought a pole for you."

"That only makes more work for you," she said.

"I don't mind." He baited the hook, threw the line into the water and handed her the pole. "It's more fish if you catch any."

He took his pole and walked a short way up the riverbank. Leah appreciated the peaceful beauty of these moments. There had been a time when she couldn't imagine herself doing something so ordinary, a time when she'd longed for life and a home in the city. Recent years had shown her days like this were the true treasures. The sun warming her through her dress and the water lapping against the bank combined to lull her into a sense of contentment. Within minutes Daniel caught the first fish, a glistening trout, and strung it on a line in the water. He turned, his handsome grin earning her notice.

She came dangerously close to letting down her guard. She was feeling emotional. It was normal, what with the baby and with all she'd been through, now with finding an old friend—someone who shared her good memories. But she couldn't afford to get her heart involved when it came to this marriage. She was smarter than that.

Right now Daniel was her rock, seeing her through

this pregnancy, through this difficult time in her life. She'd put her trust in his friendship. Eventually she would be able to pull her weight. Once the baby came she'd be a full partner and help him in his dream of building Cowboy Creek. But caring too much about a person was risky.

She caught a small fish on her line, and he got a couple more. He stored them all in a pail of water under the buggy and spread a blanket in the shade.

"Shall we drop by and see what Noah's doing this noon?" Daniel asked.

"I guess we had planned that, hadn't we?" She unpacked the hamper. "Do you think he'll mind if we interrupt his work day?"

"He'll mind. But he doesn't accept our invitations and he sure won't invite us, so we'll go uninvited."

"He must get lonely out there on his land all alone," she remarked. "Had you hoped he might show interest in one of the brides?"

"Will and I discussed the possibility. Pippa is too outgoing and..."

"Overstimulating?" she supplied.

Daniel nodded. "She's great fun, smart, talented— I'm sure she'll make a good match soon—but I don't think she's suited to life on a farm."

"I think you're right. Prudence hasn't shown interest in much other than work. She's had dinner with a few of the locals."

"What of Hannah?" he asked. "I rarely see her."

"The poor girl's been under the weather much of the time. I've made a point to check on her at the boardinghouse, just to make sure she's eating and taking care of herself. Aunt Mae is doing her best to watch after her, as well."

He looked concerned. "I hope it's nothing serious."

"It seems like exhaustion, and she assured me she's gone to seek the doctor's care."

"Will and I spoke briefly about bringing it up to the council to send for more brides. We need to talk about it again."

"You've had a lot on your mind," she reminded him.

He accepted the jar of lemonade she handed him and unwrapped a sandwich. "You seem to be feeling well."

"I am." She rested the hand holding her sandwich on her lap and looked up. "I feel surprisingly well, actually. I never felt this way before. I can't explain it."

"You don't have to. It's one of those mysterious woman things I wouldn't understand."

She shrugged and smiled.

"How did it happen, Leah? If you don't mind telling me. The babies you lost before?"

She set down her sandwich and brushed her palms together. She'd told her mother about the first baby, of course, but she'd never told anyone since. Her stomach fluttered nervously, but it was time. Daniel was her husband, after all.

Chapter Fourteen

"We changed locations a couple of times. Some forts were large, but most were small and rustic. I never knew if I'd be better off staying back in Pennsylvania or traveling with Charles. Most of the campaigns required the wives to stay behind anyway, but I guess the army thought it was good for morale to have the women waiting at the fort. It was unbearably hot that summer, and the wives stayed in small wooden structures strung together right out in the blazing sun." She brushed bread crumbs from her skirt and paused a moment.

"The army provided us servants, so the work wasn't hard, but the boredom was unbearable, so I was helping out as a teacher. We didn't have a real doctor, so the wives helped each other as best they could, and I learned a lot from one of them. Her husband was transferred and she left. It was after that I had problems." She pursed her lips as though forming her next words. "My feet and ankles swelled in the heat, so I stayed home and didn't go to school. I didn't feel well, had trouble eating, and after several false alarms, I gave birth too early."

"I'm so sorry," Daniel said.

"He was a boy," she said. "Perfect and so, so tiny." She glanced out across the sparkling river. "The next time I learned I was going to have a baby, I'd been helping the medical officers. There was one engagement after another and many were wounded. I'd seen so much and was so weary by then I insisted I go stay with my mother. I'd had enough of the suffering on those outposts."

He nodded with understanding.

She didn't go into details about her stay at home or what had happened. "I was back in Pennsylvania when I lost the second baby."

"A girl or a boy?" Daniel's question surprised her. Charles had never even asked.

She closed her eyes. "Another boy."

A silence fell between them. Finally, Daniel said, "You know your babies are in heaven, Leah."

When she opened her eyes, tears blurred her vision. She nodded. "I do. But I wanted them in my arms. I needed to hold them, love them."

He moved food aside to shift beside her and wrapped an arm around her shoulders. Snuggling close, it felt good to be able to talk about her loss, to share with someone who cared and sympathized. For the first time since the war she felt as though her feelings mattered, as though *she* mattered to someone. As though she wasn't alone.

Daniel made her feel important, and she wasn't sure she was deserving of that. Initially she'd been too foolish to recognize the nature of a good man. She'd thought she'd felt something for Will, but separation had shown her it had been a girlish infatuation. Upon meeting him, she'd imagined Charles was a good choice and she'd chosen to marry him.

She'd suspected Daniel had felt something for her, but he'd never voiced it. He'd seemed happy for his friend when she and Will had planned to stay in touch. They'd all been young, and if Daniel had experienced a youthful infatuation with her, he'd moved beyond that long ago. His kindness and concern was that of one human being for another. She didn't imagine she'd ever mean more to him than a close friend. But having a good friend was a blessing.

"It's different this time," she told him in a soft voice. "I don't feel sick. My feet and legs aren't swelling. This baby is going to be well and healthy."

Daniel touched his nose to her temple, to her silken hair, and the citrus scent enveloped him. She was brave and strong, this woman. She had endured a lot to get to this place. On top of being alone, she undoubtedly missed her husband, but she remained positive and cheerful. She didn't feel sorry for herself. She did what needed to be done. "We're going to do just fine, Leah."

They finished their lunch and sat companionably another half hour in the shade before Daniel loaded their belongings into the buggy and they headed for Noah's.

His friend had a mare tethered outside the barn near a stock tank when they arrived. Daniel helped Leah down just as Wolf bounded toward the visitors.

Leah eyed the large dog warily and tucked herself behind Daniel's shoulder.

"Hey, boy," Daniel said to the animal.

Wolf raised his nose to the air, catching scent of the newcomer.

"Wolf, go lie down," Noah ordered. The big animal moved away and obediently lowered himself into the grass.

"Wolf?" Leah spoke the word near his ear.

"Only half," he assured her. "He's not as dangerous as he looks."

"What brings the two of you out?" Noah asked.

Daniel led Leah to within several feet of the horse. "You didn't accept our invitation, so we came by to see you. We were in the area. Fishing."

"I was busy."

"Too busy for friends?".

At Daniel's pointed question Noah glanced at him from under the brim of his hat, slid a glance at Leah, and then picked up a scrub brush and pail and washed the horse with long effective brush strokes. "Not much for small talk."

"Haven't seen anything of the Murdochs since the incident at the church."

"Heard about that. Think they're gone?"

"Appears that way, but we're still cautious. Still have outlooks posted."

"If they're smart they headed out."

"I'm going to find the…um…" Leah's voice trailed off.

"Find what?" Daniel asked.

"The necessary?"

"The—oh, sure. Behind the house there."

She cast an anxious glance behind her. "Don't let Wolf follow me."

"Wolf, stay," Noah ordered.

Nose in the air, the dog watched Leah walk away.

"Fishing, huh?" Noah asked.

"Caught five good-sized trout," Daniel replied. "One was Leah's catch."

"She looks well."

Daniel nodded. "She is. She's making friends. Has the house looking nice. She's trying really hard."

"And a kid, huh?"

"Yes."

"You okay with that?" Noah asked.

"I'm perfectly okay with it. I want a family."

Noah scooped fresh water from the tank and poured it over the horse, swiping away suds with one hand, repeating the action until the animal was rinsed. "Even though it's not yours?"

"It will be mine. Leah is my wife."

Noah gave him a long, assessing look. "You'll make a good father."

Daniel grinned. "I intend to."

Leah returned a few minutes later. "You have a nice spread here," she said to Noah.

"I like it," he answered.

"I'll walk her in the sun," Daniel offered, taking the mare's bridle and leading her away. Maybe leaving Leah and Noah alone for a few minutes would break the ice. Occasionally he glanced toward them. Leah had a knack for talking to anyone. She pointed toward the rear of the house and Noah said something. The next time Daniel looked, they were gone. When he returned the horse and let her into the corral, he found his friend and his wife at the edge of Noah's vegetable garden.

"You have a knack for gardening," she was telling him. "The rows are even and your plants are healthy."

"My mama always had a huge garden. Ochre and greens and tomatoes. I can almost taste her sweet potato pie, her fried squash…and nobody makes fried chicken like her." His drawl had become more pronounced as he spoke.

"That sounds like southern cooking if I ever heard of any."

"She always made black-eyed peas with rice," he said. "Ever tried that?"

"No, I have not had that pleasure."

He gave a rueful shrug. "Wish I could cook."

"Maybe I could find some recipes and Valentine could give them a try. She's an excellent cook."

Noah glanced at Daniel and back at Leah. "That would be nice once the garden is producing."

"The mare's in the corral," Daniel said.

Noah gave a nod. "Thanks."

Noah showed Leah a few fruit trees he'd planted, took her to the strawberry bed he'd covered with netting so the birds couldn't eat the berries.

When they said their goodbyes, Daniel took Leah's hand and led her to the buggy. He gave her slender fingers a gentle squeeze. "Thank you."

"For what?"

"You know how to put people at ease. I haven't seen him talk to anyone like that since we've been here."

"He's a nice man. Smart, ambitious. I didn't want to ask when he mentioned his mother, but does he have family left?"

"He and his father didn't part on good terms when he left to fight for the Union. Both of his parents were alive then. He's mentioned three younger sisters. As far as I know he hasn't had any contact with any of them since the war."

"That's a shame if he does have someone left," she mused. "Surely his mother wonders if he's all right."

"Can't say." Daniel led the horse to pull the buggy toward town. "He has to figure things out on his own."

"Yes." She seemed contemplative for a moment. "You've been each other's family, haven't you? You and Will and Noah?"

"You might say that."

"I want to fit into your circle," she admitted in a low voice. "I don't want him to pull away from you because of me."

He reached for her hand. "It's not like that. He hasn't. And he's warming up. No one can resist you."

She smiled up at him, and he admired the curve of her cheek, the spiral of pale gold hair lying against her neck. "No one?"

"No one."

That night after Valentine set their supper on the table, Daniel suggested she go on home for the evening. "I'll clean up," he said.

"I received a lovely gift from my brother today," the woman told Leah. She removed her apron and gestured to the watch pinned to her dress. "It's near enough like the one I had before, and I had missed knowing what time it was."

"Yours was stolen by the outlaws, wasn't it?" Leah asked.

"Yes. Seems most of the women folk are having items replaced. They're not the same as the lost heirlooms, of course, like Miss Hartwood's brooch or Miss Neely's ruby earbobs, but the kind gestures are heartwarming all the same."

"That's good to hear," Leah said. "Thank you and enjoy your evening."

"I shall. Good evening."

Valentine had prepared tender veal, potatoes and beets, and Leah sliced her meat and tasted it. "You will certainly be spoiled for Valentine's cooking. I don't know I can do half as well."

"I arranged for a photographer to have a tent at the fair, and I've scheduled an appointment for us. We can have our wedding portrait done then. As long as that suits you."

"That sounds perfect."

Daniel set a small red velvet bag on the table. "This isn't going to be a surprise, but it's for you."

Leah set down her fork and picked up the bag, loosening the drawstring. She reached inside and fished out a gold wedding band and a small brooch, barely an inch wide, shaped like a dragonfly. The body was made up of deep red stones and the wings of much smaller stones. Its eyes were two tiny pearls. "Daniel, I didn't have a brooch like this."

"I know, but I thought it would look pretty on one of your dresses."

She touched one of the stones with a thumb. "Are these glass sets?"

"They're garnets, actually. It was made in Austria."

Caught off guard, she touched her hand to her chest. "Oh, Daniel. This is too much. You shouldn't have."

"I wanted to," he argued. "You deserve nice things."

His generosity made her uncomfortable. "I'll have Hannah help me make a dress that I can wear this on for the next few months. Several didn't fit when I tried them on Sunday."

"I was only thinking you might like it."

"I do like it. Very much. And I'm happy to have a wedding ring again." She held it in her palm. "Would you put it on for me? You placed the first one on my finger."

His expression showed his pleasure, and she was glad she'd asked. He smiled and took the ring from her. "'Who can find a virtuous woman, for her price is far above rubies.' I'm proud that you're my wife, Leah."

His confidence created an ache in her chest. She placed one hand over her heart as though the touch could ease her pain and looked at the ring on the hand he held. "I only want to be worthy of your commitment, Daniel. Right now I don't feel as though I'm doing my part. But I will, I promise."

"You did catch a pretty good-sized fish today." His mouth tipped up at the corners, and she laughed. "I don't want you to worry about any of that. Your job is to rest and prepare for the baby." He released her hand and turned to finish his supper. "Noah told me I am going to be a good father."

"You will be a good father," she returned. "I have no doubt."

"Leah, if you think it's right, when the time comes, will you want to tell the child about Charles?"

There was no way Daniel knew the truth about Charles. He was assuming her husband had cared and wanted a child, a family. Truth was the man had been unconcerned about Leah and her previous pregnancies. He had died before she'd even known this baby was on the way. She couldn't tell the child the truth about his father—about the way he had died. No one deserved a father like that. "Let's not get ahead of ourselves," she said. "We have a lot of time to think about it."

He sliced a piece of veal. "Well, it's something to think about."

She was beginning to feel deceptive, letting Daniel think all had been well and that Charles had been a decent man. Who was she protecting by not being honest? Charles? What did it matter now? He was gone. All at once she felt uncomfortably warm, a flush rising to her cheeks, as the truth finally dawned on her. Deep down she was protecting herself. She was embarrassed. Humiliated. She didn't want Daniel to learn what really happened in fear he might think less of her. She wasn't the person he thought she was if she couldn't even tell the truth. If a virtuous woman was as valuable as rubies, she was a lump of coal.

Eventually she would have to tell him.

Leah always enjoyed the walk along Lincoln Boulevard. The journey took her past the almost-finished schoolhouse with its red shingle roof and past an entire undeveloped block before she got to Remmy Hagermann's mercantile. Remmy wisely catered to his female patrons by carrying the items they requested and often ordering similar products and two or three of a special order. She located the catalog she wanted on a shelf, lowered herself to a chair and rested the heavy volume on her lap. Daniel would appreciate a few new books for his library shelves. She'd decided against the meager gift she had planned for him. The embroidered handkerchiefs were still in her trunk. He gave so much to her. The china he'd sent for was not only sentimental and thoughtful, but thinking of it and finding the set like her mother's had been an incredible gift she would always treasure. And he seemed to lack for nothing, so what could she possibly find for him? With every day that passed she was feeling worse and worse about not having given him a wedding gift yet.

Lost in story descriptions and titles, she noted her selections on a piece of paper and didn't pay much attention when the bell over the door rang a few times as customers came and left. The sound of women's voices discussing prospective marriages arrested her attention, punctuated by the sound of her name.

"Leah Swann did well, marrying Daniel Gardner, for goodness sake," the familiar female voice said. "Have you seen that house she lives in?"

"It's a nice house," another answered, and Leah couldn't place the voice. "But a house doesn't make a woman happy."

"It sure helps."

"I've had a dozen offers since my family moved here last fall. Robert doesn't have much. He's struggling, actually. But he's honest and funny, and a hard worker. He's the one I think about all the time. When we see each other in town my heart beats fast and I hardly know what to say."

"That's foolishness. Don't marry for love, my dear. Do what I'm doing. Marry for money. Set yourself up for the rest of your life."

"Sounds rather cynical, if you ask me."

"Why?" the woman scoffed. "Because I'm a *realist*? I've had enough hard work to last me a lifetime, and I'm done with that. I don't want to work until I'm a wrinkled old woman. Who wants to be scrubbing and cleaning and fetching water and cooking when you can live in town and have help?" A few moments ticked by, then she went on. "Will Canfield's house will be the biggest house in Cowboy Creek, and married to him I'll be the cream of society. So do yourself a favor, my dear, and set your sights higher than a dirt farmer."

Dora Edison!

Chapter Fifteen

Leah's heart pounded and indignation rose inside her. Her heart broke for Will, whom she still considered a cherished friend. She stood, the catalog hitting the floor, her notes scattering. She marched around the stack of dry goods behind her and confronted the two women idly examining spools of ribbon.

Dora looked up and her face blanched. "Leah!"

"I knew there was something wrong. Nothing about you rang true, but I believe Will cares for you."

"Leah, you can't believe I was serious. Holly and I were only joking."

Leah glanced at the other young woman and didn't recognize her. "That was not a joke. You were advising your friend to not marry for love, just as *you're* not marrying for love."

"Even if it wasn't a joke," Dora said with an unladylike sneer. "What business is it of yours? Are you an expert on marrying for love?"

Leah's neck and face burned with anger. "My situation is nothing like yours. How cruel of you to pretend to care for Will when you're nothing but a gold digger!"

"Come now, don't be so serious," Dora chided. "You're being dreadfully stuffy and pretentious. It's boring."

Leah spun on her heel, returned to grab her notes and pick up the catalog, then hurried out of the mercantile. She stood on the street for half a minute, taking a deep breath, gathering her thoughts, deciding…

There was no question in her mind what she had to do. She owed it to Will to protect him. She strode along First Street toward Eden and turned the corner. After entering the Cattleman Hotel, she perched on a bench for a minute, calming herself. She eyed the stairs, stood and started up. She paused on each landing on her way to the third floor, finally reaching her destination and locating the suite Daniel had said was Will's. After a firm knock he opened the door. He was dressed impeccably as usual, white shirt, black tie. He flashed a broad smile. "Come in, Leah. This is a surprise."

"One you won't like much," she said.

He led her past a small sitting area into his office, where he rested his hand on the back of a leather chair. "Have a seat. You have me curious now. What's wrong?"

She settled herself and smoothed her skirt over her knees in a nervous gesture, questioning the wisdom of relaying her news. He was a good friend, a decent and honest man. He didn't deserve to be duped by a conniving woman, and if she could prevent heartache in the future by revealing the truth now, it was her responsibility.

"Leah?" he asked, setting across from her. "Is everything all right with Daniel?"

She looked him square in the eye and drew a breath. "I overheard a conversation at Remmy's mercantile just now. Dora was talking to a friend. I confronted her, and she tried to shrug off her words as if they were a joke, but I don't believe they were. I think she was serious, and she has concocted a deceitful plan."

He frowned in confusion. "Well—what…? What did she say?"

Leah relayed the conversation word for word.

"'Don't marry for love, do what I'm doing and marry for money?'" Will echoed back. His expression showed bewilderment, but not the anger she'd anticipated. "'Set yourself up for the rest of your life and be the cream of society?' That's what she said? Perhaps you misconstrued her meaning."

"I just told you exactly what I heard. I didn't know the other woman. Dora called her Holly."

He nodded. "She's the daughter of one of the homesteaders, if she's the one I'm thinking of. I heard talk that young Rob McNulty, the wagonmaker's boy is keen on her."

"Well, according to Dora, this Rob fellow isn't a good enough catch."

The sound of the outer door opening and closing arrested their attention, and hurried footsteps sounded across the wood. Dora appeared in the doorway, her face flushed. "I might have known you'd come straight here," she said to Leah.

Will stood as Dora approached.

She pointed at Leah with an outstretched arm, her expression tight. "What has she been telling you?"

"I told him everything I overheard you saying to the other young woman. Everything you said about marrying for money."

"Which is exactly what *you're* doing." Dora huffed

at Leah, wielding an accusing finger under her nose. "You can't deny it is convenient you sidled up to the other wealthiest man in Cowboy Creek and got yourself hitched to him within days of arriving. It's not as though you have a life of toil and trouble ahead of you now."

"I never claimed to be anything or anyone other than who I am," Leah said. "Daniel knows all about my situation. When he asked me to marry him we had everything out in the open. He knows I came here looking for a suitable marriage."

"What other reason would a woman have for coming to this miserable state?" Dora asked with a snort of disgust. "The only redeeming qualities Cowboy Creek can boast about are the abundance of men—and the riches being made from the sale of cattle."

Leah didn't respond, and Dora's words hung in the air. She darted a glance at Will and gave her head a little shake. "This town is growing every day. Homes, businesses and even an opera house about to open." Her voice had softened to a coo. "Why, Will knows I'm excited about the progress. Everyone is profiting from the Texas cows, aren't they? That's what this is all about." She laid a placating hand on her fiancé's sleeve. "I was telling Holly just today how things are improving, and that life is getting better and better here. This is a wonderful place to settle down and make a home, start a family."

Will looked Dora in the eyes. She smiled that smile that stretched her lower lip down and showed her teeth. Her keen ability to twist words to suit her purpose gave Leah a sinking feeling in the pit of her belly. Dora would have him wrapped around her little finger and Leah would soon be accused of causing trouble.

The sound of horses' harnesses down on the street below created a muted backdrop for the drama playing out up here. Will shifted his weight before speaking. He hadn't been carrying his cane when he'd answered the door. "You told Holly not to marry for love, but to marry for money like you're doing. That was your advice to a girl who's in love with the son of the wagonmaker?"

"There are many kinds of love," Dora replied, lifting a hand to her neck. "She could love a rich man just as easily. I love you and you're rich." She gave him a sly wink, obviously meant to distract him.

Leah considered getting up and leaving. She leaned forward on the chair, but Will held a palm down to stop her.

"You're right," he said finally. "There are many kinds of love."

Dora let her shoulders swivel in a circling motion as though pleased with herself. She cast Leah a triumphant glance.

"And we don't have the kind of love that endures a lifetime. We don't have the kind, unselfish love it requires to make a marriage work. We want different things, you and I. I'm sure after you've had some time to think this over, you'll agree this was the best thing that could have happened." Swallowing hard, he fixed her with a level look. "There's a man out there for you. You're smart and pretty and ambitious. But I'm not him. The engagement is over."

Dora's nostrils flared. She inhaled and her chest puffed out. She looked from Will to Leah and back.

"You'll regret this." With stiff, controlled motions, she straightened, deliberately set her shoulders and marched out the door. The outer door of the suite slammed shut behind her.

Leah drew a shaky hand over her forehead. "That was awful. Will, I'm so sorry—"

"No," he insisted and reached for her hand. She offered it and he assisted her to her feet. "You've done me a big favor. I know because when you told me what she'd said I felt relieved. I realized something had been wrong between us, and I hadn't been dealing with it. So, thank you."

She gave his arm a gentle pat. "You deserve someone who loves you."

He agreed with a nod and reached behind his desk for his cane. "Come on, I'll walk you downstairs. Shall I find you a ride home?"

"I'm going back to Remmy's. Walking seems to agree with me and I still have shopping to do. I'm seeing Hannah for a dress fitting as well."

He took her arm. "I'll walk with you then."

"I'm feeling bad because I haven't yet given Daniel a wedding gift," she explained as they left the hotel. "I had embroidered some handkerchiefs with his initials, but then after I saw the gift he chose for me I would have been embarrassed to give them to him."

"Daniel isn't a man to care about the cost of a gift," he said. "As long as it comes from you, he'll like it."

"But I can't think of anything special, and I want it to be. I was thinking perhaps books because there are all those empty shelves in the library."

"That sounds good."

"Not really." She paused and he stopped beside her. "I want to fit in," she admitted. "I want to feel adequate."

"Daniel finds you more than adequate, my dear. You probably know he had feelings for you when we were young. When you and I imagined we might develop a relationship, he backed away for both of our sakes. But I don't believe those feelings ever dimmed."

They resumed their walk. "We were all young and carefree—foolish, actually," she replied, her voice tinged with regret. "We made mistakes. Well, I did certainly. One can't always trust feelings, because they can lead to mistakes."

"You were incensed when you overheard Dora telling her friend not to be moved by feelings, but to use reason in planning her future," he said. "Now you're telling me the opposite."

"This is different," she protested. "I didn't marry Daniel because he is one of the richest men in town. My situation is completely different from Dora's. I already made poor choices and I'm living with them now."

"Somewhere in your curly blonde head that makes sense, I suppose," Will said with a shake of his head.

She cast him a sidelong glance. "You were always exasperating."

"No argument." He gestured to the mercantile. "Here we are. Thank you again for coming to me with what you heard. You saved me a lot of grief in the long run."

"I hope so."

He gave her a brief hug. "Quit worrying about that gift. He'll appreciate anything you choose."

"Thank you." She watched him walk away, using his cane, his gait stiff.

Will deserved a woman who loved him.

She turned and entered Remmy's mercantile, her thoughts taunting her. Daniel deserved a woman who loved him, too. But it took courage to love, more courage than she could muster.

Will presided over the town council meeting in a private room at the hotel. Daniel had helped him prepare an agenda, and they kept the discussions on topic. Several homesteaders were present who hadn't been at the last impromptu gathering, so Daniel explained his and Dr. Lowell's findings about the cattle poisonings. A Texas herd was due in a week, so a celebratory atmosphere pervaded. Everyone was relieved their cattle hadn't been exposed to Texas fever. It remained to be determined who had deliberately poisoned the stock tanks and why, but since they'd uncovered the exploit, the problem had subsided. For now the cattle were safe.

They'd come to a dead end on discovering who had stolen and burned the lumber meant for the opera house. Two additional guards had been hired to take night watches, and so far there had been no further disturbances at the rail station.

Quincy Davis had reports from Morgan's Creek and the surrounding vicinity about more robberies, and another small town sixty miles north had reported stolen horses and a deputy shot while in pursuit. Apparently the Murdochs had moved their reign of terror in a northerly direction.

With that agenda item behind them, they discussed guards and measures for safety during the Webster County Fair that would be taking place the following weekend. Next Daniel brought up arrangements for a second bride train. Buck Hanley was the first to respond. "I say we go for an even dozen this time. The town coffers can afford it, right?"

"As long as the council agrees," Will replied.

"Daniel got one of the women already," Timothy Watson said. "Nobody's seen hide nor hair of the preacher's daughter since she got here. Miss Haywood don't seem none too friendly, and Miss Pippa is as busy as a one-legged man in a foot race with all the invitations she gets. We shore do need more choices."

"We agree there's a need to bring more women this time," Daniel concurred. "I guess a vote is in order. All in favor raise your hand."

Around the room hands shot in the air. Walter Frye raised the arm with the cast.

"Opposed?"

No one opposed the vote.

"More brides it is," Will said, making it official. "I'll arrange for the ads."

The men made plans to move their gathering down to Drover's Place. Amos excused himself and headed for his place over the boot shop. Daniel and Will remained behind and stood in the hotel foyer. "Are you joining the others?" Daniel asked.

"Might as well," Will replied as though weary. "Otherwise I'd just head up to my room. You're probably going on home."

"I am."

"Good for you. You got yourself a treasure when Leah married you."

"I know."

He pinched the bridge of his nose and sighed. "Did she mention what happened with Dora?"

"She did. How are you doing?"

"Well… The moment I heard what Dora had said, I felt relief. That's when I knew Leah was supposed to overhear that conversation and come to me. Otherwise I might have made a big mistake."

"Sorry it turned out the way it did."

"Don't be. I'm not. If I'm supposed to have a wife, the right woman will come along and I'll know it's right."

"Perhaps on the next bride train," Daniel suggested.

"Do you think someone from the next train will catch Noah's eye?" Will asked.

Daniel gave his head a slow shake. "He's bound and determined he doesn't need anyone. He'll likely refuse to even take a look, like he did this time."

Will adjusted his weight from one leg to the other. "Maybe we need to make sure he can't ignore a woman."

"How do you mean?"

Will's gaze traveled the lobby and returned to his friend. "By specifically requesting a bride for him. Making the arrangement."

"Without Noah's approval?"

Will raised an eyebrow. "Do you think he'll ever say yes on his own?"

"Well, I suppose not. Unless someone can manage to change his mind without him knowing his mind is being changed..." Daniel shook his head. "Leah mentioned his withdrawal. She was hoping it wasn't her he was avoiding so I took her to his place unannounced the other day and left the two of them together for a while. Once she was there and he was faced with her presence, she got him talking about his garden and he loosened up."

"That's perfect, don't you think?" Will asked with a conspiratorial wink. "If we send a bride right to his door, what can he do? He'll see she doesn't find him as hideous as he supposes. He'll relax and lower his guard like he did with Leah."

Daniel nodded. "Okay. Let's do it."

"When I contact the liaison in Chicago, I'll include a query for a specific young woman. I'd like to communicate before we choose."

"I agree. Make a list of Noah's good qualities, so the woman knows what a fine man she'll be marrying."

"Good idea," Will agreed. "Now go home to your wife."

Daniel grinned. "A few weeks ago I'd never have imagined hearing that."

Will settled his hat on his head. "Do you like it?"

"I do," Daniel admitted. After the two men parted ways, he headed for Second Street and then hurried along Lincoln Boulevard. It was a nice feeling to have a wife at home.

He entered the dimly lit house and found her asleep on the divan in the library, a book in her lap. He covered her legs with a lap blanket and seated himself at his desk, lighting the lamp wick and opening a couple of ledgers to work for a while.

Occasionally he glanced over and admired her pale hair and the soft curve of her cheek in the lamplight. He hadn't known what to expect from a marriage to this woman, hadn't had time to think about it. She wasn't the same girl who had been one of his two best friends so many years ago. She possessed a vulnerability he'd never seen before, a quiet resignation. He understood homesickness for a place and a time that would never again be. He understood feeling powerless to change the world. And he wished more than anything he could ease her burden somehow. He rested his chin on a palm, lost in thought. Not even an hour had passed when the sound of her book hitting the floor drew his attention, and she stirred.

Minutes later a muffled sound startled him, and he glanced up again. Her soft cries drew him from his chair, and he knelt beside the divan. That one as lovely and delicate as this woman carried the scars of war carved an ache in his chest. Things she didn't speak of in the daylight haunted her at night. There had been a young boy in his regiment who had cried every night in his sleep. Daniel recognized the same pain and fear in Leah's quiet sobs.

"Leah," he said softly, placing a hand on her shoulder. "Leah, you're dreaming. Wake up."

Her eyes fluttered open to focus on him. She oriented herself and moved to a sitting position, where she pushed the hair away from her face. "Oh, I—didn't know you were home. I must have fallen asleep."

"You were dreaming," he said.

Leah studied the concern on his face as he looked at her. She'd had yet another of the dreams that plagued her nights. In her dreams she saw every detail of the house she'd grown up in, just as it had been then—the furnishings, the wallpaper, the burnished woodwork... all the books lining the shelves in her father's study. But her dreams always took a turn. The rooms were engulfed in flames, the books were reduced to ashes. Her mother reached out to her, but Leah couldn't save her. *"Run! Run!"*

Leah clamped her hands over her ears, and then realized what she'd done. No one was crying out her name. A hissing fire burned cozily behind the grate in the fireplace. She sat in Daniel's library while he studied her expression with concern.

She reached a trembling hand to his cheek and touched the rough texture of a day's growth of beard. His green eyes were familiar, his handsome face dear.

"Are you all right?" His eyes were filled with compassion. "Would you like some tea?"

There it was, the kindness for which she hungered. The concern and devotion she'd missed throughout her marriage and the years they'd been apart. Humiliation and embarrassment kept her from allowing herself to divulge her feelings, from sharing the whole truth.

"I'm all right," she replied.

"I'll bring a pot of tea," he said and hurried away.

Leah adjusted her clothing and tidied her hair before he returned. He came back and set a tray on a low table, then poured her a cup and handed it to her.

"How did your meeting go?" she asked.

"Well."

"Anything new?"

He shared the news about the Murdoch gang and the plans for the next bride train. "Will and I devised another plan, as well. Will is contacting the liaison in Chicago and sending for a bride for Noah."

"Without his knowledge?"

"He would never agree."

She blew on her tea. "I understand your concern, but don't see that going well."

"I hope you're wrong."

"So do I."

"Look how well it turned out for us," he pointed out. "I didn't imagine I had a bride arriving on the first train. And here we are."

The baby must be creating havoc with her mind and her body, because she wanted to cry when he purposefully held her gaze. Sometimes when he stared at her in that sweet and tender way, when his hand touched hers or his breath grazed her temple, she closed her eyes and wished…regretted…wanted. But there were no dreams left. Her losses were so great she couldn't give up anything more. She couldn't allow herself to imagine a great love between them. She must keep possession of herself. Daniel was strength and goodness and home—and she deserved none of those things. She'd done nothing to earn his steadfast devotion, his respect or his trust.

But he deserved her devotion. He deserved respect and trust. She could give that much. Admittedly she already had, though she still felt selfish. What could she offer this man? He'd taken her in just as she was, no expectations, no demands. He'd made the utmost commitment in marrying her and promising to be a good father to her child.

Leah was afraid. Afraid of feeling more. Afraid of wanting more. Afraid of expecting anything good or perfect. Mostly she feared loss.

"Thank you for the tea. I'd better go up to bed."

"I'll bring water. It's warm."

"I'll get it." She stood and folded the throw. "Good night, Daniel."

"Good night. I'll be close by if you need me."

She paused, then left the room.

Chapter Sixteen

For the next couple of days, the talk about town centered on the Webster County Fair. The hotel filled to capacity, and neighbors brought wagons and tents and camped outside Cowboy Creek. Workers mowed a flat grassy area and constructed booths. Vendors set up tents and canopies, carpenters built a bandstand along with a wooden dance floor. Everyone became involved in one way or another.

Leah called on Opal, finding her rested and feeling stronger. "I'm looking forward to the fair," she told Leah. "I'm baking pies."

"The festivities may be just what we need," Leah agreed. "You know the rules, though. Rest when you feel tired."

"I will." She held up a hand. "Don't go just yet. I have something for you." She disappeared into the other room and returned with a small white folded bundle. "I made this for your baby."

Surprised, Leah accepted the soft blanket and unfolded it to admire the gift. "You made this?"

"Knitted it. I have a lot of time on my hands, as you

know. I already have blankets and clothes ready for our baby."

"It's so generous of you. This is the very first thing I have for the baby." Leah ran her fingers over the yarn. "It's beautiful, and such a thoughtful gift."

"You're more than a midwife to me, Leah. We're friends."

Her entire life had changed from her past experiences. She felt strong and well. She had a supportive and caring husband. She had friends. Opal's words brought tears to her eyes, and she blinked them away. "Thank you. I'm thankful to have such a thoughtful friend."

Opal gave her a hug, the girth of her bulging abdomen between them.

"I'm going to go see how Hannah is doing. The poor girl hasn't been well since we arrived in Cowboy Creek."

"What does the doctor think is wrong?"

"I have no idea. She's not forthcoming when I ask her."

"Well, here, I'll send a couple of my cinnamon rolls along for her. Tell her I'm thinking of her." She proceeded to wrap rolls and then handed them to Leah.

As Leah crossed to the boardinghouse on the other side of Eden Street, the sound of hammers and men calling out reached her from the east. "Mornin', Mrs. Gardner," Abram Booker called from where he swept the boardwalk in front of his store. She turned to wave, again surprised by her new name. The sound of clanking horseshoes echoed from the lot behind his store, making it apparent Gus and Old Horace were already busy this morning.

"Sounds like there are contenders out back," she called.

Abram nodded and she moved on. Aunt Mae answered the door in an apron and welcomed her. "Don't you look lovely! Marriage and a baby on the way agree with you, dear."

"You're too kind, Aunt Mae. I'm here to visit Hannah. How does she seem to you?"

"She came down for breakfast this morning and she appeared to have more strength. Pippa is a bundle of energy on the other hand, planning her theater troupe, scheduling lunches and suppers and picnics. Why, her social calendar is bursting while dear Hannah has only gone out with her father that I know of." She crinkled her forehead. "I'm hoping her situation doesn't become problematic. She is a prospective bride, after all. I'm beginning to hear a few grumbles."

"Let's assure the grumblers that the poor girl can't help not feeling well," Leah told her. "Opal sent her cinnamon rolls."

"Go on up. I have apples to peel and supplies to sort and pack. The fellas are setting up my booth for the fair right now."

Leah climbed the stairs and knocked on Hannah's door. "It's Leah," she called.

The key turned and the door opened. Hannah drew her shawl around herself and ushered her inside. "Come in."

"I've brought cinnamon rolls from Opal. She sends her regards."

"How is she feeling?"

"She is stronger." Leah opened the bag she carried.

"Look what she gave me. It's the first thing I have for my baby. Isn't it lovely?"

Her expression thoughtful, Hannah ran her fingers over the soft white yarn. "It's beautiful. Your baby will be blessed to have such a beautiful blanket." She glanced up. "I have a little something for you, too. I was waiting, but since you're preparing, this is a good time…"

She went to the open trunk and found what she was looking for.

Leah took the small tissue-wrapped package and peeled away the paper. Inside lay a tiny gown made of pale yellow calico. The sight of the infant garment brought a myriad of emotions to the surface. She held it with the new confidence that she would soon be dressing her baby, changing diapers, feeding him or her. Unfolding the gown, she marveled over how small it was, how perfectly the seams were stitched and how intricately the smocking was sewn in white thread across the front. "Hannah, this is a treasure. What a generous gift of your time."

"I've had plenty of time," Hannah said with a hesitant smile.

Leah reached for Hannah's hand and gave it a gentle squeeze. "It's lovely. I couldn't ask for a more thoughtful gift. Thank you."

"You're welcome. You're a good friend to me, checking on me and bringing me little things to cheer me up. I can't tell you how much it's helped."

Leah folded the gown, tucked it inside the white blanket and put them aside. "How are you doing? Aunt Mae said you went down for breakfast."

"Yes. I believe I'm finally feeling better."

Leah perched on a trunk. "That's good to hear."

"I'm still adjusting to this new place."

"I thought perhaps you'd have moved to the parsonage with your father."

Hannah sat on a chair and hugged her shawl around her shoulders. "I didn't want to be a burden until I felt well enough to help him."

"I doubt you'd be a burden. But as long as you're comfortable here, it's good you stayed. I know Aunt Mae checks on you."

"She's very kind."

"I hope you'll be able to enjoy some of the events at the fair this weekend. It's all anyone is talking about."

"Oh, I'm quite aware," Hannah replied. "Apparently there's a horseshoe competition. Gus and Old Horace have been practicing most every day."

"I heard them on my way here."

"Is it true the Murdoch gang has moved on?"

Leah nodded. "Sheriff Davis has gotten reports that they've been causing trouble farther north."

"I'm sorry they're still causing trouble, but I'm so thankful they're gone. And news has spread that Will Canfield's engagement is off, so he's eligible."

"Why, Hannah, are you thinking Will Canfield might be a good catch?"

Hannah blushed and batted a hand in the air. "Pshaw, I wasn't thinking of myself." She got up and moved to an open trunk where she pulled out a partial garment. "I have a bodice I'd like you to try on. I want to make sure I have adequate room for expansion in the side pleats."

Leah laughed and moved to insert her arms through the openings as Hannah held the piece. "Will is a good man. I trust the right woman will come along. The council is sending for another bride train."

"That's hopeful news. Let me pin a couple of places here." She reached for her pin cushion.

"I'll need a few dresses to get me through the next few months," Leah said. "Already I'm having trouble fitting into my clothing."

"Let's measure one more time to be certain my notes are correct. This looks just about right. Do you like the fabric?"

"I do. And Daniel gave me a brooch that will be perfect."

"I see he replaced your ring as well."

Leah glanced at her hand and smiled softly. "Yes."

"You're welcome to look through my trunks for fabrics and notions. We might also look through catalogs."

"How about next week? I'll see if Remmy Hagermann would allow me to borrow one or two for a few hours. He has quite a selection. You can show me the fabrics you brought along then."

"That would be perfect. I have a couple of colors in mind for you."

Leah let Hannah remove the bodice. "I'm excited to see everything you choose for me. I trust your choices. You did such a fine job with my wedding dress." She touched the other young woman's wrist. "I'd better be moving along now. I'm glad you're doing well and I hope you're able to attend the fair. I'll look for you there."

Hannah nodded and walked to the door with her. Leah didn't let Hannah's standoffish posture keep her from giving the other young woman a hug, but Hannah made the gesture awkward by holding herself back. She bid Hannah goodbye and the door closed behind her.

People were never quite what they seemed, and Hannah's evasiveness was at odds with what Leah knew about her, about her upbringing in the public eye. But she respected her privacy. The gift showed her Hannah appreciated her friendship.

Once downstairs, she found Aunt Mae with a heap of apple peels at her elbows. "Is there anything I can do to help?"

Aunt Mae glanced at the nearby mounds of dough and the remaining bucket of apples. "That's nice of you, dear. I would appreciate your help if you can spare the time. You must sit however."

Leah found a place in the dining room to store her parcels and returned to wash her hands and ask for an apron. Within minutes she was settled on a chair, peeling apples while Aunt Mae rolled crusts and demonstrated the technique at the same time.

"These pies are to sell, I've figured out, but will you enter one of the contests as well?"

Aunt Mae wiped her floured hands together and pointed to a row of prize ribbons pinned to the kitchen curtain. "Most of those are from fairs in Illinois, but a couple are from our past fairs."

"All for pies?" Leah asked.

"Pies, jellies, bread. One of them is for fried chicken."

"I've had your fried chicken. I'd have awarded you the blue ribbon, as well."

"I hear Miss Valentine Ewing is a good cook, too," Aunt Mae said.

"That she is."

"Will she give me a run for the pie ribbon this year?"

"She hasn't mentioned entering."

"I won't ask you to spy," the older woman said with a wink.

"Thank goodness."

They grinned at each other.

It was nice having friends.

Saturday morning Leah asked Daniel for help with her green-and-blue-plaid silk dress. The sleeveless dress laced up the back over a white blouse. It was difficult to lace without help, but it was one of the few dresses she could lace loosely and still wear.

"How do women do this by themselves?" he grumbled good-naturedly.

"The style is in fashion," she replied. "One does need help, however."

On the days he worked at the stockyards, Daniel wore cotton shirts and loose brown trousers with suspenders, but today he had donned a crisp pale blue shirt and a black tie.

Leah unpacked her wide-brimmed hat with ribbon and silk flowers that matched the plaid dress and settled it upon her head.

"Our portrait appointment is at ten," he informed her. "I'll come back for your dress and change into my suit."

She gestured to the two-piece ivory dress she'd hung on the open door of the armoire. "It's there."

He glanced at it. "I'm looking forward to seeing you in it again."

She made a playful grimace.

He chuckled. "You will look beautiful. No one will be the wiser if a few buttons are undone."

Cowboy Creek bustled with activity when they reached Eden Street, and excitement crackled in the air. The storefront windows previously shot out had been replaced and all of them bore new lettering and sparkled. Shop owners had swept the boardwalks and set out buckets of flowers and samples of their wares. Folding chairs and benches provided a spot in the shade wherever there were wooden awnings. The Cattleman Hotel's roof had been draped with red-and-white bunting.

"So this is the third county fair?" Leah asked.

"It's not really an official county fair because we're not the county seat," Daniel explained. "We just call it that for now and invite the surrounding towns to participate. We're basically trying it out and getting good attention directed to our town. A real county fair should be held at the end of summer when there are crops to show, vegetables and fruit to enter in competitions."

He greeted passersby and introduced them to Leah before continuing. "For now the agricultural portion of the fair is mostly informational, which is what we need anyway. We will have a few representatives and mill owners on hand to talk with farmers. The farmers want to learn about the best seed and equipment available."

"That makes sense."

"It's important for us to extend our reach and show we can handle something like this. Eventually we hope for Cowboy Creek to become the county seat. And yes, this is the third time we've done this. I hope we draw a crowd."

"A *good* crowd," she added meaningfully.

He made a face. "Yes! Lord, keep any and all troublemakers away from Cowboy Creek in Jesus's name."

"Amen," Leah punctuated.

He took her hand as they strolled east along Third

Street. She appreciated the warmth and strength of his fingers entwined with hers. She'd seen the progress of Will's house from the rear because the church sat on the next street, but she hadn't been down this way to see the front. Dora must be sorely disappointed she wouldn't be living in this house. It was an impressive structure with four giant columns reaching to roof level and supporting a catwalk.

"Mark my words," Daniel said. "That will be the governor's mansion one day."

"Will would make an excellent leader," Leah agreed. "What about you? Any political aspirations?"

"I've got all I can handle here. And as you know, I love the horses, so when Cowboy Creek is established and flourishing, if I want to expand my focus, I'll do some breeding and training."

A band was warming up as they got closer to the fairground locale. Down the center of the area booths had been constructed on both sides of what served as a midway path. A handful of the structures had protruding stovepipes with smoke puffing out the tops. Branching out in both directions from there were tents and roped-off areas, and farther out plots of land. "What happens out there?"

Daniel looked where she'd pointed. "Games, mostly. There are several competitions throughout today and tomorrow. The largest section at the outside edge is a plowing contest."

She grinned up at him, remembering their days planting the gardens. "Will you compete?"

He shook his head. "No. I'm an amateur. Wait until you see some of those farmers and homesteaders. They bring their own teams and plows and it's impressive what they can accomplish within the time limits."

"I can't wait to see that! What else? Besides horseshoes. I understand Old Horace and Gus are prepared for a competition."

"There's a course mapped out and flagged for horse racing."

She raised an eyebrow in question.

"Yes, I do have a horse I plan to race."

She grinned. "I'll cheer you on."

He squeezed her hand. "Let's start with breakfast."

"Those first booths we saw?"

"Let's check them out and see what sounds good to you. I happen to know Aunt Mae's flapjacks are prize winners themselves."

Leah tugged his hand. "Let's get you a stack."

In the center of the midway Daniel located Aunt Mae's booth. An awning shaded several tables alongside the structure.

"Mr. and Mrs. Gardner!" Aunt Mae called out when she saw them. "Don't you two look handsome side-by-side. Daniel, your bride is as pretty as a spring morning, isn't she?"

"Leah's beauty puts spring to shame," he answered and gave his new wife an affectionate kiss on the cheek.

Leah blushed. "Daniel thinks his fair experience would be for naught if he didn't have a stack of your flapjacks, Aunt Mae."

"And right he is." She turned and poured perfectly round dollops of batter into the sizzling skillets atop one of the two cast iron stoves that had been vented through the wooden roof. No wonder there had been so much activity going on the week prior to this event. Setting up these booths must have been time-consuming and labor-intensive. "Thank you for helping me peel apples and measure sugar and cinnamon, dear. I don't know if I'd have finished the pies without you. "

"My pleasure. I may be able to turn out a few on my own now. "

Aunt Mae expertly flipped their flapjacks and turned them out onto plates alongside perfectly browned sausages and then poured them steaming cups of coffee. Daniel glanced at the prices written on a chalkboard, and left a couple of bills on the makeshift counter. He used small ironstone pitchers to pour butter and syrup.

The realization of how good the fair was for the town's economy impressed Leah all the more. Businessmen from neighboring towns, farmers, homesteaders and families were spending a day or two, eating and paying to enter the competitions—a once a year event that drew a crowd, brought community together and gave the merchants and even the wives a chance to earn or win additional cash.

"Aunt Mae can make quite a profit this weekend, I suppose."

"Yes, it's a good opportunity for anyone with goods to sell."

Daniel led them out of the booth and around the side to sit under the canopy. As fate would have it, the very first person they encountered was Dora Edison. She sat at a table with a woman she resembled so much it was obvious the woman was her mother.

Leah's heartbeat stuttered. Their last encounter had been heated, with Dora attempting to downplay her words and Leah taking a defensive stance on Will's behalf. Of course it was expected they would run into each other again. Cowboy Creek wasn't a big town.

Daniel set their plates on a table, and then cupped Leah's elbow and led her several steps to the women's table. "Good morning, Mrs. Edison. Dora. Mrs. Edison, this is my wife, Leah. Leah, this is Dora's mother, Augusta."

Leave it to Daniel to forge a peace treaty. "It's a pleasure to meet you," Leah said.

Leah held her breath, waiting for a reply.

"It's nice to meet you, Leah," Augusta said finally. "Congratulations on your marriage."

"I hope you ladies enjoy the day's festivities," Daniel said.

"I'm sure we will. Thank you."

They went back to their table and sat.

Leah cast him a sidelong look. "Well, she didn't throw food."

"What can she say, Leah? Dora was in the wrong and she knows it. You did the only thing you could do with a clear conscience. Hopefully she's learned a lesson."

She picked up her fork and glanced up at him. "Do you face everything head-on?"

"Nothing gets accomplished hiding under a rock," he replied with a shrug.

Everything about him pointed out her weaknesses. She didn't know what would have happened the first time she'd seen Dora if he hadn't been with her. "I'm not as brave as you."

"You're plenty brave," he countered. "You answered the ad and came all the way to Kansas without knowing a soul until you got here. That was brave."

It didn't feel brave. It felt desperate.

She shut down that thought and worked to see herself the way he saw her. "What do you see when you look at me?"

He chewed and swallowed the bite he'd taken, and his gaze flicked across her features. His expression softened and his green eyes lit from within. "I see the most beautiful girl I've ever known."

"Really, *really* look," she said. "Deeper. What do you see?"

"I see someone with courage. Someone kind. I see someone frightened, but determined to take care of herself and her child. Someone who's lost so much it hurts to breathe some days, but she keeps going."

His directness humbled her. Leah's jaw ached with the unexplainable urge to burst into tears. She reminded herself she was teary because of the baby and took a deep, shaky breath to calm the inner confusion. "How did you get this way, Daniel?"

"What way?"

"Larger than life. Kinder than necessary. Honest. So honest sometimes it makes my teeth hurt."

He shrugged. "I guess I've always been pretty straightforward, but I learned not to take even one day or one moment for granted. Not to waste any time the good Lord gave us being superficial."

"I don't know if I want to be that person you describe or not. I want to be brave, of course. But I don't want to be frightened. Not anymore."

"What are you frightened of today? Right here, right now."

That my heart is opening, little by little. That I can't trust it. I can't trust myself. That I can't make any more mistakes. That I don't want to hurt the best man I've ever known. That I might not be good enough. That I'm flawed, and you'll see through me eventually...

She shook her head without voicing the fountain of turmoil inside. She wasn't brave. Not at all. She was too cowardly to deny being the woman he saw.

"Today I feel safe," she whispered.

His kind smile wrinkled the corners of his eyes and charmed her. For now safe was enough. They enjoyed their breakfast, waving a friendly goodbye when Dora and Augusta passed their table. Dora met Leah's eyes and nodded without a smile. It was likely they'd be living in this same town for many years to come. Leah was measurably relieved it seemed they could see each other without a problem arising.

Their appointment for the portrait wasn't until ten, so they browsed the displays, and again Leah was impressed by how much thought had gone into the planning. She lingered in a tent of quilts, while Daniel visited with a gentleman just outside. The woman who sat working on an embroidered block greeted her. "How do, Mrs. Gardner?"

A little confused, Leah returned the greeting.

"I saw you the day the bride train arrived," the woman explained. "And news travels fast, so I heard about the wedding, as well. I'm Mrs. Foster...the housekeeper at the Cattleman."

"Did you make all of these beautiful quilts?"

She chuckled. "Goodness, no. I made these few over here." She led Leah to a neatly folded stack and pointed to one hanging on a pole suspended from the beams. "This one is called a sawtooth star, and I alternated the star blocks with chintz, all in the same color. The stars are made from old clothing and curtains."

The predominant color was red, skillfully coordinated with blues, peach, ivory and green, with flecks of black here and there.

Leah studied the pattern and the stitches with admiration. "It's beautiful." She glanced aside. "And these are yours as well?"

"Yes. That one is called a kaleidoscope pattern." She opened it up for Leah's inspection. Each pastel calico block looked like a four-bladed fan, and the curved edges of the blade shapes formed larger circles. In the center of each square was a small white button, and the entire quilt was edged with green and rose calico.

Leah touched the stitches with appreciation and ran a hand over the fabric. "How long did it take you to make this?"

"A couple of winters."

Leah admired Mrs. Foster's other creations as well, but she came back to the kaleidoscope quilt and gave it a last look. "It's so beautiful. The colors are soft and pretty. I can picture it on a bed."

"Having a good day so far, Mr. Gardner?" Mrs. Foster asked.

Leah turned to see Daniel inside the opening of the tent. "Yes, the weather is clear and it's not too windy. That's a perfect day in Kansas." He turned to Leah. "I'm sorry for leaving you for so long. I met a rancher I'd never spoken with before. We were getting acquainted."

"You're fine. I enjoyed seeing the quilts and talking with Mrs. Foster. She's skilled with a needle and thread."

"We're setting up frames as soon as a couple of the other ladies arrive," the woman told Leah. "Come back later and you can see how we work on finishing a quilt.

You might want to learn how it's done. Or start one of your own. I'd be happy to show you."

"Will you be here tomorrow, too?"

"Oh, yes. We're here for the duration of the fair."

Leah glanced around the interior once more. "Perhaps I'll come back tomorrow, then."

"It's almost time for our photograph." Daniel offered his arm. "Let's go find the tent."

Chapter Seventeen

A fancily lettered sign that read John Cleve Parker Photography hung over the canopied entrance to the enormous tent they sought. The interior was sectioned off with a private studio area in the back. Just inside the entrance were framed examples of John Cleve's work as well as various trunks, chairs and drapes, silk ferns on stands and other props.

"Good day, my friends!" A man with black hair parted down the center and a huge handlebar mustache greeted them. "If you've not already signed up for a photograph, you should have. What a handsome couple you are."

"We're the Gardners," Daniel said. "Ten o'clock."

"Of course!" John Cleve shook Daniel's hand and bowed before Leah.

"We're a little early," Daniel explained. "If you have a comfortable chair, Leah will sit for a few minutes while I go home and fetch our clothing changes."

"Of course. Of course. But I'd love to do a couple of shots before the formal clothing goes on, as well, if you don't mind."

Daniel glanced at Leah and she agreed with a lift of one shoulder and a nod. "Sure. How about after Leah's rested for a few minutes? I'll be back shortly."

Daniel left the tent and John Cleve ushered Leah to a plush chair situated in one of the makeshift studio settings. He disappeared for a moment and returned with a glass of water.

"Thank you. I was thirsty." She drank half. "You certainly have quite a setup here, Mr. Parker. All of these lovely settings and props."

"This is what I do," he said cheerfully. "I bring the studio to the people. Beyond that canvas wall is my traveling darkroom because the collodion plates must be processed immediately."

"Have you done this for a long time?"

"About fifteen years, give or take," he replied.

"So…you took photographs during the war?"

He nodded, and at her expression added, "I didn't travel to battlefields. I photographed a lot of forts, horses being trained, portraits of officers. Stayed behind the scenes mostly. Still, I saw too much, as did everyone who lived through it. Did your husband fight?"

"He did." She shared where Daniel had traveled.

John Cleve studied her a moment, and then moved a few feet away where he found a cord and tugged it. The motion rolled up a window on the side of the tent and allowed air and daylight in. He glanced at her again, tilted his head, then turned and moved a boxy camera on a sturdy tripod into position. "Just as you are, please. Don't move."

She'd been enjoying the rest, the water and the relaxed conversation. His scrutiny and the camera made her self-conscious.

He fiddled with slides and a drape and ducked under the black cloth. "Don't look at the camera," he said. "Gaze away from the light for a few minutes, chin down slightly."

She sat as he asked. After he'd taken two shots he asked her to look out the window. "Think of your husband," he suggested.

It wasn't difficult to think of Daniel. He was always on her mind. Seeing him relaxed and enjoying himself was a pleasure. He had so many responsibilities and so many people depended on him, he needed days like this.

John Cleve had taken a few more shots before Daniel arrived with their changes of clothing. The photographer hung them and had Daniel pose standing just behind her chair. For another pose he asked Daniel to sit on a footstool near her knees and asked them to look at each other.

He experimented with the shade all the way up, with it down a few inches and then down halfway, finding just the lighting he preferred.

As Leah looked at Daniel, she couldn't help noticing his hair was mussed from his walk. She reached up and finger-combed the chestnut waves away from his forehead. His bright green gaze softened and he gave her a tender smile.

"Don't move. Hold still. You're going to be very happy with these portraits," John Cleve pronounced. "Mrs. Gardner, there's a changing room just through this curtain."

"I'll need help with the buttons once I have the dress on," she told Daniel.

"I will help him with his suit right here, and he'll

be ready to assist you," the photographer said with a broad smile.

Once she had changed Daniel was able to fasten most of the buttons up the back of her dress. He left a few undone.

Shy about her expanding form, she averted her gaze. "It was the flapjacks…"

"Most likely," he agreed, always the gentleman. "No one will ever know."

John Cleve had dropped a sheer valance over the open window area, filtering the light. He ushered them into a setting with gauzy drapery and swags of silk rose garlands. "It's your preference, but I suggest you both stand and I'll pose you in a few different positions."

A breeze lifted the gauze over the window. From outside came the sound of children's laughter. The photographer had them stand hip to hip, with Daniel's arm around Leah's waist. The heat of his hand radiated through the fabric of her dress, and the strength of his arm was evident across her back. The familiar scents of cedar, starch and shaving soap reached her nostrils. Her new husband smelled good. His scent made her feel safe. His closeness made her feel a little giddy. Daniel was everything good and honorable.

Daniel was home.

The sheer strength of her emotions overwhelmed her, and she fought the stinging sensation in her nose and eyes. She wanted to turn and fold herself into his warm embrace, feel safe, feel important, feel wanted. But instead she smiled for the camera and wished she was braver. Wished she'd been wiser and chosen Daniel a long time ago.

She glanced up at him and found he was already looking at her, a half smile on his handsome face.

"You're beautiful," he said in a husky voice intoned for her alone.

Even though a cool breeze wafted through the tent, her skin flushed. She worked desperately not to compare this man to Charles, but diverting her thoughts was impossible. Initially, Charles had appreciated having her appear with him at officer's functions, had bought her dresses and shoes and jewelry to wear to the functions, but the attention had quickly faded, and she'd soon felt like a china doll set upon a shelf and forgotten.

She'd told herself he was preoccupied with his career, and of course the welfare of the country was more important than her hurt feelings. It would never have occurred to him to buy her a gift for the sake of her pleasure alone. He had never whispered that she was pretty. In fact now that she thought of it, she couldn't even remember him telling her he loved her.

"These were all full-length shots," John Cleve explained, moving the tripod with the camera forward and making readjustments. "I'm going to get a few head and shoulder portraits now, and then we'll be finished and you can carry on and enjoy the fair."

"I'm enjoying myself right now," Daniel said, beaming down at his wife.

"All right, you two. Look over my shoulder at the birdcage. Soft expressions. You're in love. The day is beautiful. Birds are singing. The scent of roses is everywhere. You've just eaten delicious wedding cake with sugary frosting, and the staff will be doing the dishes."

Leah couldn't help a small smile.

"You're happier about not doing those dishes than

having eaten the cake," John Cleve teased. A few minutes later, he stood and faced them. "You are interesting and natural subjects. You may come back this afternoon to see your portraits. I won't charge you for any that don't turn out the way you hoped they would. I confess I took more than I normally would have because I was captivated by the two of you. You are a striking couple. Mr. Gardner, there will be a few surprise photographs for you, as well."

They thanked John Cleve, changed clothing, and asked him to store it until their return. The crowd had swelled, voices louder, children more boisterous. Browsing the booths, they discovered jellies had been judged, and one of the homesteader's wives had won with her blackberry. Daniel bought them slices of bread spread with butter and jelly, and they enjoyed it as they walked. A birdhouse competition was being judged at one of the booths, so they stopped to watch. Owen Ewing won with a triple story birdhouse painted in colorful Dutch designs and outfitted with multiple perches and even a mock chimney.

"I think we should get a few of those birdhouses for our garden," Daniel said.

She looked up at him. "I like the sound of our garden."

They found Will orchestrating teams for a tug-of-war.

"Come on, Dan!" Will gestured with a broad sweep of his arm. "The red team needs you."

Daniel pulled a handkerchief from his pocket and tied it around his neck. "I guess it's appropriate I have my red kerchief then."

Leah patted his shoulder and waved him off.

The teams lined up. Daniel took the lead on his side, with Amos Godwin, Remmy Hagermann, Floyd Yates and other men Leah didn't recognize.

The blue team's captain was Reverend Taggart, backed up by D.B. Burrows, Abram Booker, one of the drovers who always wore a fringed leather vest that had the shape of Texas beaded on the back, and a couple more cowboys.

Will raised a pistol in the air. "Get ready. Get set." He fired the gun, and the tug-of-war began. Leah cheered her husband's team from the sidelines, while dozens of others called out their favorites' names and cheered.

Holly, the young woman Dora had been speaking to in the mercantile the day Leah had overheard them, cheered and called out for Rob to pull harder. Holly must have ignored Dora's advice if she was cheering for the son of the wagonmaker. Leah smiled and shouted at Daniel to put his back into it.

After much cheering by the crowd and sweating by the competitors, the blue team's flag was yanked over the center divider first, ending the competition.

Daniel used his kerchief to wipe his forehead and neck. The men from both teams met and slapped each other on the back.

"I don't feel so bad," Daniel told the reverend. "You had God on your side."

Virgil Taggart smiled his good-natured smile that split his face and shook Daniel's hand. "You're just fortunate I don't have a horse to enter in the competition then, I suppose."

"That I am." Daniel laughed and found Leah.

"You probably need some refreshment," she said. "I know I do and I was only cheering."

"Let's find some lemonade," he agreed.

They drank tart cold lemonade from sweating jars and sat on canvas chairs in the shade of a canopy. Their neighbors greeted them as they passed. A horn sounded in the distance, so they searched out the event, which was a hay bale toss.

"Do you enter this?" she asked.

"I have in the past." He winked. "But I'm saving myself for the race."

A dozen or more beefy farmers lined up, ready to compete, but Judd Ernst, a local rancher, called for the first division, which were children.

Leah looked at Daniel with skeptical surprise.

He nodded. "Wait until you see these kids."

They were fun to watch, and a strapping eight-year-old lad won with a twelve-foot toss.

The next division was called, and six women lined up. A rancher's wife won with a spectacular throw of twenty-five feet.

Leah clasped her hands against her cheeks. "That was amazing. She didn't look like she could have done that."

Finally the men lined up and threw the bales one at a time. The winner's bale landed a remarkable thirty-three feet away from the line. Dressed in denim overalls and a faded red shirt, he accepted his ribbon and his prize money.

Leah looked up at Daniel. "I might need a nap."

He laughed and guided her away to visit the livestock pens, later to watch the plowing competition, and then left her under an awning with Hannah while he went to the livery for his horse.

Hannah wore one of her ruffled creations that had to

have been hot. Her fashion choices still puzzled Leah, because she was so skilled with a needle and thread, but chose dreadful ensembles for herself. They chatted and walked together to the outskirts of the fairgrounds, where bystanders gathered for the race.

"Where are the horses and riders?" Leah asked.

A tall, thin youth with dark hair turned to reply. "The start is a couple o' miles out, ma'am. This here's the finish line. Judges are posted along the route to watch."

"I see. Thank you."

"Simon, ma'am. I work at the hotel. I know you're Mrs. Gardner."

"Pleased to meet you, Simon."

"You'll hear the starting pistol," he told them.

The crowd was unusually silent as people waited for the sound of the start of the race. A tingle of apprehension ran up her spine at the apprehension in the air. Hannah fanned herself with a paper fan painted with roses.

In the distance a gunshot volleyed across the plains. A murmur went through the crowd. A few at a time the bystanders gathered along the roped-off track that bracketed the path leading to a wide white ribbon strung across the finish line. Leah and Hannah positioned themselves to be near enough to see the horses and riders cross the line, and others closed in on either side.

"I don't even know who the competitors are," Leah said.

"I read the list posted at the rail station this morning," Hannah said. "One of the horses is Walter Frye's but he can't ride because of his broken arm, so someone else is riding. There were several names I didn't recognize and a couple of the drovers. James Johnson is one of them."

"I don't know him," Leah said.

"He always wears that fringe vest with the Texas beadwork on the back."

"Oh, yes, I've seen him." She glanced in the direction from which the riders would be coming. "Is this sport at all dangerous?"

"Well, I don't know. I suppose a horse could fall or a rider could be thrown."

"Lord, protect Daniel today," she prayed aloud. "And all the other riders, of course. Let them have fun and no calamity befall them."

"Amen," Hannah said. "Just so you know, my father's been praying for this event for weeks."

"That's good to know. I like your father. He's a kind man. Always smiling. He encouraged each of us on our way here."

"I see dust!" someone shouted.

Attention riveted on the wide cloud being stirred up from the ground. Silhouettes of the riders came into view. It was difficult from this distance to distinguish individuals, let alone tell who was in the lead, but news passed from those viewing with spyglasses.

"Gardner and Johnson are in front!" someone called.

Leah clasped her hands together beneath her chin and strained to see.

Cheers went up and the crowd called out for their favorites. As the riders drew closer, it was plain two were well ahead of the others.

Leah stood on tiptoe and leaned out as far as she could as others crowded over the ropes. Daniel's distinctive brown-and-white skewbald pulled ahead, its powerful legs in captivating motion, and he leaned over its neck, his hair blowing away from his face.

The powerful animals' hooves created a cloud of dust and flung clods of sod into the air as the lead competitors neared the finish line and raced past. The white ribbon stretched and broke as the brown-and-white skewbald tore through it, and the ribbon fluttered against Daniel's legs. He sat back and slowed the horse.

Wild with excitement, the people clapped and cheered. James Johnson accepted second place with a breathless shrug and slid from his horse. Daniel dismounted and, with grins on their faces, the two men slapped each other on the back and shook hands. Daniel's green-eyed gaze immediately panned the crowd, and he found Leah on the sideline.

She gave him a broad smile, and he led the horse over to where she stood. Several people reached out to touch the horse's forehead and sweaty neck. "I'm going to walk him back to the stable to cool off and then brush him down. Will you be all right until I get back?"

"Yes, I'm fine. What's his name?"

Daniel rubbed the horse's nose. "This is Woodrow. Woodrow, meet the prettiest lady in Kansas."

The horse merely snuffed and bobbed its head once.

"He might be more impressed if you had four legs and a tail." Daniel glanced at her. "Think you'll want to go home and rest a bit before this evening?"

"Yes, I think that would be best." She turned and spoke to Hannah. "I'm going to leave for a while. Will I see you this evening?"

Hannah nodded and Leah turned back to Daniel. "Why don't I walk as far as the livery with you and Woodrow, and then I'll go on home while you take care of him?"

They stopped to grab their clothing, and John Cleve

showed them their portraits. He had framed several and others had been placed in decorative display folders. There were at least a dozen. "I want all of them," Daniel said.

"*All* of them?" Leah questioned.

"One day our children will treasure our wedding portraits. Perhaps I'll send one to my father."

She thought of all the sentimental things that had been lost when her family home burned. It would be nice to have photographs to leave their children. The thought of more children was too elusive to consider for more than a moment, but she appreciated Daniel's projection. She could never have seen herself living here, imagined this day—beheld the future that was now possible. She was learning every day to trust God for her future—for their future. She felt exceptionally fortunate in this moment.

She carried the flat, wrapped bundle. The horse plodded beside Daniel as he led him with the reins. They parted at the livery, and Leah continued home for a much-needed rest. She washed away the day's grime and napped on her bed.

It was nearly dark when Daniel rapped on her door. She rolled to get up and padded to answer his knock. "Are you rested?"

She blinked and pushed her hair back from her temples. "I didn't think I'd sleep so long. Give me half an hour."

"Take all the time you need. I'll put on some coffee and make us some eggs."

After they'd eaten, they left the house. Daniel had brought around a buggy this time, pulled by a horse she didn't recognize. "Woodrow has the night off, I assume."

"He wanted to come see you, but I told him to rest."

She laughed and smoothed her skirt over her knees as he led the horse toward the fairgrounds. For the evening festivities she'd worn her two-piece sprigged blue-and-white cotton dress with blue trim and had secured blue-and-white silk flowers and stemmed pearls in her upswept hair.

Again they heard the band, and this time they followed the music to the huge wooden dance floor that covered a portion of prairie grass. Lanterns had been strung from posts to illuminate the wood floor and the band of cowboys and pioneers with their fiddles, guitars, accordion and two musicians at upright pianos.

"How long since you've danced?" Daniel asked.

"A very long time," she answered softly.

Chapter Eighteen

They watched as couples paired off and took the floor one at a time. Every woman who lived within a hundred miles soon had a dance partner, while men lined up by the dozens and waited patiently for turns. "Will you honor me with the first dance before the cowboys compromise your time?" Daniel asked.

She took the hand he offered and he led her onto the smooth wooden planks. He led the steps effortlessly, and she soon remembered what a good dancer he'd been. "We've danced together before," she reminded him.

His fingers tightened briefly over hers. "I remember well."

"You do?"

"The last time you were fifteen, and you were the prettiest girl at the cotillion. You had on a pink dress with ruffles at the shoulders and a sash that hung down the back of your skirt. You wore your hair in long curls that hung over one shoulder, and it smelled like…"

"Like what?"

"Like it does right now. Like lemon and honeysuckle."

She leaned back to have a good look at his face. "You remember all that?"

Daniel lifted one side of his mouth in a self-deprecating grin and her heart swelled with appreciation for this man. He'd made her life so rich and full, she was able to forget the things she didn't want to remember for hours—sometimes a day at a time. She'd taken to counting down the minutes while he was away, appreciating the moments they spent together more than she'd anticipated she ever could.

This was dangerous territory, this evolving relationship, this expansion of all that she'd diligently tried to keep carefully contained and manageable. His handsome face was dear, his strong arms a haven of hope around her. She'd found more here in Kansas than she'd ever dreamed possible, but part of her—a very real, very hesitant part of her—remembered to use caution. She didn't like herself for using Charles as a measuring stick, but if she'd learned anything, she'd learned that people weren't who they seemed, and once a man got what he wanted, the bubble burst.

Daniel glanced over her shoulder and then led her toward the edge of the floor, where Will stood. "Would you mind finding Leah a seat while I get us refreshments?"

"My pleasure." Will offered his arm and guided her toward unoccupied wooden benches.

Seating herself, she watched her husband make his way from the dance floor.

"Do you think you're going to be happy in Cowboy Creek?" Will asked.

She turned her attention to him. "I can't help but

think the Lord's hand of provision was guiding me. I don't believe in coincidences."

"Nor happenstance," Will added.

"No," she agreed with a smile.

"When you showed up, he was determined you would have a good match. I doubt he slept until he'd decided he would ask you to marry him. He didn't trust anyone else as a husband. At his insistence, Noah and I went through dozens of prospects. None of them were good enough."

She couldn't resist a smile. "I guess he thinks he's the best."

"He's right, isn't he?"

At his direct question, Leah glanced into Will's eyes. "I believe so, yes."

He smiled at her. "I'm glad we can be friends, Leah."

"So am I. It looks as though we'll be seeing a lot of each other from here on out."

"I don't suppose you'll be much of a bother."

Will chuckled and Daniel returned with three sweating jars of lemonade. "Appears as though Will is amusing you."

Leah enjoyed the refreshingly tart liquid. "He can be amusing when he applies himself."

She and Will exchanged a friendly glance.

A cowboy with a fresh haircut and new dungarees approached. "Sure would like a dance, ma'am, if your husband approves."

Daniel acquiesced by gesturing to indicate it was Leah's choice. She accepted and enjoyed a turn around the floor.

Fittingly, Pippa was the belle of the ball, dancing every dance, laughing, accepting outrageous compliments and so many flowers, she had a heaping bouquet at the corner of the wooden flooring.

Leah finally spotted Prudence, her stance stiff as she danced with Nels Patterson. Hannah sat with her father on the outskirts, watching the merriment, smiling as the dancers whirled past. Daniel asked Hannah for a dance, as did Deputy Watson, who showed up off duty. Leah danced with half a dozen drovers and ranchers before Daniel came to her aid.

"I'm thinking you might need something more to drink and a break," he said, turning her in a circle and managing to move them toward the outskirts of the throng.

"That sounds good, thank you."

He found her a chair and brought her a fresh jar of iced lemonade.

The music changed, dancers paired off and formed squares for a quadrille.

Leah spotted Valentine partnered with the photographer. "Daniel, look at Valentine and John Cleve."

He settled comfortably on the ground at her knee and together they enjoyed the music and revelry.

"What happens tomorrow morning?" she asked. "It's Sunday, and the fair is still underway."

"We will have services under the big canopy over there," he answered. "The musicians have been asked to attend and play, so it should be a lively service."

"Yes, indeed."

Leah slept like a rock that night. The fresh air, walking and activity had worn her out, but she woke refreshed and ready for a new day. She chose a dress Hannah had helped her alter, this one in a rose shade with a white eyelet overskirt and a V-shaped neckline with an eyelet collar. The dress called for a necklace, so she found one she'd worn since she was a girl that her father had given her. The drops of coral interspersed with filigree nestled against her collarbone and filled the open space nicely, even though the coral didn't perfectly match her dress.

She smiled, remembering the sentiment behind the necklace, and thankful she had it.

Sunday morning service was lively, with all the musicians present, as well as men and a few wives and several children from outlying farms and ranches. Reverend Taggart did a fine job of preaching about healing and forgiveness after all the country had weathered over the past several years. He spoke of the pride of the people of Webster County and new beginnings, tying it to forgiveness and new life in Christ.

Pippa sang in her lovely, clear soprano voice:

"I hear the Savior say, 'Thy strength indeed is small;
Child of weakness, watch and pray, Find in Me thine all in all.'
Jesus paid it all, All to Him I owe; Sin had left a crimson stain,
He washed it white as snow."

There wasn't a dry eye under the canopy when she'd finished. Reverend Taggart asked if anyone wanted prayer and several went forward and he prayed for them.

Afterward people had a noon meal on their own, some with picnic lunches, others at the vendors' booths along the midway. Daniel located seating and brought plates of chicken, potato salad and buttered rolls from Aunt Mae's booth.

"Did you see Noah came to the service this morning?" he asked while they ate.

"I didn't, but I heard a couple speaking about the vicious-looking black dog outside, so I assumed he was there."

"That dog is part wolf, but his bark is worse than his bite, just like his owner."

They lingered after the lunch crowd had moved on, talking about this and that, enjoying the breeze and the distant laughter.

"That necklace looks familiar," he said. "It's lovely."

She touched the coral and silver, warm against her skin. "My father gave it to me on Christmas Eve when I was thirteen. I wore it to parties and dances. I felt so grown up."

"You haven't worn it since you've been here."

"I wore it under my clothing on my journey here. It has good memories, but it has bad memories as well." She didn't bother to keep the pain from her voice. "Those are the ones I'm trying to forget, but it's impossible. They're with me always, so I may as well wear the necklace."

"Do those memories have anything to do with the dreams?"

She blinked, uncertain about the direction of this conversation, but she answered honestly. "Yes."

He didn't question her further. His patience and understanding had no limit. No doubt he would wait if it took her years to tell him, but she couldn't keep her secret pain to herself any longer. She was hungry for kindness, hungry for the caring and concern Daniel so freely offered. "I was wearing it when I returned to Pennsylvania before the war ended."

"So you left the place you'd been where your husband was stationed and went home?"

"Yes. And I soon discovered the situation back there had become desperate for everyone. Our families, Daniel, all of our neighbors who remained. Women and children, elderly folks, everyone just trying to survive and praying for their sons and brothers and husbands to come home, but learning one by one that they weren't." She swallowed hard as the memories assailed her. "Winter was miserable. Confederates cut off supply routes, confiscated wagons, and people ate whatever they had left, holding on to only a few chickens and cows because the animals needed to eat, too, and there weren't enough workers to grow the crops. Those who could, planted gardens for themselves."

"I know, Leah," Daniel said, his tone somber. "We saw it all, too. We were the ones cutting off supplies so the southerners could no longer survive."

"We hid from the rebels." The words came easier now that she'd opened the floodgate. "We made sure the house looked unlived in, but in order to stay warm we burned furniture that wasn't essential and then started on Daddy's books."

Daniel closed his eyes as though her telling pained him. "Go on," he said, his voice hoarse with emotion. The present fell away, and he was in Pennsylvania with Leah seeing the big old house slowly being disassembled, feeling the bitter cold, smelling the books burning, sharing the pangs of hunger.

"Mama and Hattie and I slept with our clothes on to stay warm, and we wore things we didn't want to lose if we had to run. Like this." She touched her necklace. "Do you remember Hattie?"

He opened his eyes. "Your cousin."

"Yes. She'd lost both my aunt and uncle, and had been staying with Mama when I went back to Pennsylvania, thinking it would be safer there. We holed up by the fireplace in Daddy's study to stay warm. Mama took sick. She had a fever and a bad cough." A lump rose to her throat, but she managed to go on. "One morning the rebels approached the house. We heard them coming from the orchard. We ran to the ice house and watched through the cracks in the chinking as they set fire to the house."

Daniel had done the same damage as those men, looting and burning as ordered. He'd displaced innocent women and children, destroyed homes, stolen food. While those Union soldiers had been the enemy, they'd only been men just like he, hungry, frightened men with families at home waiting for the war to end. Leah's chilling words were spoken to his heart, as though he was hearing the accusations of his enemies, but he had to listen. There was no escaping the facts.

"Mama couldn't keep up," Leah said, her voice cold now, matter-of-fact, as though she was reading a book, a tale of someone she'd never met and with whom she had no personal connection. "She coughed something fierce."

He heard Mrs. Robinson's painful cough, felt the women's fear and panic, and his heart seized. He knew what was coming next, and the hair on the back of his neck stood up. He didn't want to hear the rest, but he had to listen.

"'Go,' Mama said." Leah's voice was no more than

a guttural whisper now, but he heard every nuance and syllable. "'You have a chance without me,' she said. 'Make it for me and live.' She was so brave. She picked up a rock and crouched, ready to stop the first man who came after us. So brave."

Daniel covered his face with his hands and inhaled a shaky breath. He remembered Leah's mother, graceful and happy, cooking and serving guests and enjoying her family. That she'd died in such a manner was a shame to this country and to the people the war had turned them all into. He was almost thankful his own mother had passed away when he was young, so she hadn't lived through those years, so she hadn't met a similar fate.

"We heard the gunfire, but we waited where she'd told us to. In the bushes where we could see that big flat rock that hung out over the stream. The place where we used to jump in and swim in the summer. She didn't come and we had to leave."

He knew the spot. Daniel saw the frozen water, heard the gunfire, felt her terror and grief.

Leah stood and moved in front of him, peeling his hands from his face and placing her own palms on his cheeks.

"Leah, I'm so sorry," he managed to say, and swallowed hard.

"I know." She rubbed his cheekbones gently with her thumbs. "I know."

He wrapped his arms around her expanding waist, and she flattened herself against him. Her clothing smelled like fresh air and starch. "There was nothing you could have done to save her. If you had stayed with her all of you would have died."

"I know," she said again. "Hattie just gave up once we got to the city. She took sick and died."

"Your mother was brave," he said around the rasp in his throat. "But you're brave, too. It takes courage to go on when life looks hopeless. When we look around this town, at our neighbors and friends, we're seeing the people who had the courage to go on, no matter how hard it was. I'm proud of you, Leah, and I'm thankful you fought to survive." *Because I found you.*

"So am I."

"Out of all the places you could have ended up," he said as though he'd spoken his thoughts aloud. "You're here."

This was the most she'd opened up to him since her arrival. She was more vulnerable now than in their youth. Every day he wondered over what she *didn't* say. He wondered about her husband. He heard every sound that came from her room at night, had trouble sleeping with her in there, knowing how close she was, yet they had remained a world apart. Until now. Until she'd been brave enough to tell him what gave her nightmares and woke her crying in the darkest midnight hours.

No one had entered the seating area alongside Aunt Mae's tent since they'd begun this conversation. It seemed as though they'd been divinely afforded these precious minutes of privacy in the midst of bustling activity. It didn't matter that he embraced her where anyone passing by could see them. She was his wife. He wanted to be completely honest with her about his feelings, but he didn't want to put any pressure on her. She'd begun to open up to him and this was a sign of good things to come.

He cradled her jaw, ran his thumb across her impossibly soft, pale cheek. She grasped his wrist and smiled at him through the sheen of tears. Leaning close, he brushed a gentle kiss against her lips.

Her lips trembled, but she said, "I'm glad I'm here, Daniel. I'm so thankful I found you."

Daniel kissed her again, hopeful that this was only the beginning.

The fair was a success. At the council meeting Monday evening, business owners shared that the effort and the investment had more than earned out in revenue and good will. The council rented a railcar in which to store all the lumber, the tents and awnings until the next occasion. Cowboy Creek was putting itself in the running as an excellent prospect for county seat.

After the meeting, Will caught Daniel before he left. "I sent the query for Noah's bride today."

"Are you going to tell him?"

"No," Will said. "I'm not giving him a chance to veto our efforts. I asked for someone smart and friendly. Once the prospective bride gets here and they get acquainted, he'll recognize he needs someone and see that people don't judge him by those scars."

"Did you mention the scars in the letter?"

"No. Those scars aren't who Noah is. I wrote about the kind of man he is."

"You could have written a letter for yourself."

"You did all right without trying," Will replied. "Perhaps someone on the next bride train will be perfect for me. If not, I can wait."

"Don't get your hopes up for perfect," Daniel told him. "There are always things to work through."

"Coming from the one with all the experience?"

"I have a little experience," he said almost defensively.

Will chuckled. "Well, I'll know her when I meet her. She'll bat baby blue eyes at me and twirl her fringed parasol, and I'll be besotted."

"I can't wait for that."

"I wired money for train fare and expenses," his pal said. "Hopefully a prospect should be here in a few weeks."

"I'll be looking forward to that," Daniel drawled.

"Won't we all?"

Chapter Nineteen

That week work began in earnest on the nursery. Daniel and Leah ordered an iron crib and wallpaper from one of the catalogs at Remmy's store. One afternoon Daniel came home early with a rocking chair he'd had Mr. Irving make. It was sturdily built with a padded seat and back, delightfully comfortable. Daniel carried it upstairs and set it in the room that only held a bureau and a few crates.

He pointed to one of the crates. "That came a week or so ago. Noah told me to open it when we were preparing for the baby."

"I wondered what that was."

He got a claw hammer and pried open the lid to find straw packing. After digging through the straw, he discovered items and uncovered them. "It's a carved wooden horse," he said of the wooden animal he held.

Leah took the miniature from him and examined it. "Look at the detail," she said in awe. "Where did he get these?"

"I've seen him carve. It's a hobby of his."

"Noah made this?"

Daniel nodded and searched the packing, finding a bear and a raccoon, then another bear in a different pose. As he uncovered more and more figures, it became clear there were two of each. Two cows, two goats, two pigs, two eagles, a pair of mountain lions and a pair of beavers.

"That's a big crate. How many animals are in there?" She knelt and helped him unpack. "Why, it's the animals from Noah's ark!" Leah exclaimed. "He carved two of every animal." She stood and arranged the creatures atop the bureau and admired the craftsmanship of each piece. "Can you imagine the hours that went into making these?"

Daniel shook his head. "He spends a lot of time alone."

"I do wish he'd come join us on occasion. I can't wait to thank him. Perhaps we can take a drive out to his place?"

"Of course we can." Daniel discovered a couple of large objects on the bottom and hauled them out, straw spilling to the floor. "Look, Leah. It's the ark." He set the boat-like bottom on the floor and placed a hinged box on top. It had been painted and was storage for all the animals. "He's painted a dove with an olive leaf on the top."

Leah wiped tears from her eyes. "It's beautiful, isn't it?"

Daniel moved the ark to the bureau and Leah arranged the animals on and around it. In the bottom of the crate Daniel found a few birds, two small snakes and two frogs. He and Leah smiled at each other.

Leah sat in the rocker and surveyed the room, imagining where the crib would go. Through the open window came the distant sound of hammering. "Where is that coming from? The school is finished, isn't it?"

"That's construction on the opera house over one street."

"Pippa is certainly excited. Still no idea who burned that first shipment of wood?" she asked.

"No idea, but the mayhem has died down since the Murdochs moved on."

"Just doesn't seem like something dangerous criminals would do," she mused. "Sounds more like someone with a grudge against the town or against someone in the town. Who has enemies that you know of?"

"We've all probably made a few waves, but I can't imagine anyone wanting to stop the progress of the town. This town is a joint effort for the good of everyone."

"Who might have something to gain if there are setbacks to the progress?" she prodded.

He set the crate with the straw near the doorway. "I've wondered the same thing, Leah, and I honestly don't know. It takes hard workers to create a terminus like this and aspire to the county seat. People don't come here if they're not ready to work."

They grew silent for a few moments, both lost in their worrisome thoughts, contemplating the uncertainty facing their small close-knit community.

"Valentine left early today," she remembered to mention. "She's having dinner in town. I can fix us something."

Daniel glanced at her resting comfortably in the rocker. She'd had a busy day and he'd rather she didn't go to the trouble. "Why don't we have supper at the hotel?" he suggested. "We haven't done that for a while."

"That sounds nice."

Later she changed and they strolled hand in hand to the hotel. There were quite a few diners in the restaurant. Will entered a few minutes after they'd taken their seats and Daniel waved him over.

Will took a chair and hung his cane on the back. "You look lovely this evening, Leah."

"Thank you."

"I remember that necklace you're wearing. Your father gave it to you."

She rested her fingertips over the coral stone and silver filigree and smiled, as though pleased he'd remembered. "Yes, he did."

"You wore it to dances and parties."

Daniel felt a niggle of discomfort at Will's fond remembrances. He certainly had an accurate memory about things regarding Leah. But he had an acute memory about most things. The man was polite and respectful to Daniel's wife, paying her a compliment, making social conversation. His uneasiness was only his own insecurity flaring up, he told himself, and he refused to allow the jealousy a foothold.

Will turned to him. "Today I got wind of something you should know."

"What is it?" Daniel asked, assured of his conclusion. Will had come to talk to him and had politely greeted Leah first.

"A railroad representative will be arriving soon."

Daniel narrowed his eyes. "We've met a lot of them before. What's this visit about?"

"A potential opportunity may be opening up. Obviously the railroad is still expanding. It seems we may be given the opportunity to invest in the Union Pacific."

"How did you learn this?"

"You remember Gideon Kendricks, one of the men we worked with when we sold land?" When Daniel nodded, he went on to say, "Well, we keep in touch and I got a telegram from him."

"As stockholders we could make a difference," Daniel said, warming to the idea.

"How?" Leah asked.

He turned to answer. "Stockholders can form companies and their influence makes a difference in controlling the storage and shipping rates. By investing, we may actually be able to help the farmers and ranchers keep their costs down."

"It would definitely help me on the level of state legislature when I'm ready to run for an office," Will explained.

She looked from one man to the other. "It sounds like a good thing for the economy in the long run to have two levelheaded men helping set legislation."

"Three," Will told her. "Noah has as much say as we do in investments and town concerns."

"And it could help grow the town, too, don't you think?" she asked.

Will nodded. "I do." He reached behind him for his cane. "I'll leave you two to your supper now and excuse myself. I just wanted to share the good news."

"You're welcome to join us," Leah offered.

"Thanks, but I've already eaten. I'm on my way up to my office to work for a few hours. Have a good evening."

"I always pictured him doing something like this," she told Daniel after Will had gone.

"His aspirations keep him motivated."

She leaned toward him. "But you're a surprise."

He absorbed her words, wondering what to make of them. Had she believed he had no ambition? "I guess I surprised myself when I got excited about starting a town like this."

Leah noted his tense expression and realized her words may have sounded less appreciative than she'd intended. "And yet you're still hands-on with the stock, so it makes sense," she said. "Now competing in that race yesterday—and winning? That was not a surprise."

He shrugged, but finally gave her a lopsided smile.

"You looked so happy when you jumped off Woodrow and waved your hat in the air. That was the Daniel I remember."

He gave her a tender look. "I'm that happy right now."

Meaning being here with her. She was happier than she'd been in a long time, too. Finding Daniel meant safety and security of course, but beyond that she'd found more than her old friend. He was a man she admired, a man of conviction and courage and principle. He was a trustworthy companion. He was the man with whom she would spend her life, and it wouldn't be a burden or a sacrifice.

Charles had never been a kind or a caring man, but when he'd returned after the war she hadn't even known him. He'd taken to leaving for days at a time. Between Charles, the losses she'd suffered and the state of the country, she'd lost her faith in mankind, but Daniel had gathered a community of men and women who were willing to work hard to start over and make this a place where they wanted to live.

She was happy, too, but she didn't want to admit it to herself let alone to Daniel. Caring was risky. Being happy was dangerous. Life was too fragile, and joy an elusive notion. An uncomfortable feeling grew from deep within her and she fought it down.

She was being unfair to Daniel. He was giving everything. Sharing his home, all he'd worked for, giving all. And she was holding back, protecting herself.

She'd never felt worthy of him. Every day pointed out the differences between them. Regret and a tinge of anger—directed toward herself—made her eyes sting with tears, and she looked away.

"Leah, what's wrong?" he asked.

She shook her head. "Not here. Not now."

"Do you want to leave?"

"No." She composed herself. The waiter came and they ordered their meals. She noticed Pippa having supper with a young man wearing a shirt and tie, his hair slicked back and his tanned face scrubbed shiny.

Garnering composure and resolve, she forced herself to look at Daniel. "You're using all the gifts and abilities God has given you. You're enjoying the fact that you survived the war and you're set on making this a better country to live in."

"You make me sound pretty grand." He gave a modest shrug. "I'm just doing the best I can to set things to right again. Yes, I was fortunate enough to live through something many, many men didn't. I have to believe there's a reason God spared me—along with Will and Noah—and you. I don't want to waste precious days of life when I could be enjoying them…and doing something worthwhile."

She looked at him. "I used to feel a similar desire, but that was before. Now I've become focused on survival—

on me. It's all about *me*, about how I can take care of my baby, about what's best for this child. I've been so selfish."

He placed his hand over hers, surprising her. "That's what you're supposed to be doing. It's nature's way. It's instinct. God made you a woman and gave you these protective feelings for the survival of the human race. Where would we be if women weren't brave enough to have babies and protect them?"

"I'm not a baby mill, Daniel. I want to contribute more than that. What gifts do I have that will help restore our country?"

"What about your passion for being a midwife? That's a gift to all the women coming west and having the very same concerns you have for your child. Opal for example. You probably don't know what a blessing you've been to her—and to Amos." Tightening his grip on her hand, he gently stroked his thumb over her knuckles. "And there will be more women and more opportunities as Cowboy Creek expands and the new brides marry and have children. Here you'll be, waiting for them. Families will have you to rely on, and you'll train others."

She couldn't help it—she wanted to cry—but instead she laughed. She laughed and tears trickled down her cheeks at the same time.

Daniel reached into his pocket and pulled out a handkerchief.

She dabbed her eyes and nose. "You just won't let a girl feel sorry for herself, will you? Even when I'm a big baby and a worrywart, you tell me how great I am and make me feel better."

"Do you feel better?"

She did. She had something to offer. She had a way to contribute to the lives of their neighbors and friends.

Now if she could think of something to offer Daniel, some way to deserve him, she might feel worthy of his devotion—and of his confidence in her.

Chapter Twenty

The dream came that night, but as it began Leah woke herself. She got out of bed and lit the lamp on her bureau. A light rain pattered on the roof, and she moved the curtain aside. Rivulets trickled down the panes of glass, sparkling in the moonlight shining in. "Thank You for the rain," she said softly. "Thank You for waiting until the fair was past."

The gentle rain would do wonders for their vegetable and flower gardens, as well as the fledgling rose and lilac bushes in the side yard. In a few years, they would have a lovely place to sit and have tea or lunch. She could invite the other ladies for get-togethers during fair weather.

She smiled, liking that she was thinking like a domesticated woman, someone who was settled in and part of a community again. She liked that the nightmare hadn't taken hold and stolen her peace of mind. Perhaps telling Daniel about that time and her mother's death had allowed her to face it, to grieve, to fully understand she'd done the only thing she could have and still survive. She'd lived to pick up the pieces, to start over.

She sat in the comfortable rose-printed chair, picked up her Bible from the stand and held it to her breast, her arms crossed over it and she closed her eyes. Very soon she would have a new baby to hold. She had the courage to believe it now. Only a matter of weeks now and she would be cradling her baby in her arms. She had so much to be thankful for.

She thought of the preparations they'd been making. The nursery, the ark Noah had carved, the blanket Opal had knitted and the delicate yellow calico gown Hannah had sewn. Friends were truly a blessing, and even more so when one didn't have family. If things had been different her mother would have loved to share this time with her. She and Daniel would make sure the baby had influences like Aunt Mae and Valentine in its young life. She had adored her grandparents and this child needed similar substitutes. Will and Noah would make fine uncles.

As she so often did, she thought of their families when they were children. Daniel's mother had died when he was young.

She opened her eyes and sat forward, the Bible resting on her knees. Daniel's father was still alive. She tried to remember what Daniel had mentioned about him. Had he ever said specifically where he was living or what he was doing? It would be good if he could visit.

Rain played a staccato melody on the roof. Leah stood and set down her Bible before moving to the bureau where one of the new framed portraits sat. They were all lovely, but this one was her favorite. It was one that had been taken before they'd changed into their formal clothing. An untidy lock of hair trailed down her neck. Daniel's hair was windblown. She vividly remembered the moment it was taken. She had just reached up to smooth a strand from his forehead and paused with a hand on his shoulder as he looked at her with that expression...

She loved the masculine angles of his face, the arch of his brow, the fine, straight column of his nose. He had nicely shaped lips and defined cheekbones, each feature striking on its own, the combination a riveting masterpiece. But it was his countenance that stirred the cold ashes of her heart and coaxed a steady white-hot new flame, created a disturbing jumble of nerves and breathed hope and life into tender new feelings.

Of all the things he'd given her—a home, security, his name, the china, both gold rings, the garnet brooch—this breathless new treasure was the most valuable. Expectation. Anticipation. She'd forgotten what optimism felt like.

She'd forgotten what—

The idea that struck her was an answer to her prayer. She finally knew what she could do for Daniel. The perfect thing guaranteed to please and surprise him. Leah felt altogether giddy with excitement over the plan she was forming. First thing in the morning after Daniel left for work, she would visit Will at his office and get his help in carrying out her strategy.

She focused on the portrait again, skimmed her fingertips over Daniel's image, then turned down the wick, plunging the room into darkness. She found the bed, determined to sleep now so she'd be rested for the following day.

"Thank You, Lord."

Daniel rode out to meet the trail boss who'd driven a huge herd to the stockyards the previous day. The healthy-looking longhorns milled in the pens, drinking fresh water and eating hay and grain before being shipped out. It would take a couple of days to get the cows weighed, loaded and shipped. He invited Mannie Southworth to a meal at the hotel, as he did all the bosses and their head drovers.

Waiting in the lobby for a table, Daniel glanced at the stairs as two pair of feet, trouser legs and the hem of a familiar skirt came into view. As the couple descended, he recognized Leah and Will. They didn't see him, absorbed as they were in their conversation.

Leah wore an animated expression and nodded at something Will was saying as they exited the front doors onto Eden Street. Daniel gravitated toward the front window and watched them through the pane of glass. They stood in plain sight of anyone walking past or viewing from a store window and they were doing nothing but talking.

Leah hadn't mentioned going to see Will.

The same unease he'd felt before rose in his chest. He didn't like the feeling. He'd gone through this in his younger days. Leah had chosen Will over him. Did those strong feelings ever really disappear? His hadn't.

The two certainly had a lot to say to each other. Leah's vibrant face was practically shining with excitement over whatever they were talking about. She gestured with one hand and Will smiled indulgently. Daniel's gut clenched in a visceral response. She was his wife now. He could go out there and let them know he'd seen them.

"Daniel, our table's ready," Mannie said.

"Yes," he replied, but he couldn't look away. Leah had once had strong enough feelings for Will to believe she wanted to one day marry him. They'd all been close as children, but as they matured, her feelings for Will changed while Daniel stayed a friend.

Will hadn't shared a lot of what she'd written in her few letters after they'd joined the regiment. He'd eventually told Daniel the separation wasn't working and they were calling it off. They'd learned later about Leah's marriage to Charles Swann.

Will had been engaged to Dora when Leah had arrived, so resuming their relationship hadn't been an option. Daniel had been so relieved to see her, so absorbed by her presence and concerned for her welfare, he'd barged ahead and made it his business to find a match for her.

She'd been vulnerable. She'd been through harrowing experiences and loss, and had come to Cowboy Creek seeking a solution to her dilemma. Of course Daniel had thought he was the answer. *He wanted to be the answer.* She'd come to start over, and perhaps he'd placed her in an awkward position and forced her hand.

Had she felt *obligated* because they'd been friends?

"Daniel?" Mannie called.

He turned and joined the drovers, walking into the dining room on leaden legs and taking a seat. Maybe he'd been kidding himself all along and his boyish infatuation had fooled him into thinking he and Leah could make more of this marriage than she'd ever promised.

She'd told him flat out this was a convenient arrangement. She cared for him, but she treated him as a friend. Those surprising kisses they'd shared... Perhaps she was fulfilling an obligation, acting on something she didn't feel but knew he wanted—doing what was expected of her. The thought made him sick.

The smells of the food made him queasy. His stomach burned and his chest felt heavy. There was surely an innocent explanation for why his wife had been to visit Will. She would tell him all about it tonight. She was honorable and honest, and she would never involve herself in anything inappropriate. He trusted Will with his life. They'd always been as close as brothers.

He didn't for a heartbeat believe anything was going on behind his back.

But people's hearts didn't follow the rules. Love chose a person, rather than the other way around. If Leah still loved Will, his friend was now free. Daniel may have jumped the gun by marrying her first.

The special of the day was porcupine meatballs and a mound of mashed potatoes and red gravy. He ate a few bites and pushed the rest around on his plate, forcing himself to join the conversation and be polite.

All he cared about was her happiness. He would have to do the right thing. He would have to make sure she knew he understood and apologize for being impatient. If things were as he suspected, he would have to let her go, even if the thought ripped him apart.

After their lunch, Daniel went to his office at the stockyards and buried himself in paperwork for the afternoon. Eventually he headed home, his heart thudding with dread.

She had set the dining room table, and together with Valentine prepared a meal. Valentine left and they ate in silence. Eventually, he asked, "How was your day?"

"It was fine. I picked up a few things at Remmy's."

He waited for her to speak of her meeting with Will, but no mention was forthcoming. Finally he set down his fork. "How do you feel about me, Leah?"

She glanced at him in surprise. She rested her fork on the edge of her plate. "I'm not sure what you want me to say."

"It doesn't matter what I want you to say," he said in a hollow tone. "Just be honest. Nothing more."

"I'm very fond of you. You know that. I always have been."

He pushed his plate away and folded his hands on the table. "I've made you a lot of promises, and I want you to know I will keep every last one. I will take care of you. And I'll see the baby is taken care of, no matter what happens."

She frowned. "What could happen?"

"I won't hold you against your will. You're not obligated to me. I'll do anything I can to make things easy for you—for the both of us. We've both had some time to think about things and the situation has changed since you first arrived. I can arrange for an annulment if that's what you'd prefer."

"Daniel," she whispered with tears in her eyes. "What are you saying? Why would you suggest such a thing?"

"You didn't marry me for love, Leah."

She flattened a hand over her heart. "I've made some stupid and selfish mistakes, but—"

"You're neither stupid nor selfish."

"I've been a coward."

He pushed back his chair and stood, laying down his napkin. "I won't hold you."

"Daniel."

He raised a palm. "Don't make it any harder. Just don't. It's my fault. I apologize for pushing you into something we weren't ready for. I got ahead of myself. I always have to fix everything. Maybe this time I rushed us into this marriage without waiting to see what God was going to do." Clenching his jaw, he shoved a hand through his hair, and his next words came out a strangled whisper. "This is hard for me, Leah. Hard. But it's not the kind of marriage or the life I want. I want more."

He turned and left the room.

The front door closed and Leah sat stunned in the silent dining room. She wasn't quite sure what had provoked Daniel's pronouncement or his hurt and anger, but she was pretty sure her cowardice had something to do with it. She had taken the compassion and security he offered and made marriage sound like a business contract.

He was the kindest, smartest, most generous and noble man she knew, and she'd held him at arm's length because she wasn't ready for more. Because she wasn't ready to commit. She been too afraid to open herself up—and too cowardly to let herself be vulnerable. As if holding back had worked.

As if this pain felt any better than the pain she'd have felt if she had said the words—if she had listened to her heart.

She'd been so hopeful the night before, certain she could do something that pleased him. Today she'd put her plan in motion, but now she didn't know what was going to happen.

What had she done?

Feeling as though the life and light had gone out of her plan, she cleared the plates, washed the dishes and put them away. She walked through the still house, aching with regret. She had never intended to be a burden. She had fully meant to be a wife, make Daniel happy.

But she'd mistakenly believed that marrying for sensible reasons, marrying a good friend and having security, was more important than love. What was so terrifying about love anyway?

A marble-topped bureau had been delivered that day, and she'd had it placed in the foyer and hung a mirror over it. She opened the top drawer and took out the only item she'd placed in it—a shawl. She draped it around her shoulders and left the house.

For a few moments she stood on the porch, contemplating her choices. It struck her that she had no idea where to find Daniel. He often worked at his office at the stockyards, but that was east of town and he rode a horse to get there. She didn't know what she'd say to him if she found him anyway; she simply needed to clear her head.

Normally, she took Lincoln Boulevard south, but she headed west on Fourth Street, which had very few structures, save a laundry and, on the next block, the skeleton of the opera house. What this town needed was a park, a place with benches and somewhere to sit and think. She walked farther and found a dirt road intersection surrounded by nothing but grass and crickets.

She turned south and came to a corner where she made out the silhouette of Will's house. At the end of that block she came to the church, but kept going all the way until she reached the railroad tracks. She knew exactly where she was because of the tracks and the darkened station.

"Who's there?" a male voice shouted.

She started and peered into the darkness. "It's Leah Gardner."

Cinders crunched under his boots as a tall, slim form

approached, a rifle in hand. "Ma'am. What are you doing out tonight?"

"I went for a walk," she answered. She'd forgotten the sentries. This probably hadn't been such a good idea.

From the other side of the tracks came the sound of piano music and laughter. No, she really hadn't been thinking when she'd headed this direction.

"Does Mr. Gardner know you're out walking in the dark?" His voice held a distinct Texas accent.

"I wasn't thinking," she said quietly. "Sorry if I disturbed you."

"Why don't I walk along with you to Lincoln Boulevard?" He motioned for her to walk beside him, and she recognized him as the drover who usually wore the beaded vest.

"You're James Johnson."

"Yes, ma'am."

"You've stayed in town for a few weeks now."

"I'm growin' fond of the place. I'll likely head south and ride with another drive b'fore winter. Usually ride with the Stone outfit, but we had a partin' of the ways."

"Sorry to hear that. Something you can fix?"

"Don't seem likely." They drew up at the lumber yard and he pointed up the boulevard. "Can't leave my post, ma'am, but you'll be fine from here on home. I'll watch from here."

"Thank you for the escort, James. Have a good night."

"Yes'm. You, too."

She walked passed Remmy's mercantile and on, seeing the schoolhouse ahead. She had big dreams, plans to see her and Daniel's children attending this school. Her lack of commitment, her inability to open up and admit to herself that she loved Daniel had moved all of those dreams to the edge of a cliff.

She'd made a lot of mistakes in the past, made poor choices without thinking things through, but Daniel didn't feel like the wrong choice.

She stopped in front of the school and sat on the new wooden steps. "Help me fix this one, Lord. Show me what I need to do. I do love Daniel. I believe he loves me, but I think I've hurt him. I thought there was so much time ahead, but I know now that every day I held back was painful for him."

She glanced up the street to the big house that was built angled to the southwest on the corner of the block. She hadn't lit lamps before she'd left, and the house was dark, which meant Daniel was still gone.

She wasn't going to let anything stand in the way of what she wanted now. She'd lost too much. She'd come here for a husband. Daniel was still the one she wanted. He believed in her, and she wanted to be the person he deserved. She had a yearning for the tenderness and acceptance he offered. And now she knew for sure—knew she would move a mountain to make this marriage work and create the family they both needed. She hadn't known this longing could be so powerful.

The sound of hoofbeats met her ears, and the brown-and-white skewbald came into view, its rider slowing the horse at the corner where the house sat. Daniel had ridden in from the east, and would ride Woodrow another block to the livery and walk home.

He continued past, headed for Eden Street.

Leah got up. She would go to her room and he wouldn't even know she'd been gone. She felt foolish for heading out without a plan and circling the town, ending up being discovered by James Johnson near the railroad tracks. She stepped off the bottom stair and lost her balance.

Twisting her ankle on the way down, she caught herself with both hands and landed in an ungainly heap. Her wrist smarted, and her ankle hurt. She sat up, pushed to all fours and got to her feet, testing her ankle. Pain shot through the joint, and she limped the rest of the way to the corner, across the street and to the house. She took the stairs slowly and let herself in.

She'd be sorry if she didn't take time to chip ice from the block in the chest, so she went into the kitchen, lit a lamp with a tin reflector on the wall and filled a dishtowel with ice chips. She washed her face and hands with the wet rag at the basin, turned down the wick, and slowly made her way up the stairs.

She spread a towel on the bed and lay down with the ice on her throbbing ankle. She was more embarrassed at her clumsiness and mad at herself than anything. It took her a long time to fall sleep.

This time when she dreamed, she envisioned herself lying in this bed, but she wasn't alone. A bright warmth pervaded her arms and breast, and she looked down to see her beautiful dark-haired infant snuggled against her, wearing the precious yellow smocked gown. Gently she touched her newborn's silken cheek, felt tiny gusts of breath on her finger. Joy overwhelmed her, and she never wanted to look away from her baby's captivating face. The dream embodied everything good and perfect, but also pointed out how very fragile and precious life was. She woke gently, a smile on her lips, assured that moment would be hers. "Thank You, Father," she whispered. "Thank you for this baby and for Daniel. I'm trusting You with both of them and my marriage."

For the first time she didn't go down to join Daniel for breakfast. She heard him leave and a little while later there was a soft knock on her door.

"Are you well, Leah?"

"Come in, Valentine."

The woman pushed open the door and carried in a tray. "Mr. Gardner said to make sure you eat."

"Of course he did."

"Are you all right? Do you want me to go for Doc Fletcher?"

"That might not be a bad idea."

Valentine's forehead creased in concern. "What is it, dear?"

Leah threw back the lap blanket to show her the foot she had propped on a pillow. Her ankle was swollen and bluish.

"Oh my stars! What did you do?"

"Something very stupid. I went out in the dark and took a little tumble."

"Do you hurt anywhere else?"

She held up her arm. "My wrist."

"I'll go get him. First I'll bring you some ice."

"Thank you. I'm sorry to be a bother."

"It's no bother. Don't move." She returned with a supply of ice and then hurried to collect Dr. Fletcher.

"You should have sent for me last night," he scolded her, after examining her wrist and ankle. "You could have broken a bone. You might've hurt yourself worse."

"My hands and wrist hurt because I caught myself,"

she explained. "I sort of rolled onto my side, very grace-fully I assure you. I feel perfectly fine."

"That baby feels perfectly fine," Doc said. "He's an active one, isn't he?"

She agreed.

"No other bruises or cuts?"

"That's it."

"I'm going to wrap it loosely, and I want you to stay off that foot for a few days."

Daniel was going to find out and he'd probably be angry with her. She nodded.

Valentine brought up books from the library. After lunch Opal showed up.

"Leah, what on earth happened to you? Valentine mentioned your accident to her brother this morning when she saw him going into the barber shop."

"Beside Doc Fletcher's office."

"And Owen told the barber and the news is all over town now. Amos came up and told me a little bit ago."

Which meant Daniel would hear it from someone else. Leah rolled her eyes in exasperation and blurted the whole horrible mess to Opal.

Opal sat in silence for a few minutes. "Honey, that man is so besotted with you, he can't look away when you're in the room. When he gazes at you his face lights up like the sky on a cloudless night. Whatever this business is all about, it's not because he doesn't love you. It's because he does."

"I let him down," she blurted. "I was too cowardly to admit how I feel about him. And now this."

"Be honest with him—about everything. Get it all out in the open."

"I would have liked to be able to stand and face him."

"Don't you dare. You stay off that foot."

"Yes, ma'am."

Opal turned to a bag she'd carried in and set on the chair. "I've brought something to help you pass the time while your ankle is healing." She produced a skein of blue yarn and a crochet hook. "Crochet is easier to learn than knitting, and I have a feeling you're the impatient sort."

"I appreciate that. Did intuition perhaps prompt you to bring me blue yarn?"

"No, that's what I had left from a sweater I made for my sister's little boy. I'll show you how to start."

An hour and a half later, Leah had a lopsided bootie started. Opal had nearly finished one and now pulled all the stitches back out to roll the yarn back up into the ball.

"I could have used that one," Leah said.

"You will make your own," Opal assured her.

"Maybe by the time the baby is three he'll have a pair of booties."

They both laughed.

"Go on home and rest, Opal. Thank you for everything."

"You're welcome. You rest, too."

Leah had been asleep for half an hour when the sound of heavy boots coming up the stairs woke her. She opened her eyes.

Daniel stood at the entrance to her room. "Why did I hear from Walter at the livery that you'd been injured?"

Chapter Twenty-One

She flinched at Daniel's severe expression. "It was last night and I didn't want to bother you."

He came close to look at her wrapped ankle. "You did this last night?"

"Yes."

Some of the steam left his posture. He turned and pulled the chair close to the bed and sat on the edge. "I suppose you didn't feel like you could tell me after what I said and the way I left."

"It's not your fault. I was the one who went out walking in the dark."

He frowned his displeasure. "You went out alone at night?"

"I know it was foolish."

He stared down at the comforter, a muscle ticking in his jaw. "I'm sorry about last evening, about the things I said and the way I said them." He met her eyes. "I saw you at the hotel with Will yesterday."

She thought that over. "You saw us…doing what?"

"Talking. You were coming down from his office, and then you walked outside together."

Thinking back over the things he'd said the night before, she remembered he'd asked her how she felt about him. She'd assured him she was fond of him. *Fond of him.*

He'd said the situation had changed since she'd first arrived and she hadn't known what he meant. He said they'd both had time to think since then, and he wouldn't hold her against her will. He would arrange for an annulment if that was what she wanted. Her heart sank at the memory.

"When you got to Cowboy Creek Will was engaged to Dora, but he's free now. It's possible I pushed you too fast, got ahead of God's timing and you were meant to end up with him. I saw the two of you together and you looked so happy."

"I was not meant to be with Will Canfield," she said, indignant at his misinterpretation of the scene he'd witnessed. "I was happy because we were talking about you, you big oaf."

"You chose him once, Leah. Things didn't work out when the war started, but maybe this time, maybe now…"

"And I have regretted the choices I made back then," she assured him, her voice taut with fervent emotion. She hadn't known this much regret was inside her. "I regret them more than you can imagine. I was focused on what seemed the safe choice, and at the time you scared me. You were always planning something and trying something new. You wanted to come west and start a ranch. Little did I know the whole country would disintegrate, and your plan would be the most levelheaded of all. Only you came west and started a whole town."

"With Will," he bit out. "And he has political aspirations. I'm still planning on those horses."

"I don't want anyone else, Daniel. I don't want anyone but you."

"I may have pushed you into this," he said, scrubbing a hand over his face.

"You didn't push. I made my own choice, just as I've *always* made my own choices. Only this time I made the right one. Selfishly I took the security you offered. But I made one mistake. A big one. I made marriage sound like a business contract."

He rested his corded forearms on his knees and leaned on them, steepling his fingers under his chin as he studied her.

"As though I could keep from ever hurting again if I didn't let myself admit how I felt about you."

He said nothing. It was apparent he listened with every fiber of his being.

"And then I fell in love with you."

His green eyes showed wariness, but betrayed a glimmer of hope as well.

"I didn't want to admit it to myself," she whispered. "I didn't want to admit I've probably loved you for a long, long time. But I was so wrapped up in being practical that I didn't let myself feel. It was only the past couple of days I thought I could let myself love you the way you deserve—the way I want to."

He lowered his hands. "You're saying you love me, Leah?"

"Why should you believe me? You shouldn't. I'm the woman who does whatever it takes to stay safe."

"But you don't lie."

She pursed her lips for a moment and then released

a sigh through them. "No. I don't lie. I've hurt you. You don't have to forgive me for that."

"You haven't hurt me, Leah."

"But I have. I've been holding back."

He sighed. "Can we just say this is all new to us? Neither of us has any idea how to transition from friends to—to—whatever we're becoming."

She raised her chin. "Man and wife."

His eyes held so much love and hope, her heart gained momentum. "Yes?"

She nodded. "People who love each other?"

"Yes, Leah. A hundred times yes."

Her gaze blazed into his and she reached toward him, palm up, the back of her hand resting on the bed. "Yes."

He placed his hand over hers, engulfing it. "It took me a while to realize it, but I never stopped loving you. When I believed you loved Will, when I thought Charles would make you happy, I made peace with that, but I never stopped loving you." He swallowed hard and his eyes glimmered with emotion. "Then you showed up here. When I asked you to marry me, I did so willing to live my life without your devotion, because I only wanted your welfare and that of your child. I was prepared for us to be friends, but I realize now how foolish that was. I want your love more than anything."

"But you would have let me go if I had loved Will instead?"

"It would have killed me, but I would have given you my blessing."

She adjusted herself on the bed, already weary of the lack of activity. He leaned forward to arrange the pillows behind her shoulders. Hooking an arm around his shoulder, she pulled him close. He sat at her hip and threaded his fingers into the hair at her temple.

She cupped his jaw and held his head so he had to look into her eyes. "I want you to say you won't let me go."

His eyes fluttered closed, but he opened them again and drank in her earnest expression and her plea.

"I want you to say you want me for yourself."

"I do want you for myself." The words came out gruff and low. "I always have. No one has ever taken your place in my heart. No one ever could."

He leaned toward her until their lips met. He'd kissed her before, but this kiss filled her with the renewed discovery of first love.

Daniel didn't want this moment to end. She loved him. Beautiful, gentle Leah loved him. He'd watched her grow from a young girl to a woman, all the while longing for the day they would be old enough, the day he could declare his love and ask her to marry him. This was the woman who had filled his days with longing and his nights with dreams. Her delicate fingers dug into his shoulder as she clung to him.

For so long he'd believed it was never to be. He was destined to live out his life without her, all the while knowing no other woman could fill the place she held in his heart. And now here she was, all soft and warm, and wanting to kiss him.

Loving him.

He could hardly believe she was here in the house he'd built while hoping against hope for a woman to love. She was here in his arms.

He framed her lovely face between his palms and leaned away to look into her eyes. "I love you."

Her lips curved into a smile. "I love you, Daniel Gardner. I'm going to make the best wife you can imagine."

Footsteps sounded on the stairs, and Daniel reluctantly released his wife and moved back to the chair. He'd almost forgotten Valentine was downstairs.

The woman carried in a small wooden folding table and set it beside the bed near the chair where he sat. "I've made supper, and I thought you'd like to eat together up here."

"That's thoughtful of you." He glanced at Leah and they shared a secret smile.

"I'll be right back."

"Can I help you?"

She waved over her shoulder. "I can handle it." A few minutes later she returned with plates and cups on a large tray. "Don't bother yourself with the dishes tonight. I'll take care of them in the morning."

"Thank you, Valentine." Leah gave the woman an appreciative smile. "You're a blessing."

"Don't let her get up," Valentine said to Daniel.

"I won't."

He got the lap tray from the end of the bed and set Leah's supper on it. They enjoyed the meal. He hadn't had an appetite for nearly a day, so he ate all of his food and everything Leah left on her plate. "You sure you're full?" he asked.

"I'm sure. She brought me breakfast and lunch, too."

He carried all the dishes down, and she was dozing when he returned. He went to wash and change into a clean shirt, and he carried a book back with him. The sun was setting, casting its last pink rays across the bed and turning her hair and lashes to gold. Daniel seated himself in the chair and reveled in looking at her. His wife. His heart.

She opened her eyes.

"You're beautiful."

She smiled.

Later, once the sun had disappeared over the horizon and the katydids had begun their nightly song, Daniel pulled the curtains closed. "Will you be able to sleep tonight?" he asked in the darkness.

"Will you stay close?" she asked.

"Always." He stretched out atop the covers beside her and stacked his hands behind his head.

"I'm sorry I avoided the question when you asked how I felt about you," she said. "I should have just come out and said what I was feeling. From now on that's what we'll do. We'll tell each other how we're feeling."

"I was always a little jealous over Will," he admitted. "He's my best friend, and I wanted to be happy for both of you, but it hurt."

"And then Charles…" she said.

"I never knew him, and I didn't have to see you with him. Knowing you loved someone else left me empty, though."

"I never felt about Charles the way I feel about you," she confessed. "I had high hopes and dreams, but they were shallow. There was never substance between us."

"He was a fool if he didn't know what he had," Daniel said.

Leah took a deep breath. "I was a fool, too. I thought a life as an officer's wife would be fulfilling, glamorous, safe. At first he paid attention to me and showed me off. I suspected then, I guess, that it was all for show. Had he loved me he would have cared about my welfare. He would have made an effort. Whenever he returned from the field I pretended things were all right. While he was gone I kept myself busy. And the babies..."

"What, Leah?"

"It was as though he had no part in them, as though they didn't exist for him. The first time he acted as though it hadn't happened, and to him it didn't matter. So the second time I insisted I go home to Pennsylvania."

"And that time?"

"When I told you about Mama, I never told you that I was pregnant then."

"I didn't figure it out, either."

She released a sigh. "When Hattie and I left Mama and escaped through the woods, I was about eight months along. Travel was dangerous and we didn't get any rest. I'd been eating poorly, not sleeping well. Before we reached the city, the baby had started making its way into the world. I was too weak. The baby was too weak. He didn't survive."

Daniel reached for her hand and brought it to his chest. "I'm sorry, Leah."

"Yes." She rolled her head toward him, though she couldn't see him in the darkness. "I recuperated. But Hattie died. I made my way to Chicago, where Charles kept our place. When the war ended I was there waiting for him. He came home and there was no baby. He never even asked me about it."

"And you didn't tell him."

"No. I was trying to pick up the pieces without dealing with all that had happened." She released a sigh. "I guess I imagined the end of the war would somehow change everything for the better. It didn't."

"And you stayed because there was nowhere else to go, and he was your husband."

"He stayed gone for days at a time. Once I hadn't seen him for an entire month. I started to worry what I would do if he never came back. I started to form a plan. Then I got news that he'd been killed."

"Killed?" he asked.

"I never told anyone. I was too humiliated. He was shot by an angry husband."

Daniel took a deep breath and seemed to absorb that news.

"I wasn't surprised," she confessed. "And weeks later I realized I was expecting again, and I felt like the biggest fool in the world."

"It's not foolish to hope," he responded. "To give people chances."

She shook her head against the pillow. "There was a pittance of his army pay left after he'd squandered it on who knows what. I used it for room and board, and then I got desperate. I scoured the newspapers for jobs and found the ad for mail-order brides."

"Thank You, Lord."

Silence folded them in its comforting embrace for several minutes. "Now you know it all," she said. "I didn't tell you before because I was ashamed."

"You don't have to be ashamed. You were doing your best. You were being a wife and hoping to be a mother. His mistakes aren't yours."

"I didn't believe I deserved you, Daniel," she said. "I kept so much hidden and I was embarrassed about my past, about my choices."

"You deserve the best, Leah."

She smiled into the darkness. "That's fitting then. Because you're the best."

He raised her hand to his lips and kissed her fingers. "Sleep now."

Within days, Leah was able to get up and walk with the aid of a crutch, provided by Dr. Fletcher. By the end of the week their schedule had resumed normalcy, so it was a surprise when over breakfast Leah asked Daniel if he would stay with her that morning and fetch a buggy to take her to the train station.

He widened his eyes. "Are you going somewhere?"

"No, silly. We're meeting someone."

His features relaxed. "Who are we meeting?"

"Well, this has something to do with the meeting you saw between Will and me at the hotel. We were collaborating on a plan. He was helping me."

"A bride for Will?"

"No. You'll just have to wait and see."

He raised a questioning brow. "I thought we had no secrets left."

"Just this one, and it won't be a secret for long. Trust me."

Daniel was impatient, wondering what Leah had cooked up and what Will had to do with it. She had dressed in a new dress, one created by Hannah, with a pretty green-and-white print. She wore the garnet dragonfly brooch on her collar. In the foyer she took a hat from the rack and adjusted it on her head. She would always be the prettiest woman he'd ever laid eyes on. He would always be the most fortunate man in Kansas.

Pippa waved from the corner near Remmy's as they passed.

"Remmy said his business is flourishing since you requested additional catalogs and he stocked more of the items you and Hannah shopped for," Daniel told her.

"He's selling knitted items for Opal, too. He's a smart businessman," she replied. "The place doesn't smell like pickles or salted pork, either. More women are on their way. He'll do even better when they arrive."

Daniel drove the buggy up between the station and the railroad office and helped her down. A lanky cowboy sat on one of the chairs outside the office building, a cup of coffee on his knee and a hat shading his eyes.

He touched the brim of his hat. "Mrs. Gardner. Mr. Gardner."

"Good morning, James," Leah replied.

Daniel nodded at him, lifted her down and handed her the crutch. "How do you know the Johnson fellow?"

"He's been in town for weeks now. We've met."

He helped his wife up the stairs to the platform and ushered her to a bench in the shade. Leah didn't have any family left, so he couldn't imagine who she was expecting to meet getting off the train, unless it was another bride. "Will told me he'd know his bride when she batted big blue eyes and twirled her parasol."

"That sounds like Will."

"Is that what this is about?" he prodded.

"You'll just have to wait and see. Were you this impatient waiting for my train?"

"Yes."

A dog chased a rabbit across the tracks and away, its bark fading. One other person came to wait on the platform, a Chinese man who worked at the laundry on First Street.

After twenty minutes, a train whistle blew in the

distance and a cloud of black smoke rose into the sky. Daniel glanced at Leah, who waited calmly and smiled up at him. He walked to the edge of the platform and paced back.

Finally the platform trembled as the train rumbled closer. The engine slowed, steam hissing, brakes squealing as the locomotive slowed to a halt. Steam rose into the blue sky. A conductor in his blue uniform climbed down and lowered the stairs.

A well-dressed couple emerged from the passenger car. "This here's Cowboy Creek?" the man asked.

"That's right," Daniel answered, wondering if he was supposed to know the fellow. "Welcome."

"Thank you, sir. The missus and I are doing some traveling. I heard there were good business opportunities here."

"You heard right. What's your business?"

"I was a surveyor for the army. I've done some banking. The missus is a teacher."

"It's a pleasure to meet you. I'm Daniel Gardner. The Cattleman Hotel is a fine establishment, and the town may have another hotel soon. With all that and cattle money, we can't have enough banks." He shook hands with the gentleman. "Tell Mr. Rumsford to put your meals on my tab and your first night's stay is on me."

"That's quite generous of you, Mr. Gardner. Thank you."

The couple moved on and Daniel noticed two young Chinese boys of maybe fifteen or sixteen greeting the man who'd been waiting. He turned and walked back to Leah. "Was that the surprise? A teacher? Did you know there was a teacher arriving? Or the banker?"

She shook her head. "I had no idea. But that's good news, right?"

He put his hands on his hips and strode back toward the passenger car. Leah got up and joined him, leaning on her crutch.

A man in a fawn-colored suit, a straw hat pressed to his chest and a bag in the other hand climbed down from the car. He was tall, with broad shoulders and a short-cropped beard. His hair was a distinctive chestnut brown, but instead of golden highlights, strands of silver threaded the front and temples. It took Daniel a full minute to connect what his eyes were seeing with his brain, and another thirty seconds to make his feet respond. He shot across the platform. "Pa!"

Chapter Twenty-Two

The man stepped onto the planks, unceremoniously dropped the bag and opened his arms wide. Daniel ran to him and the two men stood in a rugged embrace, joy throbbing into Daniel's bloodstream. He took a step back and looked at his father's tanned face, lined from experience, but still firm and familiar.

"It's good to see you, Daniel."

"It's good to see you." He turned and found Leah watching from a distance with tears in her eyes. He motioned her forward. She limped to join them and Oliver Gardner crushed her in a fatherly embrace.

"Leah, dear. It's been a long time." He patted her back and she gave a little sob against his jacket.

Daniel swiped a hand over his eyes. "Well, this is quite a surprise. This is what you cooked up?"

Oliver straightened. "I was surprised to get Leah's telegram."

"Will told me where you were living," she explained.

"I knew you were doing well here in Kansas, but I had no idea you boys had built an entire town—and I sure didn't know Leah had found her way here."

"I was going to send you a wedding portrait," Daniel said.

"You might have sent me a wedding invitation."

"It all happened so quickly," Daniel explained.

Leah supported his rationale. "And then things got a little rocky, but everything's sorted out now."

Daniel reached to draw Leah near. "We're going to be parents."

Oliver placed his hand over his heart. "I can't think of better news! I guess you did invite me for the best part."

Daniel slapped his father on the back and leaned to hug his wife. "Best surprise ever, Leah. Thank you."

"You're welcome."

Daniel went for Oliver's bag and Oliver clapped his straw hat on his head. "I have a town to see."

"When we exchanged letters, it sounded like you were busy," Daniel said. "Working with an international company in New York?"

"Just staying busy," he agreed. "And you. You were setting up a stockyard and getting into construction."

Daniel shrugged. "Building a house. Maybe a railroad investment soon."

"Maybe you'll need help." Oliver paused, his expression uncertain.

"If you're asking do I want you to stay, the answer is yes. And there is plenty of work to do. Opportunities arise every day."

Daniel's father fell into step at Leah's side. "What is the story about this crutch, daughter?"

"It's a pretty long story," she replied. "We'd better save that for over supper. I'm sure there will be plenty more catching up to do."

James Johnson tipped his hat from where he still sat in front of the railroad office. They reached the buggy, and Oliver went straight to the brown-and-white horse. He let the horse smell his hand and sleeve and then rubbed his knuckles down his forehead. "What's this magnificent animal doing pulling a buggy?"

"He won a race last week," Leah told him.

"I'll bet he did."

Daniel settled his hat on his head with a nonchalant adjustment. "I bought a quilt with the prize money."

Oliver raised a brow. "A quilt?"

Leah turned to her husband. "A quilt? What kind of quilt?"

"I don't know what kind. It's pink and green and has white buttons on it."

She caught his sleeve with excitement. "The kaleidoscope quilt Mrs. Foster made?"

"That might be the one."

"And you didn't tell me? Where is it?"

He grinned. "I was saving it."

"For what?"

"For a special occasion."

She waved her arm. "Well now you've spilled the beans, so you have to show me."

He laughed and helped her up to the buggy seat.

Oliver glanced at them, his expression pleased. "Daniel, are you spoiling your new wife?"

"I might be."

"Good."

Daniel handed his father the reins and Oliver flicked them over the horse's back.

"Head over this way, Pa. We call this Eden Street, because it marked the beginning."

"I like that, son." He grinned. "The two of you have a new beginning, as well. If you have a son, you can name him Adam. Or a girl could be Eve."

Daniel looked at Leah, and she met his eyes with a hopeful smile. "I like Eve," she said.

"Over there is the bank."

Oliver looked away, but said over his shoulder. "I know you're kissing your wife."

The three of them laughed.

Daniel had everything he needed. Helping to form Cowboy Creek had fulfilled his burning desire to create order. Finding Leah and rekindling an enduring love brought the inner peace for which he'd been searching. He couldn't control what happened next, he could only plan and pray. The future was always uncertain, but the certainty he relied upon now was that tomorrow was in God's hands. Whatever happened next, he and Leah would face it together.

He surveyed Railroad Street, seeing the people and the storefronts through his father's eyes. It was a good place to live and work. Leah squeezed his fingers. He gazed down at her, and his heart swelled.

Cowboy Creek was their future, their destiny, their hope. Their hearts and lives, as well as those of their countrymen, were being restored one day, one bride, one baby at a time.

* * * * *

Dear Reader,

I'm confident you're going to enjoy the *Cowboy Creek* continuity. It's been a pleasure to collaborate with Sherri Shackelford and Karen Kirst during the development of this series. We had a lot of fun with these characters, bringing three Civil War veterans and their prospective brides to life set against the vivid backdrop of a Kansas boomtown.

Daniel and Leah are both starting over, both seeking a better life and hoping to change things for the better, not only for themselves but for their community. Neither of them believes their reunion in Kansas is by chance or that abiding love and happy-ever-after is an accident. They're thankful for each day and appreciative of the opportunities afforded them.

> This I recall to my mind, therefore have I hope:
> It is of the Lord's mercies that we are not consumed, because His compassions fail not. They are new every morning; great is Thy faithfulness. The Lord is my portion, saith my soul, therefore will I hope in Him.
>
> —*Lamentations* 3:21–24

I hope what you take away from *Want Ad Wedding* is that life is all about second chances. No matter what we are going through, God's faithfulness, love and mercy is there for us. That knowledge gives me hope every day and in everything I do. I believe it's an encouragement to you as well.

I would love to hear from you: SaintJohn@aol.com!

Cheryl St. John ☺

REQUEST YOUR FREE BOOKS!

2 FREE INSPIRATIONAL NOVELS
PLUS 2 *FREE* MYSTERY GIFTS

Love Inspired® HISTORICAL

*Town founder Will Canfield has big dreams for
Cowboy Creek—but his plans are thrown for a loop
when a tiny bundle is left on his doorstep. With a
baby to care for, the last thing he needs is another
complication. But that's just what he gets, in the form
of a redheaded, trouble-making cowgirl who throws his
world upside down.*

Read on for a sneak preview of
Sherri Shackelford's
SPECIAL DELIVERY BABY,
the exciting continuation of the miniseries
COWBOY CREEK,
available May 2016 from Love Inspired Historical.

"The name is Will Canfield," he said. "Thank you for
your assistance, Miss Stone."

"You sure picked a dangerous place to take your baby
for a walk, Daddy Canfield. Might want to reconsider
your route next time."

The measured expression on his face faltered a notch.
"Oh, this isn't my baby."

She hoisted an eyebrow. "Reckon who that baby
belongs to is none of my business one way or the other."
She gestured toward the child. "I think your girl is getting
hungry. Better get mama."

"That's the whole problem." The man spoke more to
the infant in his arms than to her. "Someone abandoned
her. I found her on my doorstep just now." He glanced
over his shoulder and then back at her. "The woman—
the one who spooked the cattle. Did you see which way

she ran? I think this child belongs to her. If not, then she might have seen something. She was hiding in the shadows when I discovered this little bundle."

"Sorry. I was focused on the cattle."

Clearly frustrated by her answers, Daddy Canfield muttered something unintelligible.

He grimaced and held the bundle away from him, revealing a dark, wet patch on his expensive suit coat.

Tomasina chuckled. The boys were going to love hearing about this one. They'd never believe her but they'd love the telling. Her pa always liked a good yarn, as well. At the thought of her pa, her smile faded. He'd died on the trail a few weeks back and they'd buried him in Oklahoma Territory. The wound of his loss was still raw and she shied away from her memories of him.

"Fellow..." Tomasina said. "As much fun as this has been, I'd best be getting on."

"Thanks for your help back there," Will replied, his tone grudging. "Your quick action averted a disaster."

The admission had obviously cost him. He struck her as a prideful man, and prideful men sometimes needed a reminder of their place in the grand scheme of things.

"Daddy Canfield," she declared. "Since you don't like guns, how do you feel about rodeo shows? You know, trick riding and fancy target shooting?"

"Not in my town. Too dangerous."

"Excellent," Tomasina replied with a hearty grin.

Yep. She felt better already.

Don't miss SPECIAL DELIVERY BABY
by Sherri Shackelford,
available May 2016 wherever
Love Inspired® Historical books and ebooks are sold.
www.LoveInspired.com